MW01267960

Demon Reign

DW SHENEMAN

JAZZERA

CHAPTER 1

If not for the rain, the forest would have been deathly still. No birds twittered about in the trees. No rodents scurried around on the forest floor. The only thing that hung in the air was the thick aura that slithered through the trees like a deadly serpent.

A demon's aura wasn't an object humans could detect with their senses. They couldn't smell, taste, feel, or see it. It was a heavy darkness that forced itself onto a person's very soul. All the anguish, fear, and sorrow of every victim the demon had claimed— pushing down on the most sensitive of humans.

I felt this pain, and my stomach lurched. This was no ordinary demon we were hunting, no weak imp or shadow dweller. This was something more, something much more powerful. I paused for a moment as I reached the edge of a small stream and looked over to my protector, a Demon Slayer named Ermek. A man bound to me since we were both small children, sworn to give his life for mine.

"We should go back," he stated as he slowly pulled an arrow from his quiver.

1

Shaking my head vigorously, I placed a hand on his strong arm. "I can't go back empty-handed."

As if feeling our doubt, a voice echoed through the woods. It came from nowhere, yet everywhere. "Run away, little Priestess. Run away."

I gripped the handle of my katana tightly in my hand, easing the blade gently from the scabbard. I knew better than to reply. Demons liked to play games. Cautiously, I stepped into the small stream, my boots soaking up water as the white frills of my Priestess robe glided through the ripples. The rain had picked up as if the demon was controlling the weather. The rain would make visibility low. I would have to be at the top of my game if I wished to capture this creature.

My foot slipped, and, for an instant, I was plummeting toward the cold water. I braced for impact until I felt an arm wrap around my waist.

"He knows we're here.. the last thing you need to do is break an ankle," whispered Ermek.

"Oh, isn't that adorable," mocked the voice. This time I felt like I could pinpoint which direction it had come from. Stepping out of the water, I slipped from Ermek's arms and pushed through the thick undergrowth until I reached a clearing.

Within the clearing sat a single log with a raven perched on an old, dead limb. It ruffled its feathers and cawed loudly, glaring at us with three black eyes. Even as the rain poured down, the creature opened its wings and took flight, circling the clearing and shrieking loudly. Ermek drew his bow back and aimed, firing an arrow that missed the creature by mere inches.

"Don't kill it!" I urged.

"Kill me? Oh, Priestess, don't make me laugh," it was the voice again. Like before, it seemed as if it were bouncing off the trees and not coming from the bird itself. It made me wonder if the aura was so strong because there was not just one demon but two.

"Force it to transform!" shouted Ermek after missing the beast with a second arrow.

I nodded and reached for my satchel.. inside were tiny white prayer beads. I could force the demon to shift into its true form with the proper incantation and good aim. It would make capturing the monster much easier if I had a larger, slower target to hit.

Pulling out the beads, I whispered an incantation into my palm. When the bird came close, I tossed them as hard as possible, hitting the bird with three of them. Instantly the creature fell to the ground, writhing and flopping as if possessed, the demon ripping its way out of the body.

I watched with wide eyes as the creature began to shift. The sickening sound of bones snapping and rearranging made me want to vomit. Feathers began to melt away, exposing a mound of muscle that finally grew into a human form.

Staggering back a step, I gasped. This was no grotesque creature that lay before me, no twisted beast of Hell. In the place where the raven once flopped around was the body of a man.

The naked being had skin as pale as the moon with long black hair that covered part of its face. As it stood on shaky legs, I looked away, trying to force the blush off my face.

"Do I make you blush, Priestess?" teased the man.

3

I tried to keep my eyes above his midsection. His body was slender and hard as stone.. every muscle was chiseled as if God were the artist. He was handsome with a strong jaw, high cheekbones, and a shadow of facial hair surrounding his lips and chin. His eyes gave him away. There was no white to his eyes, only pools of blackness pulsing with evil.

"Reveal yourself!" I commanded, throwing a second handful of beads at the creature.

The man winced as the tiny pearls struck his naked body and growled, "This is my true form!"

"You lie!" shouted Ermek. "Demons don't have a natural human form."

The man shrugged and grinned wickedly. "And yet here I am." He smiled wider and then began to swing his hips back and forth.

Ermek drew his bow and nocked an arrow. "Cover yourself in the presence of the Priestess!"

"I think she's enjoying it," replied the demon as he turned to me, "I bet you want to feel every last inch of it. Don't you?"

Before I could respond, Ermek let loose the arrow. It soared through the air, hitting the creature directly in his left eye. The demon cried out in agony and dropped to his knees. Black blood poured from the wound as he tried to pull it from his skull.

"I will drill a hole in your skull and fuck your brain!" he screamed, still trying to pull the arrow free.

I took this as my opportunity to strike. Pulling my blade from its sheath, I ran at the man and swiped, cutting him from the groin to the sternum. Standing back, I watched as his intestines fell from the gaping wound and lay on the floor in a steaming black heap.

This demon was strong. What Ermek and I had just done to it would have killed a lesser demon.. it would have melted into a pile of green or black ooze and returned to Hell, but not this one. It was only wounded. I could sense it. He was far more dangerous than I first gave him credit for. Eventually, the demon managed to pull the arrow from its eye socket, gushing black blood down his cheek.

As the beast sat there, gasping for breath and clutching his insides, I pulled a small silver chain from my satchel. Drawing a long black hair from the top of my head, I wrapped it around the chain and whispered a prayer. With all my strength, I threw the chain at the demon. It swirled around him several times before wrapping itself tightly around the man's neck. He screamed in pain as the chain embedded itself into his skin, leaving a small scar around his neck. It opened its mouth to speak, but only blood came out.. he coughed and fell face-first into the wet earth.

I stood still for a moment, marveling at the sight before me. I had never seen a naked man before. When a person reaches adulthood, they are never meant to be naked in the presence of the opposite sex, especially in the presence of a Priestess. The physical intimacy needed to procreate is only permitted in the sanctity of marriage. Even then, strict modesty rules must be adhered to. I wanted to touch him, to run my fingers along the fine lines of his perfectly crafted body. I was tempted to reach out but then recoiled. Lust was a sin, especially lust over a demon.

Feeling guilty, I turned my back to it and glanced at Ermek.

"So, you captured it. Now how are we supposed to get it back?" inquired Ermek.

I glanced back at the man and sheathed my sword, "We could see if some of the younger Demon Slayers from the temple could help carry him until he's conscious."

"You would leave this demon alone here in the woods? He would follow us back the moment he could stand and kill us all in our sleep."

I knew he was right. I hadn't thought this far ahead. When I had asked Ermek to come with me to capture a demon, I had never dreamt I would find one like this. The most I had hoped for was a shadow dweller, one easy to bring down and control, but this one was something else entirely.

Ermek scooped the demon up in his arms and began walking the way we had come. The man-beast lay limp in his arms and looked as light as a doll. As hard as I tried, I couldn't suppress my smile. A shudder ran down my spine as I imagined Ermek carrying me in the same way, taking me from the temple to a faraway land—to a place where we could have children and grow old together.

Watching his long black braids sway as he walked, I sighed quietly. I knew that could never happen. Not only did he never look at me in the desirable way I looked at him, but he would be castrated if he so much as affectionately touched me. If I went to him, I would be seen as a traitor to God and stoned to death. A Priestess could never lay with any man.. she would lose her angelic mark, thus losing her ability to capture and control demons.

The walk back had been long, but at least the rain had let up, partially allowing the sun to shine through the trees. The demon was still unconscious and bleeding in Ermek's arms, but it was still breathing. I thought it odd that demons breathed.. they were beings from Hell, and Hell was a place that housed souls. Why would a demon need to breathe?

Young Demon Slayers were training in the temple yard. There were six of them in total, each waiting to be paired with their Priestess. The oldest couldn't have been more than ten, but he wielded his weapon as if he were a man who had fought countless battles.

Sitting in prayer under a young oak tree were three other Demon Slayers. The eldest of the trio was seventeen years old and already paired with a Priestess. The other two were only a few years younger and were also paired. A Priestess wasn't allowed to leave the temple until she managed to capture her own demon. Once they did, they would go to a private prayer ceremony and be sent to a village to help protect it and its people.

A large smile grew on my face. I was the eldest at twenty-three years old—the only one out of my original group not to have my own demon. The High Priestess had forbidden me from leaving the temple, claiming that my power was too great and that I would need much more training than the others to control it.

As we crossed the courtyard, the young men abandoned their training to come and see the body that lay in Ermek's arms. The black blood told them the being wasn't human, but instead of frightening them, as it should have, they seemed to be transfixed on it.

When we reached the temple's front steps, they stopped short. High Priestess Lady Ester stood with her arms crossed firmly in front of her, her old, wrinkled face twisted with disapproval. The young Demon Slayers scattered, returning to their training.

"What have you done?" queried the Priestess.

Ermek stopped and laid the demon down at the first step. "The Priestess Jazzera has captured this demon, my Lady."

Lady Ester stared at the naked man with a hanging jaw. After a moment, her mouth closed, and her thin lips quivered. Making a sign of the cross, she recoiled from the creature at her feet as if she were afraid of it.

Before I could explain, I spotted the tall brown headdress of the High Priest. He rushed down the narrow steps, almost tripping on his long brown robes. The man was tall and thin, with a rather long nose and nostrils so large a person could practically count every grey hair that hung from them.

"What is the meaning of this?" he demanded. Ermek and I bowed.

"I captured this demon," I replied without looking up.. a woman was never to look a Priest in the eyes.

"You have been forbidden from leaving this temple and, you bring this back with you? Why is he naked? Have you fornicated with this creature?"

My eyes widened, and I looked up at the Priest in shock. "No, your Grace. I would never."

"Then why is he naked?"

I looked back down to the ground, "I forced the demon to transform.. this was the form he took."

Ermek spoke up, "He claims this is his true form."

The Priest stepped backward, away from the creature, and almost lost his footing.

"What have you done? You have put every person's life in danger by bringing him here!"

Without warning, the Priest untied a horsewhip from his belt and began striking me.

Instinctively, I wanted to raise my arms to protect myself, but this wasn't the first beating I had ever taken. I knew better than to put up a fight, but this one seemed to be more brutal than the others. I could feel my skin split, blood dripping from my wounds. Without conscious thought, my body moved on its own. Raising both of my hands, I held them out to the Priest. He went to swing again, and I pushed him. When my hands made contact with his body, my angelic mark glowed a bright blue, and energy snaked down my arms, exploding from my fingertips. The Priest flew through the air, landing several steps above me.

Pulling back, I covered my mouth in horror. I lost control, just like everyone always feared I would. The last time my angelic mark glowed was when I was a child during a tantrum.

All my anger, rage, and frustration came out at once, almost killing my mother. After that, I was sent to the temple to be trained. This was far worse.. not only had I struck a man, which was bad enough, but I hit the High Priest himself. I trembled as I realized this could very well mean my death.

My eyes frantically searched my surroundings for a way to escape. They landed on Ermek, seeing his hand on the hilt of a knife hanging from his belt. His body language told me he was ready to defend me, but defending me meant that he would lose his life. He would be brought to the hills and crucified, where the animals and demons would pick at his bones until nothing remained.

I held my hand out to Ermek, trying to ease him down. My actions were my own, and I deserved to take the punishment. He deserved to have a Priestess who was more submissive, as God demanded every woman be. He didn't deserve to die because of my selfish impulses.

The Priest gradually got to his feet, and I bowed low, ready to take any beating that would come with my actions.

"Demon Slayer," he said, referring to Ermek. "Take this demon to the stables." He looked over to Lady Ester. "Place a barrier spell on the bars so he can't escape."

Several temple guards gathered near the Priest, ready to do his bidding. As I watched Ermek scoop the wounded demon in his arms, I heard the Priest order, "Take her to the whipping pole."

Two big men instantly grabbed me, forcing me to the opposite end of the courtyard.

Against the tall stone wall surrounding the temple were the gallows with four hangman's nooses blowing gently in the wind. In the center stood a large wooden pole with chains attached. I didn't fight as the chains were fastened to my wrists. There was no point.. they would only hurt me more if I struggled.

Though this was called the whipping pole, I knew I wouldn't be thrashed. Whippings were typically done to men.. women were branded with a cross. It was to help purify their souls and send them on the correct path back to God. I had already suffered through one branding, the memory causing an ache in my back. When I was fifteen, a visiting Priest put his hands on my backside, and I struck him across the face. Naturally, nobody believed me, so I received my first cross branding on my left shoulder blade.

I closed my eyes tightly as the two men tore the back of my robe open, exposing my naked back. I kept them closed, even as I heard the heavy footsteps of the Priest advance toward me. When the heat of the metal cross came close to my skin, I clenched my teeth and sucked in a deep breath. I screamed when the hot iron touched my skin, and the smell of searing flesh filled my nostrils. My pride wanted to keep me from screaming. I hated feeling so weak in the presence of these men, but my logical side told me I needed to show my pain. If a woman didn't scream or cry when being branded, it was assumed that she felt no pain. If she felt no pain, the Priest branded her as a witch, and she would be hanged shortly after.

Although it felt like hours, the metal only touched my flesh long enough to leave the mark and was pulled off. My shackles were released, and I was allowed to cover up.

Without saying a word, I limped to the healer who put medicinal herbs on my wound. I shambled into my chambers, locking the door behind me, and threw myself down on the bed.. I wept until the searing pain became a light throbbing.

I gingerly got to my feet and gazed at myself in the mirror, looking closely at my angelic mark. The mark itself was strange.. dull red, like a birthmark that started from the top of my forehead and snaked its way past my brows and cheeks, down my neck, and around my right arm. When it hit the arm, it branched off and crawled down my rib cage onto my hips and down my leg, stopping at my little toe. The strangest part about my mark was that it looked like it was spelling something out in strange symbols or letters that nobody had been able to translate. At least, that was what I had been told. Women weren't allowed to read, and it could say I was a selfish little twit and wouldn't be the wiser.

I had been told my mark was the largest of any living Priestess.. even the High Priestess at this temple didn't have a mark half as large. Her mark traveled from her forehead and only made it to the top of her right shoulder and no further.

When the Rapture occurred, people feared the mark, and since only women ever got it, people began to believe they were in league with the demons that emerged from Hell. It took quite a while until people realized these marks were blessings from God. Gifts were given to a select few to help protect the human race from the evils of Hell.

Although I was still in pain, I knew I couldn't hide in my chambers all night. I wanted to see my demon. I smiled at the thought—my demon. As the picture of him floated through my mind, my thoughts moved to Lady Ester. I wanted to know why Lady Ester and the High Priest seemed so afraid of it. He wasn't that hard to defeat. The battle was short and quick, and he was worse off for it.

After getting dressed in a new robe, I rushed out of my chambers as fast as my burned body could and headed to the stables where the demon was being kept. When I reached his stable, I gasped. I was expecting him to be lying naked, with his guts hanging out on the floor.

Instead, he was leaning against a wall, fully dressed as if nothing had happened. His clothing was like nothing that any person would have given him. He wore a black V-neck shirt and pants with a long black jacket with bright red silky lining. His long black hair no longer looked matted and wet but freshly combed and silky smooth. Had it not been for his terrifying black eyes, he would be shockingly handsome.

"Well, that must hurt," he stated, scratching his chin. I didn't respond. Grinning slightly, the demon stood in front of the bars. "The cross they seared into your skin. I could smell it from here.. it smelled delicious and made me hungry."

I cringed but continued to be silent.

The demon leaned against the bars. They began to glow red and sear his skin, but he acted as if it didn't bother him. He even placed his hand on the bar and pressed his face tighter against them.

I gagged and pinched my nose at the smell.

He chuckled and pulled himself from the bars. The grotesque scar left behind from the hot metal began to fade within seconds.

"I've lived in Hell for eons, sweetie. Do you think a little fire hurts me?"

I didn't know how to respond, nor did I know how to react to him in general. I had seen Priestesses with their demons, and they were utterly submissive. Only speaking when spoken to directly, never asking questions, and standing by their master's side, waiting for a command.

Then again, I had never been in the presence of a freshly captured demon. Perhaps they had to be broken like a horse.

"Do you want me to kill him?" asked the demon, breaking my train of thought.

I stared into the black pools of his eyes, and that's when I saw it. The High Priest- lying dead on the ground in a pool of blood. The demon, my demon, holding his still beating heart in its pale hand.

I shook my head and stepped back. "No. I don't want you to kill anybody."

"Well, you're no fun."

It was hard to tell since there was no white in this creature's eye, but he seemed to be rolling his eyes. He leaned casually against the stall wall and began twirling his long black hair with his finger.

"Nobody would blame you if you wanted him dead. First, he beats you, and then he has you branded." He paused, then grinned, "How very Christian of him." The last bit was obvious sarcasm.

"And what would you know about being Christian?" I hissed through clenched teeth.

He grinned wider and leaned up against the bars. He wrapped his hands around the metal, and they made a sickening hissing sound. The stench of burning flesh wafted through the air again. He stayed like that for a moment before pulling back and shaking off the burns.

"Okay, this is getting old."

He took another step back and held out his arms, which began to retract into his shoulders. His body started to shrink, and his legs began to fuse. The transformation only took a few moments, but when it was done, the largest snake I had ever seen slithered on the ground where the demon once stood. When I was a child, a band of performers came to the temple with a snake that looked just like this one.. they had called it a cobra.

The creature slithered up the stall door and through the bars coiling itself at my feet. In a panic, I retreated, falling hard on the ground. I winced as pain shot through my upper body from where I had been branded.

The creature began unhurriedly slithering its way up my body, staring at me with dead eyes. I was frozen in place, afraid to breathe.

"Fear not, Priestess. I can't kill you." The voice didn't come from the snake itself. Like in the woods, it came from every direction, reflecting off the walls into my ears.

As I sat frozen in terror, my eyes locked on my would-be assassin, I felt the snake's tail creep its way into my robes and down my pants. I gasped as the snake hissed, slipping its tail between my legs and over my underwear, caressing me.

"Do I make you wet, Priestess? Do you want me to fuck you hard or soft?"

Frantically, I grabbed the snake and pulled it from my body, throwing it against the wall.

I rolled over and eyed it, watching it change shape again into its human form.

"Don't act like you didn't like it. I felt you throbbing down there."

"You're disgusting!" I shrieked, trying to get to my feet.

The demon tossed his hands up. "I'm a demon, and I thrive on pleasure. Nothing in this world can compare to a good fucking and sucking."

"You will watch your words in a lady's presence, beast," ordered Lady Ester as she entered the barn. Her ice-blue eyes fixed on the monster with a hateful glare.

He slumped back against one of the stalls.

Lady Ester turned her harsh gaze toward me. "Why did you let it out?"

15

The demon broke into laughter. "You think your stupid little spell was going to hold me?" he taunted, pushing himself off the wall toward her, his dead black eyes flashing menacingly. "I am not one of those petty little demons your pathetic little girls capture.. I was once a god."

"There is only one God," stated Lady Ester, shrinking back.

The demon smirked, "Perhaps, but I was strong enough that the humans didn't know any better. They built temples and sacrificed virgins for me…" His smile turned lecherous. "I had to stop that one.. it was a shame to waste great virgin pussy."

"Enough!" I shouted.

That got his attention. His mouth closed, and I could see the small scar around his neck light up. The necklace embedded in his skin was making him obey. I would have to keep this one on a short leash. He was absolutely the vilest being I had ever encountered. Some of the words he muttered would cause me to lose my tongue.

"What is your name, Demon?" asked Ester through pursed lips.

The creature smiled and turned to me. "Am I allowed to answer her, my Lady?" his tone was sarcastic, with absolutely no respect behind it.

"What's your name?" I demanded as I gritted my teeth.

"Dagon."

JAZZERA

CHAPTER 2

L ady Ester's eyes widened at the sound of his name.. she knew it, that was for sure. I had never heard of him.. his name was never brought up in any teachings, but then, only a few demons were ever actually named. Most feared that if they were spoken out loud, even in the church, it could summon the creature to which the name belonged.

Swallowing hard, Lady Ester turned to me. "Command your demon to return to his stall, and I will send Ermek to watch over him until you return."

I nodded and instructed Dagon to enter the stall, and he did as he was told, grumbling the entire time. Once the demon was secured, Lady Ester turned on her heels and hurried out of the building. I reluctantly followed her. For an old woman, her pace was brisk, and I couldn't help but wince with each step I took trying to keep up with her.

We found Ermek sitting on the steps of the main temple. Ermek would have come to me after my branding, but having him rush to my chambers to

check on me might make people think we were
having a love affair. Lady Ester explained the
situation and relayed his new duties.. without
hesitation, Ermek followed her orders.

Wrapping her wrinkled hand tightly around my
wrist, the Priestess practically dragged me up the
stairs. It was insane how strong she was for a woman
of her age. She was a stout woman, standing just
below six feet tall. Nothing was frail about her and
had it not been for the white hair and wrinkled skin,
I doubted anyone would wish to get into a
confrontation with her.

We went through the large iron double doors
and into the temple lobby, gliding over the perfectly
polished white marble floor and down a flight of
emerald-green stairs to the lower floor of the temple.
This was the first time I had been to this part of the
temple. As far as I knew, the only thing down these
stairs were the archives and library, and, women
weren't allowed to use either of them.

"Should we be here?" I whispered as we stopped
at a large oak door.

Lady Ester didn't respond as she pulled a key
from a chain hanging around her neck. She unlocked
the door and pulled me through. My jaw dropped..
lining every inch of the four walls around me were
books of all shapes and sizes. As my eyes explored,
I noticed, with surprise, several old scrolls.

"We can't be here," I stated anxiously as a chill
ran down my spine.

"It's fine, Jazzera," she assured, using her
mother-like tone as she sifted through some books
on the wall to my right.

It didn't feel fine.. women were not supposed to
be down here. Women were not supposed to read

books. The punishment for reading was losing a finger. The words of God were not meant for the daughters of Eve. The descendants of the very first sinner.

My breath was becoming increasingly shallow as Lady Ester pulled a book from the shelf and rested it on the long wooden table in the center of the room. Hearing it thud against the wood made me recoil, and I held my breath as the Priestess opened the cover.

After flipping through a few old, tattered pages, she looked at me. "Breathe, child. I told you nothing will happen.. you won't be punished."

"We aren't supposed to be here," I murmured again, fighting back fearful tears.

The old woman smiled and walked over to me, gently running her hand through my thick black hair. "No ordinary woman is supposed to be down here, but we are far from ordinary, you especially. Every High Priestess is taught how to read once they capture their own demon." She caressed my cheek, "You are to replace me when the time comes. You are to be this temple's High Priestess.. you will learn about the different demons in this world. There are far too many for one person to memorize. It's why a High Priestess is allowed to learn to read."

It took me a moment to get my shaking under control and actually understand her words.

It came to me gradually.. I would take her place as High Priestess. There was absolutely no more tremendous honor given to a woman. My heart fluttered when it dawned on me that I would be able to read the same words men could. I could finally read the holy gospel for myself instead of hearing them secondhand. However, the smile quickly faded, and I pulled away from her grip.

"If I was meant to capture a demon anyway, why was everyone so upset that I captured one?"

Lady Ester sighed heavily, "With your demon so close, I dare not utter the truth. When you can control him better and have him as obedient as a dog, then I will explain everything. For you to leave the temple grounds is extremely dangerous, not only for you but for everyone, and, furthermore, you bring *him* back of all creatures."

She moved away and returned to the book she had been flipping through. Eventually, she stopped on a page and turned the book to me so I could look at it. The words and pictures meant nothing to me. Looking up at her, I shrugged slightly, not knowing what else to do.

"This is Dagon."

I reached for the book and pulled it closer to me. The sketch in the book looked nothing like the demon I captured. It was of a muscular man with the lower half of a fish, and its hair was wild and flowing in every direction. Instead of the neatly trimmed facial hair he had now, the drawing showed a long scraggly beard flailing about like tentacles. In this depiction, he held a giant pitchfork in his left hand. Below that picture, after several words I couldn't understand, was another drawing of a man. He also looked nothing like the demon in the stall. This one was dressed in long robes with long hair and a beard.

"Dagon is what is known as a Demon Lord. A very powerful, very dark creature. He wasn't lying when he said that people worshipped him as a god. He was even mentioned in the Bible for killing a king loyal to the one true God. In the end, however, Dagon kneeled, but there is nothing to say that he won't try to oppose God again. To have a demon such as him within the walls of this temple could be catastrophic."

"I don't understand," I muttered, wrapping my arms around myself. "I captured Dagon.. he should be no threat to anyone aside from other demons."

Lady Ester shook her head. "Which is why, starting tomorrow, you must train with him and get him under your absolute control." She smiled softly, "Regardless, I am impressed.. I never dreamed it would be possible to capture a Lord of Hell."

I wished the Priestess would explain to me what was going on. Why was it so important that I stayed in this place? Why would it be so bad to capture a powerful demon? The stronger a demon is, the more useful it could be. Or at least, that was my logic. He was certainly better than an imp.

"I will stay here and try to find as much as possible on this demon of yours. Go get some dinner, and, don't forget to feed your demon."

I turned to her and gave her a questioning look. "A demon needs food?"

She nodded, "There are different plains to this world. Heaven, Hell, and the Mortal plain.

Demons may not be able to die very easily, but they do seem to have some mortal needs. Most of the time, they feed on humans. To keep that from happening, I suggest you keep your demon well-fed with something else that would satisfy his hunger."

I was ashamed of how little I actually knew about demons. Unlike the other girls who had passed through the temple, I was taught little about them. Instead, I was taught how to fight like a Demon Slayer. That was one thing I noticed no other Priestess had been trained to do. I knew spells and prayers to capture and repel demons, but as far as how to keep a demon, that was something I was never taught. It was almost as if they had expected me to live my entire life without ever having one.

I had hundreds of questions to ask Lady Ester, but I decided to keep them to myself... for now. I pushed my boundaries far enough for one day. What was supposed to be a good day only turned out to be a day of pain and humiliation. I guess it was God's way of punishing me for being so prideful. I gave the Priestess a slight bow and returned to the stables.

ERMEK

CHAPTER 3

With my bow gripped firmly, I made my way to the stables where the demon was being kept. The aura around the stables had become putrid, but the horses didn't seem unsettled.

Usually, a horse would warn those not so sensitive to the demonic energy, openly showing fear and giving the rider time to flee along with it. However, these horses seemed calm, as if this creature of darkness was nothing more than a mere mortal. Maybe it was because this demon was injured, and they deemed it no real threat. Or perhaps, the horses were calm because they could sense the demon's impending demise.

When I reached the stall where the creature was being kept, I nearly fell back from shock.. instead of a half-dead man lying on the hay in a pool of black blood, the demon stood, healthy and whole. He was free of any blood or injury. More so, he was clean and dressed in fresh clothes.

"Didn't mommy ever tell you it isn't polite to stare?" It teased with a slight smirk. I gave it no response, only glared. "Did she send you down here to babysit?"

Standing up straight, I cleared my throat. "I was instructed to ensure you didn't try and break free."

The demon smiled and stepped closer to the stall bars. "Then maybe we should pass the time by having a little fun?"

I looked away. "I want nothing to do with you."

It grinned wider, winding its long hair between its fingers. "But I want something from you."

"Leave me be, beast," I ordered, looking toward the stable's entrance.

The creature leaned its face on the bars, and his skin began to sizzle. "But I really want some of that BBC."

I tossed him a confused look.

"Big. Black. Cock."

"Hold your tongue!" I shouted, barely able to control my anger.

He grinned larger, then shrugged his shoulders. "I know. I shouldn't be so stereotypical. I tend to cling to the twenty-first century. It was the last time you humans were any fun, them and their cute little acronyms like 'BBC.'" He paused as if waiting for a response.. he didn't get one. "It's sad, really. Men were finally able to start showing their affection to each other in public, and then the Gates of Hell opened up and kind of ruined it."

Scowling at him, I declared, "It was that grotesque nature that caused this Hell on Earth."

The demon laughed sarcastically. "Oh yes, it was totally the butt fucking. It couldn't possibly have been the war, murder, and rape that you humans loved to partake in. Nope, the Gates of Hell opened up because of the butt fucking."

"Close your mouth, Demon."

I knew I was only egging him on. The more irritated I seemed, the more he would try and pick at every last nerve I had. Typically, I would ignore him, but what if someone walked past the stables and heard him speaking to me in such a way? A simple rumor of me having sex with a human man would get me stoned to death, but a rumor that I slept with a demon would get me burned alive.

Turning on my heels, I went to the stable entrance to meet the Priestess when she finally came for her demon. The sky seemed oddly graygrey, and fog settled throughout the courtyard. Off in the distance, I heard shouting. Young Demon Slayers formed a line on either side of the path that led to the gallows. Their shouting voices clashed with the loud clanks of metal armor the temple guards wore. The only word I could make out for sure was "sinner."

Several Priestesses assembled near the Demon Slayers and began shouting along with them. Their tones were filled with hate and vitriol, as if they were cursing the poor bastard being escorted to their death.

Guards came into view, escorting a naked man down the path.. his face was hung low, covered by blond hair, and his body was thin yet muscular. It wasn't until he was almost directly in front of me that I could spot his face.. my blood ran cold. His icy blue eyes locked onto mine, and he smiled at me with soft pink lips. I reached out for him and tried to scream his name, but the words were caught in my throat.

A hand landed softly on my shoulder, and I blinked. Jazzera stood next to me with a somewhat confused look. I glanced past her to the courtyard, but everything had changed. No Demon Slayers or Priestesses stood by the gallows, and no guards dragged the young man to them. The sky was clear, and the sun was setting, covering the yard in a beautiful orange hew.

"Are you alright, Ermek?" she questioned sweetly, worried.

I didn't answer, turning to glare at the demon. He just stood there, arms crossed, smiling softly.

"I'm fine," I replied. The words were a complete lie.. I had never felt so shaken in my entire life, not since that day.

I know your sins, Demon Slayer, and, you will burn for them. The words echoing in my head made me look around frantically.. the demon's mouth hadn't moved, and the Priestess looked unfazed. The demon spoke directly to my mind. How could we ever tame a creature that was capable of that?

***

The dinner hall was filled with several younger Demon Slayers and Priestesses. Every one of them was younger than Jazzera and me. As they ate their bowls of goat stew, they filled the halls with questions about the demon and the battle we had to fight to capture him.

It wasn't long into dinner before Dagon—Jazzera informed me of his name after leaving the stalls—began his vile and perverted conversations. Most of the Priestesses left the hall of their own free will, deciding that going hungry was better than listening to the creature's filth.

"Stop with your filth!" yelled Jazzera as she stood, slamming her fists onto the table.

"Turn yourself into a raven! I command you."

Dagon narrowed his eyes at her but complied, perching on the chair he had been sitting on. He cawed loudly in annoyance but jumped to the table and began pecking at his plate of raw goat leg.

We sat silently for ten minutes until the large dining hall door swung open, and the High Priest strode inside. As a whole, we got up from our seats to bow. Dagon took flight.. cawing wildly, he swooped onto the Priest, pecking his face until the old man fell to the ground.

Instinctively, I rushed over to help the old man. Grabbing the bird by his wings, I pulled him off, but that didn't stop the demon from pecking me.

"Dagon, stop!" shouted Jazzera. Her voice was filled with panic. "Sit on the chair and don't move! I order you!"

The bird went limp, and I tossed it, letting it fly. The creature perched itself on the chair, staring down at the Priest and cawing repeatedly. It sounded like the bird was laughing rather than making random sounds.

Jazzera and I helped the old man to his feet. His face was scratched, and blood dripped from every wound. He pushed us both away and glared at Jazz, opening his mouth to say something but was cut off by the eerie floating demon voice.

"Be careful, Priest. If you kill her, I'll be set free, and, I will pluck out your eyeballs and eat them whole if you harm her. Then I will eat your tongue so you can't scream while I disembowel you and devour your insides."

The Priest closed his mouth and shrunk back.

"She's a witch!" accused one of the younger Priestesses from the table.

I glared at her, willing her to keep her mouth closed.

Dagon spoke again, focusing his three eyes on the young girl. "A witch, you say? What on Earth would give you that idea, little Priestess?"

The girl swallowed hard and said, "Why else would you protect her from the Priest. Any punishment the Priest hands out is sanctioned by God."

The raven cackled. "My dear, sweet child. The Holy Spell that binds me to this woman forces me to protect her. Even from the hand of your Priest. So, if I am forced to kill this Priest because he harms my Priestess, isn't it God's will?"

There was an awkward silence in the room. Even the Priest remained quiet, not offering any words to contradict the demon. I wasn't sure if it was because the monster was right or if the Priest was taking the demon's threats seriously.

"May I use the dove cage, your Holiness?" I requested, trying to get everyone out of this tense situation.

The old man's head bobbed tersely.

Addressing Jazzera, I murmured, "We will keep him in there overnight."

She hummed an agreement, and we rushed out of the dining hall to the dove cages just outside the horse's stalls. It took little effort to move a few doves out and place Dagon inside.

"We shouldn't leave him out here." Jazzera reached for the cage.

I grabbed the handle first. "As a Demon Slayer, I would feel more comfortable if he stayed in my quarters tonight."

"But he can't hurt me." The worry in her voice was evident. I knew she didn't want any more harm to come to anyone else because of her demon. However, I was also all too aware that Dagon could get into people's heads. The last place he needed to be was in her mind, planting some evil seed in her subconscious as she slept.

"I would feel better if he spent the night with me until he becomes more obedient."

She frowned but agreed. "You will not leave this cage until I come and get you in the morning. I command it," she stated firmly to the bird.

He said nothing, not even a rebellious raven "caw" in response.

I escorted Jazzera to the Priestesses' residential building to the left of the grand temple. It would be improper for me to accompany her to her room, so I left with a quick bow and went to my room. I shut the door quickly behind me, placing the cage on the floor in the corner as far from the bed as possible.

Usually, demons were dismissed to Hell and summoned by their Priestess when their assistance was needed. Jazzera knew how to banish them.. I had witnessed her expel several imps and shadow dwellers ever since she could use her power, but since she had never captured a demon, she didn't know how to recall one.. she hadn't been taught that trick yet.

I had never seen a demon like Dagon before. I thought Priestess Ester had control of the most powerful monster, but even that creature, with its immense size and power, couldn't get into people's heads, and it couldn't toss its voice around like an echo. If this demon were to remain in the stables, what could Dagon tempt some of the younger people to do?

That was the reason he had to come with me. I had already witnessed what he was capable of with his visions, and, I was confident that I had the willpower to resist any temptation he would send my way.

I began taking off my armor, polishing the emerald, green plates. There were specific colors for every official member of the Followers of the Horsemen, and Demon Slayers wore green. I had worn it honorably since I became an official Demon Slayer at fifteen.

I slipped into a thin, white night shirt and pants and crawled into bed. Rest didn't come easy to me.. I couldn't get the vision of the blond man out of my head. The crowd's screams echoed in my ears.

When sleep refused to come, I tossed the blanket off my body and walked to the door.

The demon sat still with all three eyes closed, its breathing soft. Ignoring it, I went out into the hall. I heard chanting in the distance, and out of curiosity, I followed them. Pushing the main doors of the building open, I could hear the screams. *Sinner! Sodomite! Deplorable!* A wave of horror washed over me as the same scene from before unfolded once more. Demon Slayers and Priestesses gathered together, chanting and spitting while guards escorted a naked, blond man to the gallows.

Grabbing the doors' metal handles, I slammed them closed, causing a loud echo to ring throughout the empty halls.

"I'm dreaming. I must be dreaming."

"Are you, though?"

I whirled around to see Dagon in his human form. "The Priestess told you to stay in your cage, Demon!"

"But you want me to stay here, don't you, Demon Slayer?"

I swallowed hard and forced myself to look at him. He stood with a sly smile, letting his long black jacket fall to the floor and slowly pulled the shirt from his body. As much as I wanted to, I couldn't look away. This creature mesmerized me. He was the embodiment of evil but beautiful at the same time. His pale white skin seemed to shine in the flickering candlelight.

My fingers itched to run through the tiny patch of chest hair between his two perfectly shaped pecks and down the outline of his chiseled yet slender frame.

Pulling the string on his pants, he let them fall. My eyes were drawn to his hanging cock, large and hard.

"Do you like it? I can make it any size you like." He grinned. "Perks of being me."

Dagon disappeared, reappearing directly behind me. His nose ran gently along the back of my neck, and his hands reached down into my pants. I gasped as his hand squeezed gently around my member, giving it a few strokes. My body went rigid as he circled me. His lips gently skimmed along my jawline, his stubble tickling my smooth skin. My breath caught as he bit down on my lower lip, giving it a gentle tug.

"Come on, Ermek. Don't act like you don't like this," he whispered soothingly.

My eyes finally shifted to his. "I don't want to do this," I responded, though we both knew that was a lie. My throbbing cock and pounding heart gave me away.

"Yes, you do." He forced my pants down, exposing me. "That gigantic shlong of yours is saying otherwise." He got to his knees, the tip of his nose only centimeters away from the end of my manhood. His face ran along it, then suddenly looked up.

"Though I do have to know. Did Lazlo suck you before he fucked your brains out or what?"

I woke with a start. The sheets of the bed were soaked in sweat. My cock was painfully erect, begging to have the tension released. It was a dream. Nothing more than a dream. I searched the room for the raven, expecting him to have escaped. Expecting him to be staring down at me, bewitching me. I was disappointed when I found him in his cage, sound asleep. Was it him who made me dream that, or was it my own sick lust?

Jazzera

Chapter 4

I hated the idea of leaving Dagon alone with Ermek. I captured him.. he was my responsibility. With the spell I cast on him, Dagon wasn't allowed to harm me. There wasn't much I could do about the situation, so I decided now was as good a time as any to get some shut-eye. I was desperately tired from the events of today, and, now that I was near my bed, every mark on my body throbbed.

Pulling myself out of my robes, I tossed them recklessly aside. I pulled on a long, white nightgown and blew out the candles. Carefully, I crawled under my blanket, making a conscious effort not to scrape my wounds on the scratchy sheets. I yawned heavily and closed my eyes.

The feeling of something touching my leg woke me from my sleep. Alarmed, I pulled the pale blue blanket from my bed to catch the intruder who made its way into my room. I expected to see a rat crawling up my leg, but the reality was far worse.

33

"I told you to stay in the cage!" I exclaimed at Dagon as I kicked at him, almost hitting him in the face. He dodged my kick easily and slid his body on top of me. The worst part was that he was completely naked.

"Get off me!" His hand covered my mouth, cutting off the rest of my shout.

"You don't want me to leave, do you, Priestess?"

I opened my mouth to respond but stopped as his hand ran between my legs. My back arched, and my breathing became shallow as his finger moved in a circular motion over my clit.

Sitting up, he grabbed my nightgown, pulling it open to expose my bare breasts. I wanted to cover up, but I seemed to be frozen in place. I was under this demon, fully exposed.

"Roll over," he urged as he moved his arm to give me a little nudge.

Reluctant, I did as requested, thankful to have my breasts covered. Panic filled my mind as he tugged at my panties, exposing my body's lower half. He lifted and arranged my body so that I sat on my knees. Part of my soul screamed for him to stop, while the other part begged him to keep going. I felt him rub himself between my cheeks, hard and warm. My body begged him to put it inside me, but he only rubbed on me. Up and down.

"Are you ready, Priestess?"

I couldn't respond.. my mouth opened in a silent gasp. I just sat in that position, head nearly buried in the pillow. Abruptly, I felt his hand slap down hard on my burn, and I screamed in agony.

The pain startled me awake.. tears welled in my eyes, and I wiped them away. I looked around my room, and Dagon wasn't there. My clothes were never touched. As I sat there, I realized my burns didn't hurt.

I pulled out a candle from my nightstand and lit it. I undressed and walked to my mirror to look at my back. My burn was healed.. there were no scars, and both crosses were gone. My question now was, why would a demon heal me?

DAGON

CHAPTER 5

T he humans took far too long to get me out of that pitiful cage. When they finally did, I remained perched upon the Priestess' shoulder like a good little demon. Internally, I pictured all the horrible things I would do to them if given a chance. Neither of them mentioned the events of the night before, and I was sure they were questioning whether or not it was their own dream or something I conjured up. In the depths of her heart, the Priestess had no desire to be a humble servant. She longed for the adventures that could come with being a Priestess yet yearned to be in the arms of a man.

The Demon Slayer was the same. He would much rather be in the arms of a man than fight demons next to a woman he was forced to protect. Even as a demon, I knew it was human nature to love and be loved. Denying that to anyone was asking for disaster, and disaster is what I would bring. If I aligned the pieces just right, I could bang both of their brains out, expose them as dirty little sinners, and have them executed. I would have my freedom by next week, and, finally, for shits and giggles, I may end up eating every pathetic little human in this silly little temple.

When we reached the dining hall, Jazzera commanded me to transform into my human form. I had half a mind to change back naked but decided against it. If I wanted my plan to work, I needed to stop being a pain in the ass. I had to walk a fine line. The duet would become suspicious if I didn't act up a little, but if I acted out too much, this little demon was stuck to only getting laid in dreams, and, this little demon hadn't had a piece of ass in weeks. This little demon was horny.

I took my seat, and a woman dressed in black placed a plate in front of me. I got a giggle out of the silly dress code this newest religion forced people into. This poor woman had been outspoken one too many times and lost her tongue. As further punishment, she was stuck serving men in a temple. She set a glass of water in front of me, and I looked down at the food in dissatisfaction. Two eggs and some goat sausage.

"God, I miss bacon," I remarked, picking at the runny eggs with my fork.

There was silence around the room, and I looked up to see every person at the table gawking at me. I remembered then, according to them, eating pork was a sin worthy of death. Or at least deserving of spending hours in a room, praying to become clean.

At this point, I would joke about wearing mixed fabrics, but it seemed every single person was wearing cotton. God damn, I missed how humans behaved before they remembered that demons were real. They were so much more fun back then. Even thousands of years ago, when humans had worshiped angels and demons as gods, they were still entertaining. For centuries, I longed to come back to the mortal realm. I would have partied hard. Picked up some hookers, snorted some coke, and danced the night away, but of course, the asshat lesser demons had to ruin everything. Once they spewed out of Hell and began murdering the human survivors, things changed quickly. Leave it to humans to start murdering innocents and controlling people in the name of God as soon as they realize Hell is real. The harsh reality is that this entire situation would have never happened if they had just done the opposite.

I wanted to enlighten the humans and explain to them that God couldn't care less which animal you ate. A big part of Leviticus was written by a raging lunatic. The other half was written by a man who despised my brother, but I knew they wouldn't believe me, so there was no point in correcting them. Humans automatically thought every word from a demon's lips was a lie. Even though, in reality, demons hardly ever lied.

Shortly after breakfast, the rather large, old Priestess hobbled into the dining hall. "Now is as good a time as any, Jazzera. Prepare your demon."

Raising my eyebrows, I gave them both a confused look. What sort of shenanigans were they up to now? Curious, I followed Jazzera and the old woman to the courtyard. A crowd was gathering, which made me think there would be a show put on, and I was the main attraction.

I stood in the center of the crowd, arms crossed, awaiting instructions. This charade was so far beneath me that it was beginning to make me sick. If it weren't for the stupid spell wrapped around my neck, I would turn into a dinosaur and bite off both of their heads.

The show began when the fat, old Priestess opened a small red portal. A grotesque creature, a glutton demon from the looks of it, crept out. It was tall, maybe ten feet or so, with a large belly that almost dragged on the ground. Its skin was lumpy, reminiscent of vomit. The demon's fat cheeks forced a toothy grin, but the more dangerous smile came from the demon's stomach. The belly opened to reveal a long tongue and giant, sharp teeth.

"Lord Dagon." The creature bowed.

"Let's get this over with." I manifested my trident even though I honestly didn't need it. I could tear this demon apart with my bare hands, but I figured it may be best to put on a show.

"Lord Dagon, you have been captured?" The demon sounded considerably less afraid.

"You are not worthy to be a Demon Lord.. you have become weak to allow yourself to be captured by humans."

"Says the fat ass who got captured by the other fat ass. At least my Priestess is hot."

Jazzera shot me a glare, her narrow eyes filled with aggravation. I blew her a quick kiss, then turned back to the demon in front of me. Before I could block his attack, the beast's stomach tongue wrapped around me and yanked me into the enormous, grotesque mouth. It slammed shut, teeth locking together.

The inside of the demon's gut was vile. It smelled worse than rotten fish mixed with pig shit and set out in the sun for days. The acid in its stomach gurgled and rose, trying to digest me alive. I moved my arms around blindly, trying to feel the mouth of the stomach.. I could stick my trident between its teeth and pry it open.

The fact that this demon actually thought it could digest me was laughable. Lesser demons can't kill a Demon Lord.. the acid in its stomach wouldn't even burn me. I would simply sit in here, constipating the creature until it eventually shit me out, and, that was not how I planned on exiting.

The smell was becoming increasingly overwhelming by the minute, and I couldn't stand being in there any longer. The only problem was that I dropped my trident. The beast's stomach gurgled, releasing a toxic gas cloud that filled my nostrils.

"That's it." I gritted my teeth as I forced my hand through the creature's flesh. There was a squeal of pain, and it danced around franticly, causing stomach juices to slosh around and get into my eyes. With my other hand, I ripped at the hole until I finally came spilling out of the beast's belly. Acid gushed out of the beast's stomach and ate at the stone beneath my body.

After taking several deep breaths, I got to my feet. The demon wobbled, and its belly tongue thrashed toward me again. It missed the first try. On its second attempt, I caught the tip in my fist, pulling with all my might. The creature pulled itself backward. Caught in a vicious game of tug-o-war, I planned on being the victor.

With one final powerful tug, the tongue popped loose from the creature, releasing a fountain of green blood and stomach acid that drenched me. The demon groaned and fell lifeless on the ground. Wiping my eyes, I walked over to the body and fished out my trident, plunging the sharp spearheads into the small head of the beast. As I pulled the trident from its skull, the demon trembled and slowly reduced to ash that floated away in the morning breeze.

With my fists clenched, I turned to Jazzera and the old woman. "I don't care whose dick I have to suck. Or even if I have to eat the old woman's pussy. I need a fucking bath, and I need it now!"

JAZZERA

CHAPTER 6

Whence Dagon was first swallowed alive, I
began to worry. Perhaps this so-called
Demon Lord was not as mighty as he
claimed to be. I held my tongue, though, when he
freed himself with his bare hands. With the battle
over, I worried that I might get into trouble. Dagon
was only meant to injure the creature, not kill it. If a
lesser demon died in the mortal realm, there was no
coming back. They ceased to exist instead of being
sent back to Hell. They were simply gone.

I wanted to be mad at Dagon for rudely
demanding a bath, but once I saw him completely
covered in slime, I couldn't help but laugh. Two
guards and a Demon Slayer escorted him to the
bathhouse. Even though he belonged to me, I wasn't
allowed to attend because he paraded around in his
human form. Had he taken the form of any other
creature, there wouldn't be a problem.

The men were afraid he would rape me, but I
doubted that would ever be an issue. I couldn't put
my finger on it, but it seemed like he would gain

more pleasure if I willingly fornicated with him. As if I were some trophy to be won instead of stolen. As I stood waiting at the entrance of the bathhouse, Lady Ester approached me.

"I no longer have a demon," she sighed heavily.

I gripped the sleeve of her robes tightly. "Please forgive me! I didn't realize he would kill it. I don't even know if he knew he wasn't supposed to."

Lady Ester patted my arm. "It's alright, child. I am too old to go and capture another demon, which means I need a successor. By the next full moon, you will become the High Priestess of this temple, and that means you and Dagon will have a lot of training to complete."

I couldn't keep the smile off my face. The role of High Priestess came with so many privileges, more than any woman could ever dream of. I would be allowed to read, and men were not allowed to strike me. There would be no more whippings and no more brandings, and, even the High Priest would have to listen to what I say.

I was about to embrace her when Dagon emerged from the bathhouse, freshly clean with his long black hair pulled neatly back into a ponytail. His clothing remained relatively the same.. however, his jacket's lining was now bright orange instead of red.

"We have company, Priestess," he announced, nodding to the courtyard's entrance.

I squinted my eyes as I tried to see past the rising sunlight—a group of horses carrying men with shining white armor came into view. Pulling up the group's rear was a single man in golden armor, a Holy Knight. One of four men at the very top of the Followers of the Horsemen and one of the holiest men to ever walk the Earth. Hand-picked by the Prophet to carry on God's great work and save humanity.

In unison, the horses galloped down the path until they surrounded our small group.

"This is the girl?" the Holy Knight inquired.

Cocking my head slightly to the side, I looked to Lady Ester for answers.

"Your Eminence. Forgive me, but I know not of what you speak," Lady Ester replied with a bow.

"The girl with the large angelic mark."

Lady Ester turned to me. "This is the Priestess, Jazzera Fukumoto."

"My mother said it means 'blessed origin' in her native tongue," I confessed bashfully.

"And where would that native land be?"

"I barely remember my mother..." I started. It wasn't a lie. I remembered very few things about her.. digging a bee stinger out of my foot as a child, pretending to eat my mud pies, and of course, when I had almost killed her.

"Japan," answered Lady Ester when it looked as if the Knight was growing impatient.

"No doubt that sword of yours once belonged to your father?" he inquired.

I nodded shyly. Even though I didn't know my father, I recalled my mother telling me that this particular sword belonged to him.

After a few moments, the temple's High Priest came waddling up. His face was covered in bandages from Dagon's attack, and I winced at the sight of them, remembering that he could still beat me for it at any time.

"Your Eminence, what an honor to see you in our humble temple. For what do we owe the pleasure of your visit?"

The Holy Knight glanced down at the old Priest from his horse. "We require this Priestess to clear out a demon in a neighboring town."

The High Priest eyeballed me for a moment, then turned his attention back to the Holy Horseman. "But your Grace, Lady Jazzera, cannot leave this temple."

"She is the one with the large angelic mark, is she not?" The Knight's face twisted with disapproval.

"Yes, but—" The Priest was cut off by the Knight's dismissive hand.

"Then she will leave with her Slayer and demon and clear the town of this abomination."

Lady Ester spoke up, "There are many skilled Demon Slayers that reside at this temple. Perhaps we could send a few to clear out the pest?"

The Knight scowled. "Are you questioning me, Priestess?"

Lady Ester took a step forward. "Indeed, I am."

Before anyone could react, the Knight swung at the old woman with his metal gloves, knocking her off her feet. The sound of metal hitting flesh made me recoil. Men were not supposed to strike the High Priestess, but then again, this was no ordinary man.

"Your grace, if I may," the High Priest sheepishly stuttered. The Knight glared at him. The Priest continued, "If this temple should be attacked, we will need Lady Jazzera and her demon."

"Did your High Priestess not just say there were several capable Demon Slayers? I will also stay behind to help protect this temple. After all, we all

45

know what is at stake here, but this particular demon will require a mighty Priestess. She is to leave with her Slayer and demon immediately." He looked down at Lady Ester, who struggled to get back on her feet. "Prepare the Priestess for her journey and send her on her way. The journey will take about a day and a half. Make sure she has what she needs."

Before I could process what was happening, Lady Ester hurriedly escorted me to my chambers. Leaving Dagon outside, she locked the door behind us and whispered, "I don't like this. How did the Knight know who you are?"

I shrugged, not knowing the answer. "Maybe word has spread? I am the only person who looks like me. From Japan, isn't that what you said? I sort of stand out. Every other Priestess is either pale skin with light hair or brown skin with dark hair."

She furrowed her brows. "You are not the only Priestess of Asian descent, Jazzera, and you are not the only girl with a mark that large. You just have the largest mark in this area, and he, of all people, should know why you are here and why it is important that you stay here."

"And why is it so important for me to stay here? I don't understand. What is my purpose here?"

Lady Ester shook her head dejectedly and pulled a fresh robe from my dresser. "As I've said, I dare not speak of it with your demon so close by. We'd be lucky if he doesn't already know why you are here, but if he doesn't, then he is the last being on this planet that should know."

Letting out an aggravated grunt, I sat heavily down on my bed. What was so important about me? Yes, I was aware that I had an unusually large angelic mark, but according to the Head Priestess, there were others like me. I was also trained as a Demon Slayer, unlike any other Priestess before me, but what did that have to do with me staying at this particular temple?

It took less than ten minutes for the High Priestess to pack up the clothing I would need for the journey. We went to the kitchen next to gather a sack full of bread and water as provisions. With our tasks complete, she practically dragged me out into the courtyard, where two horses were waiting for Ermek and me.

"I don't get a horse?" asked Dagon as he strolled over to the steeds.

"No horse in their right mind would let a demon ride it," stated Ermek as he mounted a solid white horse.

Dagon laughed and walked over to the remaining brown mare. He patted her gently on the snout, walked to her side, and mounted her. The horse didn't so much as let out a whinny.

"Only humans are afraid of me and, other demons, of course."

The shocked look on Ermek's face only caused Dagon to smile as he fiddled with the horse's mane. I was going to give him no such satisfaction.

"Turn into a raven, and you can ride on my shoulder," I instructed passively, waiting for him to dismount so I could climb up.

Dagon groaned but did as he was told. His transformation spooked the horse slightly, causing it to do a small dance, but it settled down quickly. Stroking the creature gently, I walked around and climbed into the saddle. When Dagon perched quietly on my shoulder, I gave the horse a little kick at her side, and we were off.

We took the road created by the ancients. Had it not been for frequent horse travel, the remanence of their old stone highways would have been completely hidden. From what I had learned, the stone that created the road was man-made and not meant to hold up very long throughout the years. This made me often wonder what the point was if they constantly had to repair it.

"Too bad cars don't work anymore," lamented Dagon.

I hated how his voice seemed to come from nowhere when he was in animal form. I glanced at a metal frame as we passed it. It was nothing more than an old, rusted frame with weeds growing through it. I knew nothing about it but had always been told that contraptions like these caused the Rapture. Humans and their technology had pulled away from God, making men do things they were never meant to do. There were rumors that our ancestors could even fly in large metal boxes.

"Those contraptions are the Devil's playthings," I declared matter-of-factly.

Dagon cawed in a way that made me feel like he was laughing at my comment. "With one of those contraptions, we would be at this village in a matter of hours, not days."

"Those objects are what sent the human race straight to Hell!"

Again, Dagon chuckle-cawed. "Yes, of course, Priestess. It was all the car's fault, and God forbid humans take responsibility for their own actions. By all means, let's blame the inanimate objects."

I refused to debate with him. Everyone knew that demons lied.. It was their job to tempt humans so that they could become a soldier in Lucifer's army.

It was up to me to fight the demons and return them to Hell, where they belonged.

Several hours passed without a word, and not even Dagon spoke. It wasn't until we smelled the putrid fragrance of death that Dagon finally perked up. I anxiously scanned the terrain, expecting to find some sort of demon.. A foul smell sometimes accompanies them.

However, I wasn't sensing a demon's presence. It wasn't until we reached the top of the hill that I could see where the smell was coming from.

Two men were nailed to crosses standing up on the side of the road. They were long dead, bodies bloated and decomposing.. animals had already begun picking at their corpses. Fixed to the top of the crosses were signs with a single word written on them.

"What do they say?" I questioned Ermek.

He winced as he looked at the bodies. "Sodomites."

"In other words, they liked man-on-man butt sex," voiced Dagon with a chuckle.

I looked away. "Serves them right."

"You know, I've often wondered if God didn't want men to have sex with each other, why did he put the man's G spot in his ass?"

"I have no idea what you're talking about," I stonewalled, refusing to look in his direction.

"You don't know what a G spot is? You poor, poor woman."

A loud howl broke through the air. It sounded like a wolf's cry, but so loud it shook the ground. The horses reared back, kicking their front legs in the air. It took a moment, but Ermek and I eventually got the creatures to calm down. I pulled my sword blade from its sheath, ready to strike at whatever beast was about to attack. Ermek already had an arrow nocked and ready.

The forest trees trembled and fell, revealing an enormous beast taller than most houses. It resembled a dog that was missing its fur and skin, exposing raw muscle and tendons. The teeth of the creature were as long as one of my arms.

Ermek pulled his bowstring back and was about to let loose his arrow when Dagon flew from my shoulder and snatched it in his mouth. He landed on the ground a few feet from Ermek and changed back into his human form.

"Don't kill it," he urged.

Ermek ignored him and pulled another arrow from his quiver. "It's a demon!"

"It's a hellhound. It won't hurt you if you don't attack it. There is no point in getting into a fight with this thing."

I didn't know if I could trust him. It was very likely that Dagon was setting us up for some type of trap. I wanted to tell Ermek to shoot the creature, but some part of my brain told me to listen to the demon.

"We can't have it roaming around just to eat the next traveler that passes by."

Dagon shook his head but kept his black eyes on Ermek. "It won't. Not if they leave it alone.. it has no use for humans."

"Then what does it want?" Ermek lowered his weapon.

Dagon walked up to the giant beast, and it laid down, letting him scratch it under its insanely prominent chin.

"You're a good boy, aren't you? You're just doing your job like a good hellhound."

Patting the creature on its gigantic neck, Dagon turned back to Ermek. "Hellhounds were one of the first demons created after Hell was made. Their only purpose is to track down damned souls that managed to escape. Your ancestors called those spirits poltergeists. The hellhound would track the soul and drag it back to Hell. With the Gates open, several damned souls have managed to snake their way out of their prisons." He turned back to the hound, petting it. "Sorry, Buddy. You have about five hundred more years of this endless struggle until you can go home for good."

I didn't know how to feel about the scene unfolding before me. Dagon showed compassion to this creature, the same kindness he had offered the horses, and, even seemed to care about their well-being.

Ermek murmured in a hushed tone, "I don't trust this, Jazz."

I looked at him briefly, then back to the beast. "Do you really want to get into a fight with that thing?"

Ermek was a skilled fighter, but he had barely left my side since he was assigned my Demon Slayer. If I had never seen a creature this large, I knew that Ermek hadn't either.

"If you're sure it won't harm anything, I suggest we be on our way. We only have a few hours of sunlight left."

Dagon whispered something to the beast, and it sprinted off, over the road and through a large field until it disappeared into the forest on the other side.

JAZZERA

CHAPTER 7

We were lucky enough to find an old, crumbling building as the sun set on the horizon. It was undoubtedly a building created by the ancients. Two walls were gone, and the only trace of their existence were piles of bricks, slowly disintegrating into dust. The third wall was partially destroyed, but the fourth was fully intact. A piece of the upstairs flooring was still in place, connected to the relatively undamaged corner. We decided to use that as shelter in case it rained. The inside flooring was almost completely gone, and the foundation was cracked and withered away.

The darker it got, the colder it became. We knew that demons and monsters preferred the dark rather than the light. So, the idea of lighting a fire was a questionable decision. Would we draw unwanted attention or not? Still, even with the blanket and winter robe in my pack, I feared Ermek, and I might catch hypothermia.

"We should light a fire," I suggested through chattering teeth.

"I could keep you warm, Priestess," offered Dagon as he picked at his fingernails.

"A fire could draw the wrong kind of attention.. demons or bandits may attack," warned Ermek.

I shuddered and pulled the blanket tighter around myself. "Dagon could warn us if any danger were to approach."

Ermek scoffed. "You really trust that creature to do that for us? Remember Jazz, your death means his freedom."

"Can't argue with that logic," remarked Dagon, not even trying to stand up for himself.

"If I command him to warn us of danger, he has no choice."

"Then gather us some firewood, beast." Ermek glared at Dagon.

Dagon's black eyes narrowed, but he forced himself to his feet, gave a mocking bow, and wandered into the brush. After only a few minutes, Dagon returned with a rather large log and plopped it down close to our shelter.

"That's far too big. We need kindling."

Dagon lifted his hand, his black eyes became portals to Hell, glowing red and orange.

A small blaze erupted on his palm, hovering inches from his skin. He watched it dance before throwing it at the log, which instantly caught fire.

"Every single demon can call upon Hell's fire. It will burn the entire night, and it will get quite hot." He looked over at me. "In fact, it may get a little too hot, Priestess. You may want to reconsider letting me stick my dick in—" He chortled. "I mean cuddling."

"Why couldn't you have gotten an imp or shadow dweller? Maybe even one of the stronger demons, like the glutton? Why did you have to capture him?" complained Ermek as he pulled out a blanket to stretch out on.

I didn't respond, only stared into the fire. If this was the fire of Hell, I expected to see something within the flames, perhaps demons or even damned souls. Instead, the fire was peaceful and soothing. I saw Ermek unclasping his armor from the corner of my eye. He took it apart piece by piece until only his under armor remained. I don't know what material it was made out of, only that it was skintight. I bet I could see every line of his perfect body if I looked hard enough.

Dirty girl.

My eyes immediately flew from Ermek back to the fire.

Don't worry, Priestess. He can't hear me. Think all the dirty thoughts you want. It was Dagon's voice inside my head.

"I had no dirty thoughts," I whispered.

Come, come now, Priestess. There is no need for lies between us.. I saw you undressing him with your eyes.

"I did no such thing," I growled in a hushed tone.

Why wouldn't you? He's the perfect specimen. Look at his long-braided hair, dark silky skin, flawless full lips, and those honey-glazed eyes.

"Get out of my head."

"Did you say something, Jazz?" asked Ermek, now fluffing up his pack to use as a pillow.

"Nothing," I got to my feet and gathered my supplies. "I'm going to try and sleep." I paused at the corner of the ruin before addressing Dagon, "I command you to keep watch over us tonight.. you will wake us up at the first sign of danger."

I think he rolled his eyes as he sat down on the ground. I unrolled my blanket and laid down on top of it. Dagon wasn't joking when he said the fire would burn hot. I was ten feet away from the flames and felt no need to cover myself. Staring up at the decaying ceiling, I tried to keep my thoughts away from Ermek. The last thing I needed was for Dagon to continue trying to rile me up.

Instead, I thought about Lady Ester. What secret was she not telling me? What was so important about my staying at the temple? And if they were so worried about Dagon knowing the secret, why hadn't they told me sooner? Years ago, before I contemplated capturing a demon on my own?

Somewhere amid my thoughts, I must have fallen asleep. The cold woke me. Dagon had said the fire would burn all night, but the log was now nothing more than ash. Getting to my knees, I looked around our camp. Ermek's sleeping spot was empty, and Dagon was nowhere to be found. Cautiously, I got to my feet, sword in hand, ambled to the far side of the building. There was no sign of my companions.

A snapping twig caught my attention, and I spun around in surprise. In the tall grass beyond the building stood Ermek.. his golden eyes and smile were soft. Walking toward me, he tugged his shirt off his body, revealing his perfect masculine form.

"What are you doing?"

He put a finger to his lips. "Shh."

"Where is Dagon?"

"He will be along soon enough, I'm sure. For now, we are alone."

I stepped back, tripping on his blankets, and fell hard to the floor beneath me. Ermek got down to his knees, only inches away from my body, before leaning forward to press his lips firmly to mine. We lingered for a moment, trapped in a position I had yearned to be in since I was first partnered with him. I pushed my hand against his hard chest as he moved on top of me.

"We can't do this," I whispered. "It's forbidden."

"We are all alone, Jazz. Nobody can punish us," he cajoled, sitting upright and tugging at his pants.

"I'll lose my mark."

He smiled slyly. "Then I'll make sure that doesn't happen."

Ermek abruptly pushed my robes past my waist, exposing my lower half, and with a violent pull, he practically ripped my panties off.

My heart throbbed as he yanked my legs apart. I needed to stop him—I should stop him—but my body was aching to feel his touch. I felt his fingers pull me apart, and his tongue slid around my forbidden fruit. Sitting up on my elbows, I arched my back and moaned. As his tongue slid up and down, I felt one of his large fingers slip its way inside me. I gasped and clawed at the ground beneath me, barely able to take what he was doing to me. There was a strong tingling feeling deep within my belly. The more he licked, the more I felt like I was going to explode.

"Enjoying yourself, Priestess?"

I turned my head to see Dagon lying down next to me. My eyes widened, and I looked down at Ermek, buried deep between my thighs. I tried to speak, but my voice was stuck. The pressure that had been building up within me released, and I could feel myself pulsating around Ermeks fingers, which were still sliding in and out at a rapid pace.

"And *that*, Priestess, is *an orgasm*."

JAZZERA

CHAPTER 8

My eyes shot open. The sun was barely rising, and the fire was beginning to smolder. Ermek was on the far end of the building, sound asleep on his blanket. It was only a dream. I tried to force myself to my feet, but my knees felt like they would give out from under me.

"That must have been one hell of a wild dream," jibed Dagon, appearing practically out of nowhere and startling me so much that I almost fell backward.

"I don't remember it," I lied, pulling the blanket over me.

He chuckled. "I can smell an orgasm from a mile away. You were a naughty girl in your dreamland, weren't you?"

"Stay out of my dreams."

Dismissively, he said, "I have no idea what you're talking about, and it's perfectly normal for a human to have wet dreams every now and then. Perhaps your newfound freedom outside the temple grounds had unleashed the beast." I said nothing. "I could show you what it's really like, Priestess. I could show you pleasures you couldn't conjure up in your wildest dreams."

"I would never lay with a demon!" I snapped. "I would never lay with any man. I have been chosen to bear this mark, and as a chosen woman, I must remain pure."

Dagon plopped beside me. "You really fall for that shit?"

"It's not shit," I muttered.

"It is the biggest load of shit. Don't you think God has bigger things to worry about than who you fuck?" He laughed, then continued mockingly, "I'm God. I'm going to give women special powers to fight demons. If she has a dick shoved in her, I'm going to take that power away.. because fuck her. Those demons can stay on Earth."

"I've heard enough.. we need to be on our way. Now put the fire out." My words were like venom that struck him in the face, and he recoiled with narrowed eyes as if he were challenging me. After a moment, he gave up and walked to the fire. Holding his hand over the white smoke, what remained of the flames danced up and were absorbed into his skin.

"There." He walked away toward the horses.

DAGON

CHAPTER 9

I wanted nothing more than to eat these pathetic mortals. I could almost visualize myself turning into a dinosaur and swallowing them whole. No, no, I wouldn't swallow them. I would chew them up until they were nothing more than mush. Unfortunately, the spell that the Priestess had on me would let me do nothing of the sort, and, sadly, there were only two ways to break this wretched curse. The Priestess had to release me of her own free will or she had to die.

The problem was, I needed her alive. At least until my quest was completed. After that, I didn't give a shit about what happened to her or her companion. Keeping her alive would be a struggle, though. She seemed too eager to prove something.

Why such a tiny woman would ever think to take on a hellhound was beyond me. She lacked common sense, that was for sure. It seemed getting her hands on me had made her cocky. I was convinced I would be fighting more than I wanted to by the time I ended up at my destination.

I played the good, little captured demon and helped them ready the horses. I didn't even complain about not having my own.. I just sat atop my Priestess' shoulder and enjoyed the scenery.

The ride lasted several hours, and the sun was directly overhead when I spotted smoke.

When the humans finally caught on to what was happening, Jazzera forced the horse into a full-out gallop. Being unprepared for this sudden increase in speed, I lost my grip and flailed about in the air. As I hit the ground, I transformed into my normal body and stood there, watching in amusement as the horses got further away. If the humans wished to leave me behind, it would be on them if they were torn apart by demons. After all, I still had one other option for a powerful Priestess.

Stuffing my hands in my pockets, I sauntered toward the town. Around the halfway point, I felt a burning sensation around my neck, and my body suddenly pulled toward the Priestess. Not wanting to feel the discomfort for much longer, I transformed into the fastest land mammal and sprinted.. the difference between a regular cheetah and me was that I didn't run out of stamina.

There was nothing of particular interest when I reached the gates. A few of the old buildings were smoldering, but other than that, I sensed no other demons in the area. So why the Priestess demanded that I join them, I would never know. Transforming back, I took a closer look at my surroundings. The town was created before the Rapture. Aside from the ones that were currently burning, many old brick homes were still intact. The town's barrier wall was made up of many different miscellaneous things.

Most were old tractor and semi tires that wouldn't decay for years.

I walked toward the town center and spotted the Priestess on her knees, crying. That was when I finally noticed the bodies on the ground. There was hardly any blood to be found. Every single body looked as if it had been mummified. Their jaws hung open at an awkward angle, their eyes were hollow, and their cheeks were sunken. Looks of pure terror were permanently etched on their faces. Only one demon in Hell could cause this type of massacre and leave very little blood.

"We're too late," Jazzera sniffled, wiping away tears.

I shrugged. "Better luck next time."

"Could you at least act as if you have some compassion!" screamed Ermek.

Sarcastically, I replied, "Boo-hoo, they're all dead. Here's me playing the world's smallest violin." I rubbed my fingers together and chuckled.

Jazzera stood up and violently shoved me. To my surprise, I actually stumbled back. This little bitty thing was stronger than she looked.

"You should have already guessed that these people were long dead. If there was a demon here that required my strength and your power to defeat, these people didn't stand a chance. It was a wild goose chase."

Jazzera looked blankly out into the distance. As if a lightbulb suddenly turned on in her brain, she said, "He may be right." She looked at the Demon Slayer. "Lady Ester was right."

Ermek tilted his head to the side, clearly confused.

I crossed my arms and smiled slightly.. she was catching on.

"Before we left, Lady Ester said something about the Holy Knight was unsettling. How did he know who I was? And how did he know about Dagon? I had just captured him the day before. It took a day and a half to even get here on horseback. I had never seen that man a day in my life. How did he know me? Lady Ester and Priest Embrock insisted I shouldn't leave the temple grounds. They insisted that he, of all people, should know that, but he sent us anyway.

What if he was in league with this demon?"

It was clear on Ermek's face that he didn't like the idea that one of their faith's highest-ranking officials could be a traitor.

"You think they wanted us to leave the temple?"

Jazzera nodded and began running toward the horses. "I think our temple could be in danger!"

Ermek followed.

"We're running again?" I huffed.

"We must get to the temple! We have no time to waste!"

JAZZERA

CHAPTER 10

I pushed my horse as fast as she could go. I wanted to travel into the night, but Ermek insisted we make camp, his reasoning being that the horses could die of exhaustion. As much as I wanted to argue, I knew he was right. I wondered how many creatures Dagon could turn into. If I commanded him to turn into a horse, I could have him carry me the rest of the way, but then that would leave Ermek out in the wilderness alone.

We built our camp in a place Dagon called an 'airport.' It was filled with metal contraptions that he swore used to fly humans from place to place. They weren't metal boxes like I had been led to believe but more like large cylinders with wings. It was hard to picture them as they may have been two hundred years ago, given all the plant life growing through them. Most were nothing more than frames that made an adequate shelter for animals.

I stayed up as long as possible. I didn't want another dream like the one from the night before.. I didn't need that type of distraction. Besides, I couldn't get the picture of those poor people's bodies out of my mind. Thankfully, I couldn't remember having any dreams when I woke up. It seemed Dagon had taken the hint and decided to keep to himself. At least for the night, anyway.

Within ten minutes, we packed up our camp and got the horses ready for the rest of our trip home. At midday, I spotted the temple off in the distance.. white smoke billowed from behind the tall white walls. I kicked the mare in the side, and she took off in a dead run down the old, decrepit road.

Yanking the reigns, I forced the horse to stop just before the gates. The metal bars that kept the outside world from coming in were tossed aside, broken like toothpicks.. not a single guard was at their post. Sliding from the horse, I pulled my sword from its sheath and walked cautiously past the walls to the temple courtyard.

The sight awaiting me felt like a dagger plunged into my gut. Bodies were strewn about the perfectly manicured lawn. Some of them looked like the bodies from the previous town, while others were torn to pieces. The sight of such brutality caused my body to shake violently, and I almost dropped my sword. It took every ounce of willpower to stay standing.

These people were my friends, practically family, and, I couldn't find a single movement among the bodies. A hand on my shoulder caused me to jump. Ermek stood behind me, silent as a stone.. the look on his face was pure agony. He had helped train many of the young Demon Slayers that now lay at our feet.

The Priestesses, only distinguishable by their white and blue robes, were cut down while they tried to flee. Their bodies looked exactly like the victims of the other town. The Demon Slayers, however, were different. These poor young men were butchered, and dark blood stained the grass around their corpses. In most cases, they were missing limbs.. some were cut in half or decapitated. There was so much blood that I could barely see the green of their armor.

A glimmer of light caught my eye, and I turned to the gallows across the courtyard. The four knights that accompanied the High Knight were hanging from nooses, each missing limbs. I shuddered in shock and pulled away from Ermek to get a closer look. The Holy Knight was strapped to the whipping pole in the center of the platform. His limbs were torn off, and his lower jaw was missing, which allowed his tongue to hang awkwardly out. His golden armor was the only way I could identify him.

My heart wrenched when I noticed the body tied to the other side of the pole. His old, shriveled corpse was naked and exposed to the world, and buried in his chest was the cross he branded many women with. His sex organ was removed entirely, lying uselessly at his feet.

I couldn't keep my composure any longer, and the little I had eaten the night before came back up with a violent heave. I retched for several moments until I could finally stand. Despite my urgent longing to flee the temple, there was one body that I had to find, Lady Ester. I held on to a tiny sliver of hope that my old mentor was still alive.

Wiping my face, I went into the main temple.. Ermek followed me, but Dagon lingered somewhere out of sight. I didn't care. There was no demonic aura aside from his, anyway. Whatever demon had caused this massacre was long gone.

Inside the temple was more of the same. The male servants were all butchered, and the women seemed to have the life simply sucked out of them. The stench of death was stronger within the temple's walls, and I covered my nose and mouth in a vain attempt to ward off the smell. My eyes watered, but I blinked the tears away and continued my search.

Every room I checked was empty, and my last hope to find her was the library. Gripping my sword tightly, I went down the stairs with Ermek on my heels. I pushed the door open and gaped at the destruction.. books and scrolls were tossed to the floor, and a shelf at the end of the room was flung to the ground, exposing a door behind it. The metal door hung wide open, barely hanging onto its hinges. I hadn't even known that door existed. I stepped closer to investigate and stopped when I heard a groan on the floor.

The High Priestess lay beneath the toppled bookshelf. Fresh blood ran from her thin, pale lips, and her skin was as white as her robes.

"Lady Ester!" I cried, dropping down to my knees.

Ermek rushed forward and pulled at the bookcase, trying to lift it from her old, fragile body. She cried in pain as her body shifted. When the shelf was finally removed, I gripped her hand.

"Lady Ester," I murmured, barely audible.

Her soft, blue eyes shifted to mine, and for a moment, I thought I saw a hint of a smile. "You're here." Her voice was faint.

"What can I do?"

She swallowed, then coughed. "A woman possessed the Knight's body, and, a man with long, white hair and glowing green eyes. Find the key."

"What key?" I asked, squeezing her hand tighter. I wasn't sure how anyone could find anything in this mess, but if it would ease her mind, I would do my best to find it.

"The key..." She forced in a shallow breath. "The Key of Babylon."

I tried to ask a question, but she cut me off. "You must find the key.. the fate of humanity depends on it."

"Lady Ester, I don't know of any key. We must get you to bed, and then you can tell me about the key." My voice wavered.

"No!" she insisted, letting out another fit of coughs. "You must find the key. Dagon. Dagon knows. Ask Dagon about the key." Those were the last words to slip from her lips as she let out a long, rattling breath.

Tears welled in my eyes. I tried to fight them, but they flowed down my cheeks like a river. I sat on the floor, hopeless and lost, for a long time before Ermek coaxed me to my feet.

Wiping my face, I peeked over my shoulder one last time before returning to the courtyard.

"Dagon!" I roared, not seeing any trace of the demon.

He casually strolled up to the temple's steps, whistling a strange tune I didn't recognize.

He was acting all nonchalant, as if there weren't several dead bodies lying across the ground.. it made my blood boil. I wanted to slice his head from his shoulders.. I was furious at how relaxed and unaffected he was by the carnage, but I stopped myself when I remembered what he was. a demon born of Hell. He has no care for the loss of human lives. In fact, he and his kind were the cause of so many untimely deaths.

"May I help you?" he asked, running his fingers through his silky black hair.

"What do you know of the demons who attacked this place?" demanded Ermek.

Dagon shrugged. "Absolutely nothing.. I was with you the entire time. Remember?"

Ermek balled up his fists. "Lady Ester said that the Holy Knight had been possessed by a woman, and, that there was a man with green eyes and white hair. Tell me, Demon! I shall hunt them to the ends of the Earth for what they have done!"

Dagon smirked. "Good luck with that. In fact, please let me watch. I'll even bring some popcorn."

I had to stop Ermek from swinging at Dagon. "Who were they?"

Dagon looked around as if assessing his surroundings. "Well, judging from the... artwork. I'm going to guess that the woman was Lilith. She really doesn't like human men. She's sort of the poster child for feminism. Except that she doesn't hold picket signs.. she just tears their limbs off." He snickered at that and paused as if expecting us to laugh along with him. "Right, feminism was before your time. Anyway, only one being I know chooses to take the form of a man with ridiculously long, white hair and glowing green eyes, and, when I say ridiculous, I do mean *ridiculous*. It goes all the way down to their calves, and, then they wear all white. It clashes so badly."

"They? You mean it was more than just two demons?" I was so confused.

Dagon bobbed his head. "Sort of. The other demon that was here was Legion, a Soul Eater. You know all of those stories about the devil making deals and taking souls? Well, it wasn't Lucifer.. it was Legion, and, now that they are free to roam the Earth, they can eat any soul they want."

"Why do you keep referring to him as 'they?'" inquired Ermek.

"Because Legion is many. Millions of souls in one body. They may choose to walk around as a human man, but you will hear several voices at once when they speak. Men and women. They always refer to themselves as We, and, so, the proper pronoun is, in fact, *they*."

"What about the key?" I asked, but Dagon didn't respond. "The Key of Babylon!" He stayed tight-lipped. I felt rage build up inside me. How dare he be so dismissive? After all that has happened here, how dare he look so smug? "I command you! Tell me about the key!"

My skin burned as the angelic mark began to shine bright blue. The brand around Dagon's neck began to glow, but still no answer.. he only stared hatefully at me with those dead, black eyes. "Tell me now!" I shrieked.

Dagon's brand glowed brighter, and he fell to his knees, shouting in pain. He leaped to his feet and rushed at me, stopping only inches from my face. The look said it all.. he would kill me if he could. He would do to me what those other demons had done to the poor people of this temple, but the magical leash around his neck stopped him from doing so.

"Tell me."

Eventually, he backed off. "It's the key to the Gates of Hell."

"What does that mean?" Ermek probed.

"It's what the Priestess was protecting. The key was here the entire time, and her angelic powers kept it cloaked."

I gasped. That was why I was never allowed to leave the temple and why the Priest and Lady Ester begged the Knight to let me stay.

"If that's true, how did the demons know where it was?"

Dagon smirked. "Well, you're not some cliché chosen one, Priestess. However, very few women possess an angelic mark as large as yours. The bastards keep breeding your kind." He seemed to be rolling his eyes. "For two hundred years, the mortals managed to keep it hidden. Moving it from place to place, Priestess to Priestess, and, they kept your kind well hidden. It was always just out of our grasp, moved right before we could locate one of you, but this generation was smaller. More boys were born than girls in this batch. There were maybe five of you in total, and it just became a matter of elimination."

I was dumbfounded. I wanted to ask what he meant by "my kind." But that question could be answered at another time. I knew that if I let him, Dagon would stonewall the question for as long as possible. "So what about the key?"

Dagon huffed. "God promised the Demon Lords that we would be able to walk the mortal plain again when Hell was full. A side effect was that all the other demons got to come and play as well. No big deal, considering everyone left behind were shitty human beings bound for Hell anyway. Mostly politicians and rich, greedy bastards. He promised us seven hundred years, but that's a blink of an eye to a demon. It takes longer than that for a damned soul to become a demon. The key will keep the gates open. Long after those seven hundred years have passed."

Why would God ever allow such a thing to exist? And why would God ever strike a deal with demons? They were creatures of pure evil. I know the Lord works in mysterious ways, but I couldn't seem to piece this together. "Does the key work both ways?"

Dagon sneered at me. "I suppose."

Finally, there seemed to be a silver lining. "Then we will find that key and close the Gates of Hell.

DAGON

CHAPTER 11

"You done lost your ever-lovin' mind!" I declared, trying extra hard not to laugh. "Hard pass on that, my Lady." Her cheeks flushed, and her eyes narrowed. It was so adorable that I had to resist the urge to pinch her cheek. "I am not going to fight Legion."

"Are you afraid, Demon?" The Demon Slayer stepped toward me, crossing his arms in front of himself.

I nodded. "Yes, I am." Grinning, I took a step toward him as well. The last thing I needed was for this Slayer to think he held any power over me. "I would rather become a human and have my dick torn off daily in Hell than fight Legion."

"What is so terrifying about this Legion character?" interrogated Jazzera.

I rolled my eyes. "What part of Soul Eater, don't you understand? When you kill them, a normal demon ceases to exist. You can't kill a Demon Lord. I can't kill a Demon Lord. We can beat the shit out of each other and send the other back to where they

73

came from, but in the end, we can't kill each other. There are only two ways to kill a Demon Lord completely. The first is Azrael's scythe, the Angel of Death's weapon. If he cuts off a Demon Lord's head, they no longer exist and are gone forever. The second is Legion. If they get their hands on you, they absorb you into them. You become part of the hive mind that is the demon. You no longer think for yourself, and to me, that's the same as not existing."

Jazzera put her hands on her hips as if she were about to throw a temper tantrum like a child. "You will take us there!"

I turned away, unwilling to engage with her face-to-face. "And how exactly are you going to get there, Priestess?" I couldn't help but glance over my shoulder to see her reaction.. she was scowling.

"I don't know. You tell us."

I turned back to look at her fully. Her arms were crossed stubbornly across her chest, and I had to resist the urge to grin. She was playing right into my hand. No matter what I told her, she would still use the spell to force me to take her.

There were only two ways we could make it to Babylon these days. The first would be to make the jump between what used to be Alaska and Russia. We would have to travel through three countries and over the Bering Strait. That trip alone would take years before we reached the desert. The second way would be bringing them through Hell itself.

The first option put me in contact with at least three other Priestesses with the same power as hers. So, if my Priestess met an untimely death, I could pick up one of the other three. If I remembered correctly, we were now standing in West Texas, about fifty miles from what used to be El Paso. If we veered east a bit, we could make it to Kansas, where there was a woman named Evalyn with a mark that matched Jazzera's, but she could prove challenging to get my hands on. The other two would bring me far out of my way- one residing in Mississippi and the other at the far tip of Maine.

"Babylon is on the other side of the planet, well hidden in one of the largest deserts in the world. There aren't any ships we can take these days, not with the Leviathan roaming the depths. The only way we can get there is to travel north."

"Then let's get started."

"We need to bury the dead," voiced Ermek, placing a gentle hand on her shoulder.. she nodded in agreement. It made me cringe.

"Why? They're dead, and they don't care," I huffed. I hated humans and their stupid traditions. The worst part was that they would make me take care of it. I could make an excuse like, my being a demon would taint the soil, but I doubted they would fall for that.

"We can't just leave them.. it would be wrong."

She was fighting back the tears as she spoke, and I sighed. "I'm not lying to you, Priestess. They don't care what happens to their body.. they're gone. The best thing to do is to let them become part of the circle of life. Let the animals have them. It's nature's way."

Jazzera looked at the ground as if contemplating my words. "Can you use the fire?"

I looked around at the carnage and exhaled heavily. I could summon enough Hell's fire to light a log whenever I wanted and sometimes use it in battle, but to use enough fire to cremate all these bodies was a power I didn't possess at the moment. I would have to be in an all-out rage for that to happen, an uncontrollable fit of anger.

Clicking my tongue, I thought for a moment. "I don't have the power to summon that much fire. However, you seem to have been close to that old woman.. I can cremate her."

"And what about the Priest and the Holy Knight? At the very least, they deserve a proper burial," remarked the Demon Slayer.

I couldn't help but chuckle at his comment. "Oh, they are already burning. It might be rude to burn their bodies, like adding insult to injury." I couldn't help myself from breaking into a full-on laughing fit. "They have their own personal condo right on the Lake of Fire. You can't even imagine the things being shoved up their asses as we speak." My laughter abruptly stopped when I felt something slap against the side of my head. The Priestess had thrown her shoe at me. Straightening my face, I brushed the hair off my shoulder as if I hadn't felt the object. "I'm not lying. Legion didn't eat their souls.. they are now in Hell, where they belong."

"But they were holy men," protested Jazzera.

Shaking my head, I glanced at the gallows where the bodies swung, "They were cruel men, and many innocents were killed on their orders."

"They were righteous men! Anyone killed by their orders was—"

I cut Ermek off with a disparaging, "Was what? Sodomites? Men, who liked to suck cock?" He shut his mouth, as I knew he would. Then turned to the Priestess. "Women who liked to speak their minds? Or dared to read? God doesn't like it when wicked men use him as an excuse to harm others."

The Demon Slayer and Priestess backed down. I could feel their desire to protest. Since birth, they had strict rules drilled into their brains, and they were conditioned to believe that anything a so-called "holy man" said was the next best thing to God himself speaking.

Dismissively, I walked up the steps toward the main temple. When I was about halfway, I turned back and suggested, "You two may want to start packing.. it's going to be a very long journey."

I continued my excursion into the central part of the building. Time to get this part over with and begin the quest. The longer we stayed at this temple, the longer it would take me to get rid of these pests. I looked around at the chaos before heading to the library. It felt like a waste to use their books and scrolls for kindling until I spotted the *Malleus Maleficarum.* I looked over the cover, and it wasn't one of the originals. It was a copy, most likely made somewhere around the twentieth or twenty-first century. The book was roughly translated into English and described ways to interrogate, torture, and kill so-called witches. It was amazing how this little book was the cause of so much suffering, but then I could say the same thing about the Bible. That book was even worse.

Tossing the paper atrocity aside, I waded through the sea of hardcovers and paperbacks until I stood inches from the remains of the old High Priestess. I could almost see her entire life flutter before my eyes, and, what a waste it was. She had done everything the men had told her without question. She had taken several beatings and had never known the love of another. All for fear of burning in Hell.

Closing my eyes, I tried to picture the very core of Hell, where the fire burned the hottest.

I willed it to come to me, and a bright red flame danced beautifully above my palm. Without ceremony, I tossed it to the ground, igniting the books that covered the old woman. The fire spread instantly and engulfed the entire room. Part of me wanted to stay, to watch the ancient tomes burn, but if I ever wanted to be free within this century, I would have to get this journey started.

JAZZERA

CHAPTER 12

I packed as light as I could for our journey—a few articles of clothing and some blankets. The leaves on the trees were already beginning to change color, and winter wasn't too far off.

Warmer clothing would be needed, so most of my clothes were thicker. Ermek mentioned that he would get a couple of tents to sleep in, ensuring our travel would be more comfortable. The last thing I grabbed was my wet stone set to sharpen my sword. I had never used the set because the blade never lost its edge as if it had been forged by magic.

Giggling to myself, I shook the ridiculous thought away. Believing my sword was magical was blasphemous, but wasn't it also blasphemous to teach a woman how to wield a sword? I shoved the stones into the pack and headed to the courtyard.

A horrific sulfur smell flowed through the air as black smoke billowed from the main temple.. Dagon kept his word. Though I would have preferred the High Priestess be placed on a pyre so that her soul could properly be sent off, at least the others in the temple would find peace as well.

Ermek was already loading our horses. Sadly, one of the fires that had burned while we were gone destroyed the horses' stables. Without horses, the humans would have had to flee on foot, and, no human could outrun a demon.

My horse was packed with as much food and water as it could carry. Ermek attached my bags and the two tents to his horse. As we mounted, I spotted Dagon leaving the temple.

Naturally, the fire did not affect him. His long, black hair was perfect and flowing, and his jacket swayed slightly in the breeze. He looked almost majestic as he strode down the stairs.

After saying a quick prayer of farewell, we started our journey. Dagon instructed that we must travel north first, but I wished there was another way. I had heard stories about the northern half of the world. Heathens resided there, and monstrous men captured Priestesses to use their demons against my people. The war between the Heathens and the Followers of the Horsemen had been going on since before I was born. Though women were not told much about it, the impression I got of the north was that it resembled Sodom and Gomorrah. Cities filled with sinners destined to be put down by the hand of God.

I supposed going east wasn't much better. Aside from the Heathens and The Followers, one more faction remained on this land.. they called themselves The Descendants. From what I had been told, they were another civilization that resembled Sodom and Gomorrah. I heard tales that they had witches amongst their ranks that fornicated with demons and produced demonic offspring.

We passed many ruins on our travels, old remnants of the time before. Most of them were nothing more than the outer shell of the structure. Others were barely more than rubble. Many people were taken when the Rapture occurred, leaving homes empty. Those that remained eventually congregated together. The Followers had done their best to rebuild this world.

However, a few skeletons of the past remained, cheap structures of wood that decayed too quickly and metal that eventually rusted beyond repair. Modern homes were not as cheaply made as the homes of the ancients.. they were constructed from much stronger wood with stone and mortar.

We passed through a few modern-day villages on our travels. The people of the villages were kind.. most of them were happy to accommodate a Priestess and her Demon Slayer for the night in their homes. Dagon would typically turn himself into something more pleasing to the eye. Once, it was a dog that could easily be explained. Other times it was a smaller creature, such as a mouse, that could hide within our packs.

We were about two weeks into our journey when a massive pain in my midsection woke me. Tossing my blanket from my body, I got to my feet and felt something warm running down my leg.

"Shit," I whispered. Luckily, dawn was approaching. With the tent being a light cream color, it did very little to block the sun out, so I could see without the help of a lantern.

Frantically, I searched through my pack, knowing precisely what was happening, without needing to check my underwear. My monthly curse had started. Sighing heavily, I pulled out a bright red robe, the matching face scarf, and a blood rag to keep myself from making too much of a mess.

Typically, red was a forbidden color. The only people to wear it were Heathens, Descendants, and women who had started their cycle. For the most part, women would stay locked in their rooms until the bleeding stopped, but if they could not do so, they had to show the world they were living their curse by wearing red. I had no time to spend an entire week in my tent, and, thus, I would have to deal with the embarrassment of riding along the countryside in my red robes.

After changing into the new robe, I carefully tied the scarf around my face, covering my mouth. Women were not to speak while bleeding because they were unclean. The blood was the curse Eve brought upon mankind. Anyone she spoke to would also become unclean and have to spend the day praying, forgoing their duties.

Pushing the flaps of my tent open, I gazed around. There was a faint smell of smoke from the campfire, and a beautiful creek wound its way around tall evergreens. The clear, crisp water called to me as I gazed upon it. It would be cold, but it would be nice to take a bath. I always felt extra dirty when my cycle started. As silently as possible, I made my way around the campsite, ensuring that Dagon and Ermek were nowhere to be seen.

The water wasn't deep enough to submerge my entire body, but it would be enough to clean myself up. I pulled off the bottom half of my robes, buried my underwear, and quickly splashed water on myself. The cold water made me want to yelp, but I kept quiet, not wanting to draw attention. Confident I was as clean as possible, I dressed again and returned to the campsite.

"Breakfast is ready, Priestess."

Dagon was sitting on a fallen log, tending to some small animal he or Ermek captured.

My insides twisted. I wondered if I should ignore him and return to my tent. Ermek would understand if I wanted to take a day to get these vicious curse pains under control, but I would still need food. If this journey was going to be as long as Dagon claimed, I would need plenty of food to keep my strength up. I walked to the fire and sat on a log opposite Dagon. A moment later, Ermek came up from the creek carrying a bundle of edible reeds. He averted his eyes when he looked at me and laid the bundle down on the grass.

Dagon plucked one of the roasting critters from the fire and walked over to me. He silently handed me the cool end of the stick and returned to where he was sitting. We sat there for a long while in awkward silence. Ermek was doing his best not to even look in my direction, while only God himself could tell what Dagon was thinking.

When the critter was finally cool enough to handle, I pulled my scarf from my face and nibbled on the charred outer layer of the animal. Upon further inspection, I decided that it was a squirrel. All three of us ate in silence, and when the animal I was eating was no more than bones, I tossed them to the side and pulled my face scarf back up.

"So, what's with the scarf?" asked Dagon, finally breaking the silence.

I didn't respond. I didn't know what to do. Dagon was a demon, so did it really matter if I spoke to him?

He was already unclean, and I doubted that any amount of prayer would ever change that.

"This is getting creepy, even for me."

Ermek spoke up, "The lady is bleeding, and she is not to speak until her cycle has ended."

The cackle Dagon let out almost startled me to the point of falling off the log. "You're shitting me, right? She can't talk because she's on her period? For fuck's sake, men are stupid."

"Talking to the Priestess while she is suffering through Eve's curse will make the man who speaks to her unclean. They will have to spend a day in their hut praying to God to cleanse them."

Dagon laughed even louder. It took extreme willpower not to start screaming at him. It was bad enough that I had to embarrass myself by wearing these red robes, but it was another thing to have someone laugh at my misery.

I fought back the tears of humiliation and stomped back to my tent. Once inside, I tore the scarf from my face and practically fell onto my sleeping mat. Ever since I first got the curse, I had to deal with men ignoring my presence and scowling at me, treating me as if I were nothing more than a stray dog that they simply allowed to exist in their presence. I had hoped Ermek wouldn't treat me any differently when the curse came during this journey, but his words and the fact that he refused to even look at me felt cold.

A rustling caused me to stir. I hoped it was Ermek coming to soothe some of the tension, but instead, I was greeted by a demon.

Without an invitation, Dagon plopped down on the ground, crossing his legs. "So, this is real then?" I looked at him blankly, not understanding what he meant. "The unclean thing. You can't talk because you're bleeding?"

I nodded in response.

A grin slid across his handsome face. "This silent treatment is kind of weird. Talk to me all you want. Make me unclean. I love being dirty."

I rolled my eyes, knowing exactly where his mind was going when he said, "dirty." I had put up with his filthy mouth for so long that I understood his perverted sense of humor. "The Bible says that women should not interact with anyone while bleeding."

"The Bible says a lot of stupid things."

"I wouldn't expect a demon to understand," I grumbled, turning my back to him and lying down on my stomach.

"You're right.. a demon wouldn't understand. Because a demon knows that every woman, if healthy, has a period.. animals have periods. There is nothing sinful about nature."

I sighed heavily and tried to resist the urge to cry. I jumped when his hand rested on my lower back and tried to resist, but he swatted my hand away.

"You'll thank me later."

My body tensed, not liking that this demon was intimately touching me, but after a few moments, I began to relax. He was massaging my pain away, and heat radiated from his hand, driving it directly into my tense and cramping muscles. As much as I wanted to doze off while he was doing this, I couldn't help but wonder what his motive was. Why was he being kind to me?

First, he was kind enough to get up from his seat and bring me food.. that was not something any man at the temple would have done. Now he was soothing my pain.

"Why are you doing this?"

"What? Am I not allowed to do something nice?

"No. You're a demon.. why would you do something to be nice?"

"That is a common misconception about demons. I'm not a cruel being, Priestess."

"You're a demon. All of your kind is cruel."

He smirked, then shook his head. "I could have been an angel. I could be in Heaven right now, but I chose to be a demon, and I chose to go to Hell."

This statement caused me to sit up and look him straight in those black pools he had for eyes. "How?"

"When humans were given souls, they were allowed to go to Heaven, but seeing the cruel nature of man, God decided that not every mortal should be allowed to spend eternity in Paradise. Hell needed wardens, and, some angels chose to become those wardens. Just like now, we were allowed to roam the Earth, and so were angels, but eventually, God felt that we were influencing humans too much. So finally, he forced us to stay in either Heaven or Hell. We could walk the mortal plane, but only in spirit form."

"Then, why are you here if you chose to go to Hell?"

He sighed and laid down, propping his head on his hand. "Because Hell is a horrible place, filled with pain, fear, and sorrow. God took that away from us. He took away the ability to feel those things. God made us numb. Not only could we not feel pain and sorrow, but we also couldn't feel pleasure. We couldn't taste or smell anything. We lost all ability to feel. Sometimes, I would have given anything to feel the torture the souls were feeling. Feeling pain and agony is better than feeling numb for centuries. God didn't like that his volunteers weren't happy, but he didn't want to subject us to the torture the mortal souls were getting. So, he made us a promise. Hell could only hold so many souls, and the Gates would open when that quota was met, and, we could walk the Earth and feel once again."

I tried hard to see the lies in his eyes, but they were just pools of blackness, and I could see nothing but my own reflection. I tried to think back to the many demons I had encountered.

Many attacked on sight. Others, once captured, seemed to have lost their will. Not a single one had shown kindness to any mortal. The only exception was Dagon.

Suddenly, I was struck with a moral dilemma. Demons lie, and demons are tricksters. How could I ever believe a single word to snake its way across his lips?

"If demons aren't bad, why did they kill everyone at the temple?" I shuddered at the memory of all of those bodies. I was used to seeing death, but seeing the ones I cared for lying across the temple grounds was hard for me to keep suppressed.

Dagon shrugged. "I didn't say all demons were good. Those lesser demons, the ones that you Priestesses tend to catch. The ones that look like monsters. Those were once humans. With a few exceptions, of course, like the hell hounds, for example. The ones created to be wardens of Hell have very little use for harming humans, but the ones who were once humans lived evil lives, so why wouldn't they be evil demons?"

"You said the two that attacked were Demon Lords."

Smiling, Dagon twisted his jet-black hair between his fingers. "Being able to feel for all eternity is worth a few human sacrifices."

I laid back down, turning away from him. Nothing was worth taking all those innocent lives. "Leave," I demanded, refusing to look at him.

It took a few moments until I heard him get to his feet. "I want to show you something, Priestess."

Groaning loudly, I rolled over and glared at him. "I said leave."

"I only want you to be able to see things through my point of view."

I pushed myself to my feet and crossed my arms, glaring as I waited for him to explain.

Motioning to the tent's entrance, he held his hand out as if expecting me to take it.

Instead, I bent down and picked up my scarf.

"You don't need that," he insisted.

Reluctantly, I dropped the scarf and took his hand. It was warm and oddly soothing to me. With a grin, he led me through the tent flaps. We were no longer at our campsite. Instead, we were in some strange place surrounded by roses and torches. There were dark, wooden walls with a glass ceiling showing brightly shining stars. The fact that it was morning a few moments ago would have bothered me greatly until I saw the chains hanging from the ceiling, which bothered me more.

Dagon stopped walking and turned to me. His black eyes gave me a once-over, and he tutted. "This outfit won't do." He waved his hand over me, and my robes vanished. I was left standing practically naked before him. The undergarments I was left in weren't

88

even my own. The object that kept my breasts in place was not an undergarment wrap but a red, lacy object that cupped each breast separately using shoulder straps to hold them up. The underpants I had could barely be called underpants by any standard. They were cut very high, and I could feel the back side slowly creeping into my butt crack.

My first instinct was to cover up, but it seemed like my arms were content staying where they were. My right arm hung uselessly at my side, and my left was still attached to Dagon. As he guided us further into the room, I had to take shallow breaths. He stopped in the center of the room, and I started to hear the moans. I gazed around in amazement.. it was as if people had appeared out of nowhere. Several individuals were entangled with each other, panting and groaning.

The closest group was a woman on her knees and two men.. one stood behind her, thrusting his manhood deep inside her womanhood. The other stood before her, shoving his shaft deep into her throat. I quickly looked away, but people were doing unspeakable, lustful things everywhere I glanced. In one corner was a man sitting on top of another. The man on top moaned loudly with every rough thrust inside of him. In another corner was a group of women. One of them lay on the ground with her legs spread wide as another vigorously licked up her juices while yet another sucked on her hard nipples. Across from them, a woman had two men deep inside her, each filling a different hole. People were groaning, thrusting, and sucking on each other everywhere I looked.

My thighs rubbed together as I felt a tingle between my legs. A pulsing, throbbing feeling crept its way up into my stomach. Dagon turned to me, gripping both of my arms and raising them. Helplessly, I watched as chains lowered from the ceiling, wrapped themselves around my wrists, ankles, and thighs, and gently lifted me into the air. My crotch was now almost eye level with Dagon, yet he did nothing. He only smiled and took a step back. As I hung there, unable to move, one of the men in the room sauntered to me. The chains lowered me slightly, and my eyes widened as he got to his knees. He stuck his fingers beneath my underwear and tugged hard, causing the cloth to rip and fall apart. I was fully exposed to this strange man who kneeled before me.

Unhurriedly, he leaned forward and let his tongue slide up and down my slit. After a few licks, he pulled the lips apart and began sucking on my tiny jewel. An involuntary moan slipped from my lips and seemed to signal two nearby men. One man tugged at my upper garment, ripping it from my body. Each of them cupped a breast and began sucking on my diamond-hard nipples.

As the man below became more violent with his tongue thrashings, I felt a burning in the pit of my stomach, and my toes began to curl. My body tensed, and I began to thrash. It was as if I were hanging on the edge of a cliff and couldn't take it any longer. I needed a release. I needed to be set free.

"I think you have warmed her up enough," declared Dagon.

I had forgotten he was in the same room for a moment. As if on command, the three men left, and Dagon took a step closer. He was no longer wearing clothing. His perfectly sculpted body stood before me with no shame, and his manhood hung out hard and long. Gripping my thighs tightly, he stepped closer. I could feel the head of his monster touching the very edge of my hole.

Every fiber in my body told me to scream, to fight, but the throbbing in my bud begged him to give me the release it desired. I knew what this would mean.. I would burn in Hell. I would lose my mark and be useless to the world. Ermek may even turn me in, and I would be sentenced to death, but as I felt the beast linger around my opening, I realized that I didn't care. I needed it. I wanted it.

He must have read my mind because he pushed deep inside me. I had expected it to hurt, but there was nothing but pure, raw pleasure. My insides cradled him as he thrusted deeper.

His body slammed against mine. I wanted to feel and force him deeper inside. As if reading my mind, the chains lifted until my upper body was now only inches from him. Gradually the chains around my arms and legs unraveled, and I wrapped myself around Dagon. My nails dug deep into his flesh, and my legs wrapped tightly around his waist. He looked at me as he lifted my body up and down on top of his beast. For some unknown reason, I bit his lower lip, and he let his tongue slide out and lick my lips.

Tugging at his hair, I pushed myself onto him. His tongue found its way into my mouth, massaging my own, and, then it finally hit. I finally fell off the edge. I moaned loudly, unable to control myself as my lady bits pulsed uncontrollably around his thick member.

Dagon pressed his forehead against mine and whispered, "Open your eyes."

I blinked, and I was back in the tent, fully dressed in my red robes. Dagon stood before me, fully dressed without a single hair out of place. Pulling myself away from him, I tripped on my sleeping mat and fell to the ground.

"Fear not, Priestess. I never touched you."

My lips quivered as I tugged at my robe to see my mark. To my relief, it was still there. I looked at him. "What did you do to me?"

He grinned. "Nothing. That was all just a type of dream. You would have never let me do that in real life…Or would you?"

I glowered at him. "Never!"

He shrugged. "I wanted to show you what I had gone millennia without. Not feeling is bad enough, but not being able to feel pleasure is torture. Even if I did it in a person's subconscious, I could never feel it, only remember."

"I would have never…."

"I know. You wouldn't have sex with me in real life. Yeah. Yeah. In there, your mind has very little control. Your body controls you, and your body wanted a good dick down, but in that place, sadly, I can't feel it. I can make my dick hard and do whatever you want me to, but I'm left with very uncomfortable blue balls. So, excuse me, Priestess, while I go rub one off."

I blinked, dumbfounded, as he exited the tent. It was all a dream, and, according to him, a fantasy he couldn't even feel. I wanted to feel dirty, but instead, I felt calm and relaxed, as if that entire experience was something my body needed.

"You're a lustful sinner," I muttered hatefully, wrapping up in my blankets.

ERMEK

CHAPTER 13

I hated how Dagon laughed at Jazzera. The embarrassment of wearing those red robes must be terrible, but to laugh at her misfortune was just cruel. I had wanted to protest when I saw him walking into her tent but thought better of it. Perhaps he was being decent and offering her an apology.

After about thirty minutes of Dagon not returning, I became anxious. What could they be doing that was taking this long? Was he harming her? Was she allowing him to do things to her?

I shook the thought off. Jazzera was a faithful woman and would never betray God by doing unholy things with a demon.. she was better than that. Deep down, I knew she could control her lust and was a stronger person than I. Still, it was best to check on them. I was about a foot away from the tent's flaps when Dagon stepped out.

He ignored me for the most part and continued walking until he reached the old dirt road that followed the creek.

"Where are you going?" I called.

He turned to me. "If I'm right, the Heathen border is a few miles up the road. There is a town on the other side.. I'm going there."

"You can't just leave," I said, hurrying to catch up to him.

He sneered. "Look, I haven't been laid in ages. I'm fucking horny. The Heathens aren't a bunch of prudes. Are you going to fuck me and suck me? Because if not, there are plenty of people there who will. If you're willing, I will drop my pants and let you ram it home right here, big boy." He smiled and moved closer. "Oh yeah, you're the one who prefers to be rammed." He was only inches from me. "I'm sure I could fuck you better than Lazlo ever could."

"Get away from me, vile beast!" I cried, resisting the urge to strike him.

He put his hands up and backed away. "Alright, I'll be on my way if you aren't willing."

"You're not going anywhere, Demon!"

The black pools of his eyes turned a blood-red color. "You do not control me, Demon Slayer!"

I staggered back a step. His voice had changed into something dark and devilish. The sound actually struck fear into my heart. I continued to retreat, and the red in his eyes returned to black.

"The Priestess barely controls me." He flipped his hair off his shoulder and turned back to the road, leaving me trembling.

As the day went on, I busied myself with small tasks around our camp. Jazzera hadn't made an appearance since breakfast, and instead of bothering her, I decided to catch dinner.

After whittling a spear, I stepped into the creek and tried my luck at fishing. By the time my stomach started to rumble, I had only managed to catch seven small fish. This would barely be enough for Jazzera and me.. the demon could find his own food.

I gutted and scaled the fish, stuck them on skewers, and placed them over the fire embers to cook. Then I chopped the reeds I had collected earlier and put them into a pot of boiling water.

When our food finished cooking, I made a plate for Jazzera and set it down inside her tent. We would need to leave this place before her curse stopped, but I understood why she would want to hide away, at least for the first day.

By the time the sun set, the demon still hadn't returned. I decided this was as good a time as any to make my rounds of the camp. Priestesses were more in tune with a demon's aura than a Demon Slayer. We were only slightly sensitive to a demon's presence, but I still should be able to detect something should it get close to the camp.

After searching for a while, I decided to go down the road Dagon had gone. I would stop before getting to the border, but knowing the demon hadn't completely abandoned us would ease my mind.

I had been walking for no more than ten minutes when I felt a demon's presence. Gripping my bow, I diverted from the road and began walking stealthily into the woods. Every time a leaf crinkled under my feet, I paused and listened. Nocking an arrow, I followed the creek to where the demon's presence was strongest. A creature was swimming in a large pond within a clearing of trees. It must be some sort of water demon, a powerful one by the feel of it. Pulling my arrow back, I pointed my bow at the creature, then stopped. Relaxing, I unnotched my arrow and put it back into the quiver.

"What are you doing?"

"Taking a bath. You should try it sometime."

"That water has to be freezing," I shivered at the mere thought of it.

"It is, but I'm not human. So, it doesn't bother me as much." Dagon leaned back and slightly sank his head into the water to pull his hair from his face.

As much as I hated to admit it, he was extraordinarily sexy and looked almost angelic instead of demonic in the full moon's light. He waded through the water until he got to the shore. He was completely naked, his cock standing long and erect. I swallowed hard, then looked away.

"I thought you had gone to take care of that."

"Maybe you can take care of it for me?"

I looked back at him, and he was only inches away. I opened my mouth to speak, but no words came out. My cock grew in my pants, throbbing to be set loose. "I can't."

He grinned and moved his face closer. "You can. There is nobody here to see us and turn you in." Gently, he put his hand on my face before unclasping my armor. I grabbed his arm and held it while looking into his black eyes. He leaned forward, pressing his lips firmly to mine.

Instead of fighting, I kissed him back. We stayed locked in that position for only a moment before I pulled off my shirt. His hands caressed down my body as I stood bare-chested in front of him. Surprisingly, they were warm instead of freezing like I had expected. He tugged at the buckle of my pants and dragged them down, exposing me. My cock was rock hard, and I watched eagerly as he took me into his mouth all the way to the base. I could feel it bend slightly as it went down the curve of his throat. Impulsively, I gripped his hair tightly and began pushing his head up and down. Pressing his hand firmly on my stomach, he gave me a push, and I let go of his hair. He got to his feet and stared at me. I couldn't tell what he was feeling. Was he angry? Or was his intensity growing?

Roughly, he grabbed me by my own hair and walked me over to a nearby bolder. He shoved me, and I fell hard against it. He gripped my arm, forcing me to turn and bend over the rock. I felt something wet touch my hole, and his fingers massaged me. He rubbed himself up and down my crack until he slowly began pushing himself inside. It was gentle at first, but the more relaxed I became, the harder he drove into me.

I groaned loudly with each thrust and dug my nails into the mossy stone every time he rubbed my prostate. I couldn't control myself.. with one last thrust, I felt my seed explode from my body, drizzling down the side of the bolder. Even as I finished, Dagon continued to thrust in and out until he eventually let out a moan, and his seed seeped out of me.

I nearly shed a tear as I felt him pull out. I knew I was already going to Hell for fucking a man, but what circle of Hell would I wind up in for fucking a demon? Dejectedly, I walked past Dagon and began picking up my clothing.

"Didn't you enjoy yourself?"

"You got what you wanted. I'm going to burn for all eternity because of my lust."

Slapping himself in the face with his palm, Dagon let out a chuckle. "Oh, you poor misled little bastard. Fucking me or any other man isn't what's sending you to Hell.. what you did to Lazlo will send you to Hell."

A tear slid down my cheek, and he winced. "More like a thousand years in Purgatory, but it's pretty close, and it's not as bad," he remarked as if trying to lighten the blow.

"Purgatory isn't real.. it's something the old religions made up."

"Oh, it's real. It's for those who don't quite deserve to go to Hell but don't deserve to go to Heaven, either. You may not have killed him with your own hands, but you pointed the finger that led him to the gallows. It was fear for your own life, and that could be your only saving grace. God doesn't care who you humans fuck, if it's consensual and no one is hurt, but he does care when you send someone to their death. The only time killing is acceptable is if you are in immediate danger. Or if you are protecting someone else."

I started to get dressed, and as I did, my mind flooded with the memories I shared with Lazlo. How we shared our first kiss when we were twelve. When I was fourteen, I wanted nothing more than to run away with him into the Heathen country, and, by the time we were sixteen, we were sleeping together. My memories took a darker turn, and I remembered how a fellow Demon Slayer had accused me of sodomy. He claimed that he saw Lazlo and me together in the bathhouse. In a panic for my own life, I told the Priest that Lazlo forced himself upon me and that I was too ashamed to come forward. Later that day, Lazlo was in chains. He never did try to pass the blame onto me. Nobody came to haul me away to the gallows. He kept our secret even as they threw the first of many stones.

DAGON

CHAPTER 14

I almost felt sorry for the Demon Slayer as he attempted to dress. He had a look of pure anguish on his face, and his guilt practically oozed out of his pores. I cringed at the thought. I had no time to feel sorry for these stupid humans. Still, as much as I wanted to push these feelings aside, I had to admit they had lived in a fucked-up society.

I had hoped that the remaining humans would advance when the Gates of Hell opened. That letting them remember the divine existed would help their more evolved brains work on creating a better world, but instead, like humans tend to do, they took a thousand steps backward. The Bible didn't even say man shall not lay with man, as these current humans believed. Not the original anyway. Thousands of years of playing the telephone game had turned the Bible into laughable gibberish. It was possible my brother could have caused this misled belief, but that was so long ago I doubted anyone even remembered it.

Eve's curse was also laughable. To think that a single woman was the cause of all the misery on Earth was ridiculous, but a man had written it down thousands of years ago, so it must be true. The hard reality was that men wanted to control women so they could have all the rights to their bodies.

I contemplated how hard it must be for them to exist. The Priestess, being a woman, has to do everything a man asks of her or risk physical punishment, and, then there's the Demon Slayer, who isn't allowed to love a man for fear of death.

Perhaps these two humans didn't deserve to be punished the way they were, but many humans, especially those claiming to be "holy," deserved this Hell on Earth.

I began thinking about the journey ahead as I strolled back to camp. There were so many ways humans could die on this trip. I wouldn't be distraught if the Demon Slayer died, but the Priestess needed to survive. It would be cold by the time we reached Alaska, and I needed to ensure the humans stayed warm. When it was time to cross the Bering Strait, I would have to watch out for the Leviathan. If they managed to survive the Russian wilderness, I would have to keep them hydrated in the desert.

When I reached the camp, I took my raven form and perched on top of a tree branch. The Demon Slayer wasn't far behind me, carrying his head low all the way from the road to his tent. Closing my eyes, I fell asleep until the light of dawn hit my feathers.

The Priestess was the first to exit her tent. Dressed in red, she silently began packing her stuff and pulling down her tent. When she finished, she sat on one of the logs near the old burnt-out campfire and waited for the Demon Slayer to awaken.

An hour or so later, the Slayer finally rose to greet the sun, and he was silent while packing up the remainder of the camp. Once the horses were readied, I flew down and perched myself on the Priestess' shoulder.

"We should avoid the town," I advised as we walked closer to the Heathen border. "Your robes are going to make you stand out. Heathens, especially the ones closest to the borders, don't really care for your people."

Instead of replying to me, the Priestess nodded to the Demon Slayer.

Ermek glanced at her briefly, then brought his eyes back to the road. "Do you know how we can do this?"

I assumed he was directing his comment toward me.. it was funny. This Slayer had sex with me the night before but still refused to address a woman during her period. It was adorable how humans seemed to pick and choose which sins were worth punishment and which weren't. It appeared that the Demon Slayer would rather be stoned to death than pray in a tent for a day.

"You know the whole concept of 'talking to a woman on her period makes you unclean' is all horse shit, right?"

Neither responded, and I ruffled my feathers in annoyance. Why was it that when I lied, humans believed me? But when I told the truth, they thought I was lying? That was a paradox I had yet to figure out.

They brought the horses to a halt when we reached the Heathen border. Ermek looked over at me, and I assumed he wanted me to answer the question he had asked earlier. The Heathen border was nothing more than a crudely dug trench that stretched for miles in either direction. At some point, it hit the Mississippi river, which was used as another border. There were only a few places to cross. If we crossed the rickety old bridge, we'd run into a fork in the dirt road. I knew that a town would be on the right, and, I wasn't fibbing when I said going to that town was a bad idea.

"We go left at the fork. We will hit another town by nightfall and just go past that one. By the time we hit River's Bed, the Priestess should be off her cycle, and we can get her a change of clothes and more supplies."

"What's River's Bed?"

"The biggest Heathen city for miles. If you want to make it all the way to Babylon, you'll need more supplies than you brought." Not that I cared if the humans got more supplies.. I just wanted to hit up a whore house. One of the fantastic perks of being a demon was the inability to catch an STD.

The rest of the trip was as dull as I could expect, though I did try to spice it up when I could. I spent a few nights in the Demon Slayer's tent, both in and out of his dreams. The other nights I spent in the mind of the Priestess. It amused me at how infatuated she truly was with the Demon Slayer. I almost hated thinking about what would happen if she confessed her love to him. He couldn't tell her the truth, so I wondered how he would break her heart. Or would he pretend to love her back to keep his secret safe?

It may have been cruel, but there were times I appeared to her as the Demon Slayer, and other times I materialized as myself. She fucked both forms eagerly, and, , of course, the following day, she would be ashamed of herself.

"You're back again." She stood at the edge of a lake.. we were in her dream world again.

"I enjoy our time together," I stated with a sly grin.

She turned to me. "I know it's you. Even when you're Ermek."

"And do you like it?"

Her eyes lowered for a brief moment. "I would prefer you not come to me as Ermek. I know he will never love me back. I'm not sure why, but I feel it deep within my heart."

"And does that bother you?"

She said nothing, only looked out to the lake once more. In her dreams, I could have almost complete control. A little perk of being me. I was one of the few demons that had that power. Incubi was what the old churches had once called my kind. I could control the setting, what she wore, and what I looked like, but it was up to her body if she wished to connect with me, and, so far, her body had never disappointed. She was a lustful little creature. I found that if a human is denied the touch of another, their lust will grow strong within them, and, this woman's lust was so intense, I could almost taste it.

I walked behind her and ran my fingers through her long, raven hair. It was a pity I couldn't feel anything in this dream state. For as many times as I had fucked her senseless, I would genuinely like to feel her for once.

I tugged at her robe, slowly sliding it from her body and exposing her naked form. She mutely stared at the lake, which suddenly became an ocean. We no longer stood on grass but on a white, sandy beach. Running my nose softly down the side of her neck, I stepped around her and slid my fingers between her perky breasts. Before my fingers could reach her crotch, she pushed me away.

"I want to keep looking at the sea."

For a moment, I was dumbfounded, was her body suddenly rejecting me? As if answering my unspoken question, the Priestess got to her hands and knees and crawled toward the water.

The waves barely made it to her knees when she looked back at me. Her hand reached underneath her body and began rubbing the folds of her pussy.

I took this as my cue. My cock hardened, and I got down to my knees, gripping her hips.

Her fingers slid in and out of her wet hole, making herself ready for me. I didn't hesitate.. I didn't have to worry about causing her pain in the dream world. There was no hymen to tear, so I could ram myself inside her, and the Priestess would feel nothing but pleasure. I could make my cock the size of an arm, and she'd only feel slight discomfort, but in this world, she could take it. It would only be her mind telling her that it hurt a little.

With that delicious thought, I did just that. My cock grew in thickness and length as I pushed myself in. Her pussy stretched with every inch added, and I listened to the screams of pleasure as I drove it to the base. In the real world, if I were to do this, I would be practically killing her. My cock would rupture some kind of organ, I was sure, but in this world, she begged for more.

Sitting back on my knees, I lifted her up, cradled her legs under my arms, and thrust her back on top of my shaft. Like curling weights, I lifted her up and down on top of me until I heard her climax. It was a specific moan that I knew well.

I opened my eyes. The Priestess once again had an orgasm, and I was left feeling pathetically horny. It couldn't be long before I got to feel that pussy for real. Typically, I preferred nonvirgins. I liked women and men alike to be experienced so that I didn't have to do all the work, but for her, I would make an exception.

JAZZERA

CHAPTER 15

I awoke from my slumber covered in sweat. Dagon had his way with me again. As dirty as I felt afterward, I would be lying to myself if I said I didn't like it. At first, it was horrible, terrifying even, but the more frequent it became, the more my body seemed to betray me, but now I was starting to wonder if my mind was also betraying me. Dagon had never once been cruel to me. He had been kind and generous. When every other man refused to talk to me, he soothed my curse pains. Even though they were dreams, his touch was always gentle.

"Stop it," I muttered to myself. "Dagon's a demon, and he just wants you to sin. That's all." Pushing the covers from my body, I went to my pack to get dressed. Thankfully my curse had stopped, so I could wear my normal robes. Now I could finally speak in the presence of a man. Gathering my things, I left the tent and shivered. The air was cold and crisp, but it was nice to breathe it in without my face covered.

As Ermek attended the smoldering campfire, I asked, "You did bring money, didn't you?"

He looked up at me and smiled. "Why would you need money?"

Arms wrapped around my chest, I tried to shield myself from the cold. "Dagon suggested we get supplies, and he also said I shouldn't be wearing this. I could use a new cloak."

Dagon appeared next to me, pulling off his own jacket. The inner lining was changed to a bold blue color.

"Wear this." He draped it around my shoulders.

At first, I was hesitant, but upon feeling its unnatural warmth, I slid my arms in and wrapped the jacket around myself.

"That's very kind of you," voiced Ermek.

Dagon smiled at him. "Don't thank me too much, Demon Slayer. Remember, her death means my freedom."

Reaching my hand out, I gripped his shoulder. "What if I repay your kindness by freeing you at the end of our journey?"

I kept my gaze locked on his black eyes as he contemplated what I offered. Truthfully, I didn't know if I would free him. Could I even trust that he wouldn't kill Ermek and me? Regardless, I couldn't free him now. I knew I wouldn't stand a chance against that Legion character, and I would need Dagon by my side to fight them.

After a moment, he laughed derisively. "Priestess, what's the point? If you close the Gates of Hell, I'll be free anyway and return to the spirit realm, and, you will just go back to being a normal woman."

"What do you mean a normal woman?"

"You will lose your mark. There will be no need for it anymore." His voice was flat as he spoke, and I could almost sense a feeling of sadness. Dagon quietly turned into a raven and flew over to my horse, perching himself upon the saddle.

I didn't know how to feel. This demon was the only man aside from Ermek to ever show me kindness. Yet I was banishing him away to his own personal Hell. A place where he could no longer feel. Something he said was worse than any torture given out to the souls of the damned.

Ermek and I packed up and mounted our horses. The day's trip was quiet until I spotted what could only be River's Bed. Considering that it was the largest Heathen city in the area, it was far less impressive than I imagined. The towns in the Follower territory were neat and clean, and most buildings were made of stone with expert craftsmanship. The city before me looked like it had been constructed with heaps of junk slapped together to create make-shift shelters.

The walls that surrounded the city were made out of jagged, rusted metal. Nothing was uniform.. it seemed like they nailed together any piece of loose metal they could find. From what I could see, the homes were stacked high and made of wood and other miscellaneous detritus.

Most of which was salvaged junk from before the Rapture, debris my people would call "litter."

Dirt roads wound in every direction, creating a labyrinth. Pretty pieces of brightly colored cloth acted as awnings and bathed the streets in a kaleidoscope of colors, and, the people were a different breed altogether. Women rushed about in strange clothing that would never be allowed beyond the border. Some of them even dressed like men with pants and tunics. There was hardly a single dress to be found. That is until I spotted two women hanging over a balcony. One wore a short black dress that barely covered her breasts. The other wore a light purple dress with a side slit that showed off her leg and a plunging neckline that exposed much of her midsection. We all made eye contact, and I blushed, unsure what to do.

"It's okay, sweetie. We don't discriminate.. we do women, too!" shouted the woman in the purple dress.

Dagon laughed in my head. *Go for it, Priestess. After all, nobody can touch a woman quite like another woman. Just let me watch.*

"Shut up," I groaned, causing Ermek to turn to me.

"What did he say this time?"

"You don't want to know."

"You'll want to put the horses up before we look around," Dagon suggested before flying off and perching outside a tall building with one horse tied to a rail.

He transformed into his human form and changed his eyes.. instead of the endless pools of black, they were now green with tiny flecks of blue and brown.

"Should you be transforming out in the open like this?" I fretted.

He grinned at me. "Nobody noticed, I assure you. They see what I want them to see."

"And what about the horses? What if somebody steals them?"

"The Demon Slayer here will buy them some protection."

I looked at Ermek, who was now tying his horse to the rail.

"I won't leave Jazzera alone."

Rolling his eyes, Dagon said, "The Priestess has a sword. A sharp one. I should know.. she practically gutted me with it. Jazzera is a badass, and she can handle herself. If she gets into too much trouble, I'll know."

"Just go ahead, Ermek. I'll be fine," I reassured, giving him a bright smile. Having someone tell me I was good enough to take care of myself felt nice. Even if it was a lustful, foul-mouth demon.

ERMEK

CHAPTER 16

The stories I had been told about the Heathen territory were what made me hesitate when it came to leaving Jazzera on her own. What if it was like Sodom and Gomorrah, and a group of men came to rape her?

The demon reminded me that Jazzera wasn't like other Priestesses. She had the skill of a Demon Slayer, and, if she were overwhelmed, her demon would be forced to protect her. Still, it didn't make me feel less uneasy as Dagon practically pushed me through the bright orange wooden door.

Once inside, I stopped and gawked wide-eyed. From the look of the people in the building, I immediately knew where Dagon had brought me. Women were parading around wearing next to nothing, and some even had their breasts fully exposed, sitting on men's laps. In the far corner, two women were making out.

"What are we doing here?"

"Customer parking only. All others will be towed," he replied with a chuckle.

111

I didn't really get the joke. Rather than lingering on it, I grabbed him by the back of his shirt. "I don't have the money to buy you a whore right now."

Dagon winked at me and whispered conspiratorially, "You're not buying me a whore, Demon Slayer.. I'm buying you one."

I looked around sheepishly and stepped closer to him. "You know how I feel about women."

"I know. Don't worry, Demon Slayer.. you will have a good time," he assured me.

Before I could protest further, he gripped me by the shoulder and pushed me toward the bar where several men sat, sipping on a brown liquid. Behind the bar were jugs of what I assumed was some kind of liquor. I surveyed my surroundings.. the building, for the most part, was built of wood except for the large stone fireplace that burned in the center of the room.

Brightly colored fabric hung from the rafters, and deer antler chandeliers lit the room with a dull glow from dripping candles. A man played the banjo in a far corner while a woman sang sweetly to the tune.

Dagon leaned over to speak to the barkeep, who giggled a few times before fetching a key out from under the bar. Dagon took it with a smile and turned to me.

"Well, you're in luck, but you're not." Arching my brow, I waited for him to continue. "They only have one man available right now, and it's a few hours wait for the other two. You'll have a bigger pool to choose from if you don't mind waiting for sloppy seconds, but if you want to get your dick sucked now, you have one choice."

I looked around the room, my instincts telling me to scream at him to keep his voice down. "We don't have enough money to spend on a whore. May we please go?" My voice was hushed but urgent.

Dagon tsked at me. "You aren't paying for it.. I am."

"With what money?"

"The Headmistress owes me. She told me no man had ever made her cum. I bet her I could make her cum twice, and I made her cum three times for good measure. After all, I have an image to maintain. Afterward, she told me my next visit was on the house. Anyone I chose. So, I'm choosing to get you laid."

Swallowing hard, I nervously scanned the room again.

"But I warn you, Demon Slayer…." He leaned close to my ear. "Nobody will be able to fuck you better than I can."

Shuddering slightly, I pulled away. He tossed me the key and pointedly glanced upstairs. The number six was painted on the key, and I could only assume this meant room six. "What about Jazzera?"

"I'll keep her company. Give me some money, and I'll get you two more suitable clothes." He held out his hand.

Rolling my eyes, I reached under my armor, pulled out a few paper credits, and handed them over. Even though we were practically in another country, all three factions that ruled this land shared each other's currency. Heathen money was worth less in Follower territory, but they took it, and, from what I heard from roamers, Heathen country was the same.

Snatching the money from my hand, Dagon pushed past me and headed toward the door.

My mind told me to go with him, to forget this stupid little venture and get on with our quest. But my eyes moved back to the female couple sitting close to the fire. They got up from their seats and headed upstairs. Not a single person looked in their direction, all except for me, of course. Nobody seemed bothered by it, as if it were normal, something they saw every day, and, Dagon just bought me a man. The woman behind the bar must have known that she was selling a man off to another. She giggled but didn't seem disgusted, and, I wasn't even sure if she was laughing at Dagon asking for a man or if he had made some joke.

Gripping the key tightly, I decided to take the plunge. After all, why shouldn't I enjoy myself? Why would God curse me with these feelings if I weren't meant to use them? Maybe Dagon was right. Maybe my sin wasn't loving men. Perhaps when this was all finished, I could return to Heathen country, where I didn't have to worry about getting stoned to death. Maybe I could find a man who would love me back.

All the doors on the upper floor were painted red, with a large number painted on the front. One through sixteen. Taking a steadying breath, I walked to room six, put the key in the lock, and listened for the click before turning the doorknob and heading inside. The space was dimly lit by candles resting on shelves. In the center of the room was a canopy bed with red, lacy drapes. Lying in the middle of the bed was a man about my age. He had pale, white skin with freckles speckling his thin body and slightly curly, red hair that fell just below his cheekbones.

He smiled and crawled to the end of the bed. "Well, hello, handsome."

I swallowed. "Hi." I wanted to roll my eyes. What I wouldn't give to have the same confidence that Dagon seemed to have.

"My name is Sheldon. What's yours?"

"Ermek."

"Well, Ermek, are you going to do dirty things to me?"

My jaw dropped as he shed his pants and got up from the bed. He walked around me, touching me before unclasping my armor and letting it fall to the floor. Sheldon pulled my black top from my body, lips tracing down my core muscles and back up to my neck. Pulling back, he sauntered to the bed and bent over.

"I'm prepared to take that big cock of yours. I'm all ready to take whatever you can throw at me."

His words sent heat through my groin, and my cock hardened as I watched him play with himself. Without overthinking too much, I peeled off my pants. Fully erect, I towered over him.

His hole glistened.. he must have put some ointment on to lubricate himself. Pressing the head of my cock up against him, I slowly slid myself in until he was resting on the base. He moaned heavily and pushed himself further onto me. I pulled back and thrust back in, trying to keep a balanced motion to avoid hurting him, a lesson I learned with Lazlo. You had to start off gently if you wanted pleasure instead of pain.

When I felt his walls loosen slightly around me, I thrust into him a bit harder. He clenched the bedspread tightly, arching his back and moaning louder. "Yeah, that's it. Fuck me!" he cried.

In the heat of the moment, I pushed into him hard and fast. I could feel the tension in the pit of my stomach, like when I was a child on a swing that was moving too fast. The butterflies rose, and my brain seemed to shut off for a split second before I felt my cum explode inside him.

I groaned loudly and squeezed his cheeks before pulling back. My hand prints were still visible as red marks on his skin.

Looking over his shoulder, he smiled contentedly. Sweat beaded on my brow and rolled down my neck. "Thank you for that."

"Oh no, baby, thank you." He winked at me. "Most of the time, all I ever get in here are men with tiny dicks, but you have a monster between your legs. If I didn't have to charge extra, I'd beg you for more."

Embarrassed, I looked down at the floor. I didn't know what to say or feel. There wasn't a feeling of shame like with Dagon, but it wasn't love like I felt with Lazlo. It was freedom

"So, that armor, Followers of the Horsemen, right?"

I nodded and walked over to the small washtub beside the bed.

"I don't understand. You guys worship the Horsemen?"

I chuckled. "No. Before the Rapture, the Four Horsemen of the Apocalypse came to this world. We are what followed, the descendants of those left behind."

He snorted. "Oh, well, it's kind of a silly name. No offense. When you say it out loud, it sounds like you worship the guys."

I thought about it, and he wasn't wrong. When raised around it, you don't question how the name sounds. After giving myself a quick wash, I gathered my clothes from the floor.

"Can I come with you?" he asked.

My eyes widened. "Come with me?"

Practically jumping off the bed, he rushed to me and gripped my arm. "I'm a slave here. Take me with you, and I will let you fuck this hole every night."

Tugging on my pants, I shook my head. "They would stone you to death."

He shrugged. "So just take me away from here. Just far enough so that they won't follow me. Please. I'll do anything you want."

I stood there for a long second, trying to figure out how to respond. It would be nice to share my world with someone who wasn't a demon.

Another person, like me, who I didn't have to feel ashamed around. Someone that I could be my authentic self with. Taking a deep breath, I nodded. "Get dressed."

JAZZERA

CHAPTER 17

I watched Ermek hesitantly follow Dagon into the building. The moment they were inside, I did a small twirl next to the horse. Beyond the border, a Priestess was never allowed to be alone without her escort. She was always to have her Demon Slayer near to protect her, but Dagon was right.. I had been trained to kill demons since I was a small child, and, from what I'd been told, demons were much more difficult to fight than humans.

As I waited for my companions to return, I surveyed the crowd as they went about their lives. Several women were going from one place to another, and, barely any of them walked with a man. If they weren't afraid, then why should I be?

"Enjoying your little taste of freedom, Priestess?" I spun around to see Dagon beaming at me.

"I don't know what you're talking about."

His grin grew. "Like they said in the old days, you don't have to lie to kick it."

"I don't even know what that means."

He sighed. "It means you don't have to lie to me. I know you've been oppressed your entire life, and you've never done anything alone. You're more than welcome to get a little excited over being allowed to babysit a horse."

"Where is Ermek?" I wonder aloud, glancing behind Dagon.

"He's going to stay here.. he has things to attend to. As for you and I, we're going to get you some new clothing."

Dagon wrapped his arm around mine and tugged me into the middle of the crowd. I glanced over my shoulder, but Dagon pulled me harder. He practically shoved me into a building filled with clothing, and I completely forgot that I was worried about Ermek. There were articles of clothing in every color I could ever dream of, from pink to blue, to bright yellow. There were even reds in almost every shade.

"Heathen women don't wear dresses or frilly robes when they travel. So, you're going to want to wear pants," Dagon threw a pair of pink pants at me.

I cringed at the color. "I think I'll pick out my own."

I left his side and started browsing the clothes racks. I tried to avoid specific colors that were part of my own culture. Light blue was only worn by Priestesses. Brown for Priests, black for servants, green for Demon Slayers, pink for small girls, grey for small boys, and solid white for women engaged to be married, and, , of course, there was red for the women going through their curse. This made my options limited.

After glancing over several racks twice, I decided purple was my color and began picking out several shirts with matching pants. Dagon groaned and snatched the pants from me. "They also don't color code, and you don't have to wear all one color, and, they don't follow that stupid mixed fabrics rule."

I bit my lip. "But I do follow the mixed fabric rule, and, it's not stupid.. it's in the Bible."

He glared at me. "Do you want to blend in or not?"

I didn't know what the correct answer was. I wasn't supposed to mix my clothing. It's why Priestesses wore robes.. it made it simple to keep to one type of fabric, but I also didn't want to be harassed for being a Follower of the Horsemen. After a moment, I agreed, and Dagon grabbed my chosen pants and tossed them to the side. He handed me a few pairs of black pants and two white ones.

"These will make your ass look good."

I sighed heavily. "Can you not be so crude? For once?"

"Can you not be such a prude? For once?"

Turning back to the rack, he pulled out a purple item with black strings. The garment was stiff, but the cloth was silky.

"What is this?"

"A corset," he answered as he plucked a pair of pants from my hand. "It's not an authentic corset, but you wouldn't be able to breathe in one of those."

Before I could protest, Dagon pulled me to a counter where a woman with short, spiky hair stood waiting.

"Could you help my friend put this on?" he requested, then leaned forward and whispered in the woman's ear. She looked over at me and nodded.

"Come with me, darling," said the woman, taking my hand. With great hesitation, I followed her into a small box of a room.

"Take them off," she ordered, gesturing to my robes before setting the clothing on a small bench.

"Is this really necessary?"

The woman smiled. "Not really, but your friend said he would pay me extra to help you put it on properly. I can turn my back until you need help with the top if it makes you more comfortable."

When she turned, I quickly pulled off my robes, grabbed a pair of black pants, and slid them on. They were tight yet comfortable and hugged my curves at every angle.. there was no room for modesty. Snatching the top from her hand, I opened it up and held it against my bare breasts, unsure exactly how to put it on.

"I suppose I do need help with this."

She turned to me and gave me a once-over. "We have to loosen it first," she counseled, taking the garment.

I covered myself, blushing uncontrollably.

"Don't hide those ladies.. they are amazing, and, your tattoo is impressive too."

My blush deepened, wanting desperately to get out of this situation. I supposed the tattoo she was referring to was my angelic mark.

Instead of correcting her, I murmured, "Thank you."

"Slide this over your head, and I'll show you how to tie it."

Snatching the item, I spun around and pulled it over my head. It hung loosely around my body. I turned to her, still holding the thing together.

"Move your boobs up. This is meant to lift them, not bind them."

This had to be the most humiliating moment of my life. Far worse than wearing the red robes. How Dagon managed to talk me into this was beyond me. I was tempted to call the entire thing off and put my robes back on, but doing that would take even more time. I pushed my breasts up until they rested in the tiny cups at the top. When they were positioned correctly, the woman began tying the strings tightly, sucking in my slim midsection while explaining how it was done.

"You want it tight but not so tight you can't breathe."

When she was finished, I glanced down at myself. Mostly all I could see was cleavage.. instinctively, I wanted to cover up more. "So, do I put on another top over this one?"

The woman chuckled. "If you wanted a top, you were supposed to put it under it. This outfit isn't meant to be hidden. Now come on, I have a mirror by the desk."

Trying to keep myself covered, I cautiously walked out of the tiny room, following the woman as closely as possible. When we got to the mirror, I let my arms slip away and gazed at myself.

"That looks great on you." Dagon stepped into the reflection behind me.

I scowled at him. "I look like a harlot, and it looks like I'm just begging for a man to rape me."

Dagon frowned. "No woman asks for that. No matter what the woman is wearing. Men who force themselves on women based on what they wear have a special little place in Hell that is all their own. Men aren't animals, and they can control themselves." He grinned and opened his jacket.. the inner lining was now purple. "And look, we match."

I put my hands over my chest, trying to cover the cleavage again. "How do you do that?"

He brushed a strand of hair out of my face. "I can change anything about myself. I chose to wear these clothes, and so they manifest. I allowed you to wear my jacket because we are bound together for the time being. I get bored with the same old thing every day, but I love this jacket. I've had it since the twentieth century. I enjoy changing the color of the lining frequently."

Handing the woman some payment notes, he put his hand on the small of my back and began escorting me out. I resisted. "I can't go out there like this."

Sighing, he said, "Nobody is going to say anything. Women in Heathen territory are free. If a man rapes a woman here, they are strung up on a pole naked, and a group of women beat him. Most of the time, the man survives, but he learns his lesson, that's for sure." He reached into a cloth bag he had been carrying. "And if you're still that worried about it, I got this for you. It's warm."

I took the cloth item from his hand and shook it out. It was a black cloak with a hood.. the fabric was thick and felt warmer than my other one. I flung it over my shoulders and clasped it around my neck.

Together, we walked back to the building we had come from. Ermek was standing outside next to his horse. "Good, you're here.. we have to go."

"Did something happen?" I asked.

"Please, Jazzera, we have to leave."

Dagon cocked his head. "Can't I get laid first? There are some women…or men just begging for me to fill them."

"We don't have time for your demonic shenanigans," stated Ermek as he mounted his horse.

Dagon grumbled something, but I was unable to hear it. I walked to my horse and mounted her. It was surprising how much easier it was to straddle the horse without all the extra fabric of robes in the way.

Dagon groaned, tossed the bag he'd been carrying at me, and took his raven form. As he perched upon my shoulder, I asked, "So why a raven?"

"Because, like myself, they are misunderstood creatures. They are always seen as bad omens, even though they are highly intelligent creatures who can create strong bonds. That and a group of them together is called a murder." He chuckled at the little joke.

Our horses trotted out of the main gate, and we followed the city's left side wall toward the river we had been following earlier.

"Where are we going?" I called.

"It shouldn't be too far."

Pushing our horses into a full gallop, we followed the river until I could barely see the city behind me. Around the corner, at the river bend, I spotted a man standing beside a white horse, the same horse that had been tied up next to our own.

Ermek pulled up next to him, dismounted, and waited patiently for me to climb from my horse.

"Who's this?"

"This is Sheldon."

DAGON

CHAPTER 18

I flapped my wings and flew to a nearby tree, where I could observe the trio. The Demon Slayer seemed more desperate for companionship than I once thought... this new human was none other than the man I hooked him up with at the brothel. My hopes were that I would get the Slayer some ass, dress the Priestess, and then I could have some fun of my own.

Fluffing my feathers, I watched the Slayer and Priestess bicker about the new guy.

Jazzera insisted that this new human couldn't come with us. It was too dangerous, and there were too many mouths to feed. The Demon Slayer argued, insisting that he would be no trouble. I was confused as to why Ermek was so insistent. This male wasn't even particularly interesting. He was shorter in stature than average, and if I had to guess, the Priestess was taller than him. He was thin with little to no muscle mass, with bright red hair and freckles covering his body.

"Please, my Lady. I was a prisoner at that place.. I saw the Demon Slayer and begged him to take me back to Follower territory."

"We're not going to Follower territory.. we are going across the sea," she insisted.

"Then take me as far as you can. Just far enough so the Heathens won't drag me back to that hell hole."

I swooped down and landed on the ground at his feet, letting out a small caw before taking my human form. Sheldon gasped and nearly fell on his ass.

"So, you stole a horse and ran away, assuming they won't follow us?"

"What are you?" he shouted, taking several steps back.

I huffed. "I'm a demon.. she's a Priestess of the Followers. Put two and two together."

Sheldon swallowed hard and looked to the ground. "I know where we can camp for the night." He pointed to a large hill on the other side of the woods. "The people say a mighty rock demon lives near that hill, and nobody will go near it."

I chuckled. I had never heard of a rock demon before. Demons were typically named after sins. This man most likely knew there was no demon around, which is why he suggested it.

Taking a step closer to him, I gazed into his eyes. I wondered if this was a trap but could find nothing in his eyes. No guilt, no fear. In fact, this man was practically unreadable. No shame, anxiety, or desire seeped from his skin like every other mortal. I didn't trust him. Still, knowing I would have little say in the matter, I stepped away to let the humans decide.

"He was forced to pleasure men in that place. He wishes to be absolved of his sins, and only a Priest can do that. If you send him back, he will never get redemption."

Every fiber in my mortal form wanted to slap the Slayer in the face for saying that. The Priestess had no power here to turn that human in. No Heathen was going to arrest anyone for sleeping with the same sex. Why didn't he just tell her the truth? That he preferred the company of other men as opposed to women and enjoyed a good dick down. He wanted to stay in the Heathen country, even if it was with the first man he had come across since Lazlo. Why did these idiots always have to bring God into it?

I watched as the Priestess bit her lip. "Are you sure he seeks redemption?"

Ermek scoffed. "Look at what the Heathens' land has done to you! We have barely crossed the border, and you're dressed like a harlot."

Jazzera cringed, and I spoke up. "The Priestess looks stunning. She is gorgeous. No woman should be afraid to show her body. I am a demon and have yet to force myself upon her. Even if she were to dance around me naked, I would never touch her unless she asked me to." I paused, looking over at the Priestess. She was indeed a work of fine art. "And believe me, I want to. I want to run my tongue along every crevice of her body, but I don't."

"God does not wish to have women parading their bodies like that."

"Your biggest sin is assuming what God does and doesn't like. A woman should cover their body for what reason? So that a man won't rape her? Wouldn't you think that if a demon, a creature of pure evil, as you say, can control himself, a man

127

should have a much easier time of it? Worry about your own sins, Demon Slayer."

He backed down, clearly shamed. The Priestess smiled at me and glanced at Sheldon.

"Fine. You can travel with us until you find a safe place, and, we will retrieve you once our quest has been completed."

We followed the new guy over an old bridge that crossed the river. The roadway on the other side was overgrown and barely visible as if humans hadn't traveled the path in a very long time. A strong breeze picked up, causing orange leaves to flutter and scrape loudly along the ground. When we entered the woods, I began feeling another demon's presence. I almost stopped our little caravan until I realized what it was. It was a demon, of course, but not one that I or anyone else should fear. Like myself, it was a warden of Hell and never human. It wouldn't bother us if we didn't bother it.

"There is a demon about," declared the Priestess. She reached for her blade, but I stopped her.

"Yes, but it's nothing to worry about. It's only Cronus."

"And who is Cronus?" she questioned as her body shivered.

"He's like the hellhound. He was born of Hell. Created to be a warden. He would eat damned souls, and they would stay in his belly, burning in the juices until he shit them out." I chuckled as the Priestess grimaced. "He has no use for eating mortals."

We set up camp in a small clearing at the base of some tall, jagged cliffs. Sheldon brought dried fish with him, and we all feasted on that for dinner. As nighttime came, I built a fire, and the humans pitched their tents. Before long, the Demon Slayer and the new human walked into Ermek's tent. After a moment, the Priestess decided to grace me with her presence and sat on the log next to me.

"So, they are sharing a tent now?"

Jazzera glanced over to the tent the couple had disappeared into. "It's too cold for him to sleep without shelter, and he didn't even bring blankets. It would be improper for him to sleep in my tent."

I grinned. "Sheldon was fucking men back at the place where he was found. You don't think it's more improper for him to sleep in the Demon Slayer's tent?"

She contemplated that question, then said, "Ermek wouldn't do anything with him.. he is a God-fearing man."

It took nearly all my willpower to not out the Slayer right then and there, but I kept my mouth shut.

"I wanted to thank you, by the way."

"For what?"

"For standing up for me." She turned to face me, less than a foot away. "Ermek is a kind soul, but he is strict, and, he's right.. I look like a harlot."

Brushing the hair from her face, I inched my way closer. "Don't let me hear those words come from your mouth again. You're beautiful, and even in the robes, you're still attractive.

These clothes simply complement that."

Before I could move back, the Priestess pressed her lips firmly to mine. My eyes went wide for a moment, and I had to resist the urge to pull back from pure shock, but as her lips lingered on mine, I pushed forward, running my hand through her hair and biting her lower lip before sliding my tongue into her mouth. She returned the gesture, and I let my hand slide down the front of the corset. She startled and pushed away from me.

"I'm sorry. I shouldn't have done that." Getting to her feet, she rushed over to her tent.

I stood, wanting to follow. "Would you like some company?"

She hesitated. "Could you please stay out of my dreams for one night?"

"I wasn't talking about your dreams."

She walked back to me and took my hand in hers. "I have a mission to complete."

"You will keep your mark if that's what you are worried about. They tell you that bullshit to control you. If you fall in love and have a family, you're less likely to focus on your duties at the temple."

She squeezed my hand tighter. "It's not about that.. I can't get any closer to you. As I said, I have a mission I have to complete."

She released my hand and began to walk away once more. "I should hate you."

She stopped and turned.

"Part of me does hate you. You took my freedom away." I moved closer. "But the other part of me feels sorry for you. You are just as much a prisoner as I am. Bound to the shackles of your society." Caressing under her chin, I made her look me in the eyes. "If you insist on continuing this journey, do me a favor. If you manage to close the gates, don't go home. Don't go back to the Followers."

She wrinkled her eyebrows as if needing an explanation.

"Even without your mark, they will keep you locked up like a little trinket. Go to the Heathen country. You will be free there. Free to love someone and be loved back, but don't you dare settle or put up with any bullshit. You find a man who will respect you, or you kick their ass."

Pulling away, she smiled at me. "Goodnight, Dagon." And with that, she disappeared into her tent.

I stood there for a long moment, just staring at the fire. The longer I stared, the higher it got. It was feeding off my energy. I had to calm myself, or I would burn the forest down. I supposed I could spare her life when this was all finished.. she didn't truly have to die. If she released me, I could let bygones be bygones and leave it at that. Revenge seems so petty.

Hearing some rustling from Ermek's tent, I decided to investigate. If I couldn't visit the Priestess in her dreams, I'd get some pleasure in the real world. After all, the Demon Slayer owed me. I stepped into the tent, and my instincts were correct. The Slayer was on his back, getting sucked off by our little visitor.

"What are you doing?" He was annoyed.

"You blew my opportunity to get laid earlier, so I figured I'd join in on the fun."

Sheldon let his lips slip away from Ermek's shaft. He glanced at me and then at Ermek. "Is he serious?"

"If you want him to join, he will."

The man on his knees smiled and lifted his ass higher in the air. "I don't mind." He returned to Ermek, taking the entire shaft down his throat.

My eyes moved over the little human's body. Spotting a malachite necklace hanging from his neck, I smirked to myself. No wonder I couldn't sense any guilt coming from him. What a clever little human. Humans tried to use malachite and other minerals to ward off demons.. however, they only mask guilt and fear.

I removed my clothing and got down on my knees. I did a little reach around, stroking the man's cock for a few moments. I was thoroughly unimpressed. He had length but absolutely no girth. Pulling his cheeks apart, I slid myself inside of him. A muffled moan came from his mouth as he continued to bob up and down on top of Ermek.

I closed my eyes, pushing deeper into his hole. With every heavy thrust, the vision of him I had in my mind distorted, and pictures of the Priestess now danced behind my eyelids. Her naked body wrapped around mine as I thrust deep within her. Her soft, sensual lips pressed greedily against mine. With one final thrust, I felt cum erupt from my cock and fill Sheldon's tight little ass. I opened my eyes. Sheldon removed his lips from the Demon Slayer and looked back at me.

"Well, that was quick. No offense, but I would have thought a demon could last longer."

I rolled my eyes at his snide remark.. I could have said a thing or two about him, but the Slayer commented, "Typically, he can. He never let me go without me getting mine. Is something on your mind, Dagon?"

I smirked and pulled out. "Guess I'm not exactly in the mood for all that, and I just wanted a little quicky. You two boys have fun. I'm going to go get some air." Getting to my feet, I willed my clothing to reappear and stepped out into the frigid air.

Lying down by the log, I gazed back into the fire. What was wrong with me? I had never cum that quickly before in my entire life, and, that was saying something since I was thousands of years old. My dick had seen the inside of more men and women than I could ever count, and, I never turned down a piece of ass once it was offered, but just then, I didn't want Ermek or his little plaything. I wanted Jazzera, and, what was with the Demon Slayer suddenly calling me by my name? What happened to simply calling me "demon?"

Huffing, I tossed a small stick into the fire. This was a dangerous game I was playing. In one way or another, humans always disappoint. Either they betray you, or they leave you for all eternity. Glancing over to Jazzera's tent, I sighed. Could these two humans be different? Could she be different?

JAZZERA

CHAPTER 19

I spent nearly the entire night wide awake. Part of me worried that Dagon would creep into my dreams, but I also kept focusing on the kiss we shared. I had never kissed a man in real life.. I had kissed Ermek in my dreams, and once, I kissed Dagon, but again, they were only ever dreams. Last night was real, and, it was everything I hoped it would be. I liked how soft his lips were and how the scruff on his face tickled my nose.

Secretly, I wanted him to follow me into the tent. I wanted him to ravish and fill me as he did in my dreams. I wanted to feel his real body up against mine, and, that thought terrified me. I was a Priestess who was falling in love with a demon. For years, I had thought that I loved Ermek, but my feelings for him were not the same as I felt for Dagon. The more time I spent with Dagon, the more my feelings for Ermek began to fade. Why? Because he was kind to me?

That could be a trick. Demons liked to play games, but last night didn't feel like a game to me.

He asked me to find a man who would love me and treat me respectfully. What type of game was that? He told me not to settle, and it felt like he cared about my well-being.

What if I didn't close the gates? What if I ran away with him? Set him free, and we lived quietly together somewhere in Heathen territory? Would he even stay with me if I set him free? Or would he kill me? He mentioned that part of him hated me, and I couldn't blame him.

My thoughts were disrupted by the shrieking of our horses. Frantically, I rushed over to my blade and darted out of the tent as quickly as possible. My jaw dropped as I looked toward the sky. An enormous beast dropped my mare into its gigantic maw, eating the poor creature alive. It then reached down to the white horse and did the same thing. I looked away, unwilling to watch as the poor beast suffered.

This demon was larger than any I had ever seen. It looked like its body was made of stone.. trees and grass grew from it, and, as I looked closer, I noticed its body was actually the cliffs we had camped next to.

Dagon marched up to the beast, cursing at it. "God damn it, Cronos! You ate our horses, you asshole!"

The creature looked down at him. "I no eat people!" it boomed.

"I know you don't eat people, but you ate our ride! Why did you eat our horses, you asshat?"

"Was hungry!" it roared.

"Clearly. You ate all three of them. Go home, Cronos. You don't belong here."

"Dagon no belong here."

"I do belong here. I was given permission to be here. You eat souls, and there are no souls here.. ergo, you're hungry. You keep eating livestock, and the humans will get mad."

The creature cackled. "No care about tiny humans."

"You need to care. Because if they attack you, you're going to kill them. Then God will be very upset that you killed mortals, and then poof, no more Cronos."

It looked as if the giant demon was contemplating his words. Then out of nowhere, it vanished with no other trace but a crater where it once lay.

"If God would destroy him for killing humans, why hasn't he killed the others?"

Dagon turned to me. "He won't. I just told him that to get him to go away. He's too damned big to be in the mortal realm." Dagon chuckled and poked at me. "It's cute that you thought you could do something to him with that little toothpick."

I wanted to say something in my defense, but Ermek spoke up, "So now what do we do?

He ate our horses and the supplies that were on them."

"Pack up," instructed Dagon before walking into the crater the demon had left.

I watched, wide-eyed, as he shifted. His body expanded to twice the size of a horse, growing black scales that glistened in the morning sun. His snout grew long and pointed, his eyes glowed crimson, and a long lizard-like tail jutted from his hindquarters, smacking the ground with a thunderous clap. Massive black and red wings sprouted from his back, and two large goat-like horns spiraled to the sky from the crown of his head. He had transformed into—a dragon.

At first, I was in awe, but then I was angry. "You're telling me you could turn into a dragon this entire time?"

"I can turn into anything I want, Priestess. Shapeshifting is my specialty."

"You could have stopped all of this!" I shouted, and, it was true. He could have flown us to the village where the people had been slaughtered, and maybe we could have saved them. Perhaps Lady Ester would have still been alive if he had transformed into something useful instead of a stupid raven.

"I couldn't have made it in time. The motions were all set in stone."

"How do you know?" I cried.

He took a thundering step toward me. "Because I was part of it!"

My breath caught in my throat. I was more surprised than I should have been, and, even with all my willpower, I couldn't stop the tear from sliding down my face.

"Do you really believe you captured me that easily? I practically handed myself to you on a golden platter. I didn't even fight back! Every Demon Lord has their own special abilities. Lilith can possess people in the mortal realm, including high-ranking holy men. Legion eats souls, and I transform. I can transform into anything, including Demon Slayers and Priestesses who may poke fun at a twenty-something-year-old Priestess who doesn't have her own demon. I could plant a seed in that Priestess' mind to make her think she is unworthy of the title "Priestess." And so, I baited you. I lured you away with my aura so we could tell if the key was inside."

"All those innocent people."

"And what about us? We were condemned to Hell for millennia because humans couldn't stop killing each other!"

Ermek's hand landed on my shoulder, and I turned into him, weeping. He gently patted the back of my head and said, "We still have a mission, and all of those deaths won't be in vain if we can close the gates."

Dagon let out a snort.

"How do you know it won't drop us?" worried Sheldon.

"Because he can't willingly kill Jazzera. He may have voluntarily become her slave, but he is her slave nonetheless. All she needs to do is command him."

Pulling away, I nodded. "Right. Let's close that gate."

JAZZERA

CHAPTER 20

Somehow, all three of us fit on his back with our gear attached. When Dagon left the ground, I thought my soul had departed from my body. I kept my eyes clamped shut for a long while until I heard Dagon's voice telling me to open them. I wasn't disappointed. The view from his back was the most spectacular thing I had ever seen. All the trees were turning bold, bright colors and evergreens stood tall and proud. All of them seemed as tiny as children's toys.

We had just crossed a field of wheat when Dagon suddenly thrashed and squealed. His roar was so loud it almost pierced my ear drums. I leaned back, trying to get a better grip on his scales, when I felt something abnormal behind me. A spearhead was pierced through his back.

His wings began to falter, and we hurtled to the ground in a half-glide, half-plummet.

"Dagon!" I shrieked. Though I wasn't sure if he could hear me over the screams of Ermek and Sheldon.

Dagon continued to thrash, and my body started to pull away from him. I looked down in horror as we fell. We were too high up.. we would never survive the fall. Dagon kept flapping his wings and went belly up. His tail wrapped around Ermek's waist, Sheldon was caught with his back foot, and me with his front. We slammed hard into the ground.

The wind rushed from my body as he flung me from his grasp. The world spun, and my body throbbed. Pushing myself up, I gradually got to my feet, trying to get my head to stop whirling. I looked over to Dagon. He saved us. He could have simply let us fall, but he took the brunt of the impact instead. As soon as my wobbly legs worked, I rushed over to him and dropped to my knees. Slowly, he transformed back into his human body. The spear was large compared to his dragon form.. however, in his human form, the spear was enormous. It protruded through his back and chest, propping him up so that his body could not fully rest on the ground.

I panicked at seeing the amount of black blood pooling beneath him. Cupping his face in my hands, I pressed my forehead to his. "Dagon, wake up."

He didn't respond, only lay there with the blacks of his eyes staring out into nothingness. He couldn't be dead.. a Demon Lord can't be killed that way, he said so himself. Maybe if I pulled the spear out, he could heal and be better.

A shock ran through my system as I touched the spear.. it lit up with bright blue angelic markings. A Priestess had blessed this spear, an immensely powerful Priestess.

"Are you alright, Jazzera?"

Ermek limped along with Sheldon in tow. I nodded and looked back down at Dagon.

"This was the doing of Demon Slayers. A Priestess blessed this spear."

"You can't pull it out?"

I shook my head. "It shocked me."

"Then we will wait for them. Surely, they will recognize their error and remove it for us."

I looked down at the chain that was attached to the spear. Whoever was on the other end would surely be along shortly to claim their prize. There were stories of demon dragons, as well as giant bird-like demons. So, I wasn't too surprised to find that a Demon Slayer or two may be lying in wait for such a creature to cross their path, but what would a Priestess and Demon Slayer be doing this far into Heathen territory? Priestesses were never sent beyond the border.

We didn't have to wait long before a group of men entered the clearing. I stood up and grasped my sword. They weren't wearing Demon Slayer armor.. they wore tattered green, brown, and black rags.

"Well, I'll be damned. You caught yourself a shapeshifter, Marley," declared the man at the head of the group. He was darker-toned with short, black hair and a scar along his left cheek.

"We took him down with Evalyn's spear. Shouldn't he be some fucked up creature by now?"

The man up front grinned. "There is only one type of demon who can keep human form when struck down, a demon that was born on Earth.. this is a child of Lilith."

I glanced at Dagon. Lilith? The demon woman who strangles infants in their cradles? But the stories always said that all her children were killed by angels. Was Dagon truly Lilith's son? It would make sense as to why they were working together.

Turning back to the man, I explained, "This is my demon. We were on an important mission when you shot us from the sky.. I ask that you release him so we can move on." I tried to sound as pleasant as possible, but something about them gave my words an edge.

The group laughed, and Ermek pulled his bow. More bows were pointed at us. "This is Evalyn's demon now."

"Put your bow away, Ermek," I ordered, letting go of my weapon. I knew as well as Ermek did that no other Priestess could take my demon, and I would have to hand him over with a ritual. This would give us some time to devise a plan to escape. Or at least allow Dagon enough time to heal from his wounds.

We're going to take them with us," announced the man.

"Why don't we kill her and take the damned demon, Jose?" asked another.

Shaking his head, the man named Jose laughed. "Do you want to fight a Demon Lord? If we kill her, then he is free. It's going to take Evalyn several days to get to us. By then, he may have some of his strength back, even with the spear. I've seen what these creatures can do firsthand." He scrutinized Dagon. "When I was a small child, the Demon Lord Moloch destroyed my entire village. He's a sibling to this one, a child of Lilith. If we keep this Priestess alive, she can keep him under control if she wishes to live."

I was helpless to do anything as two of the men pushed their way past me to Dagon. Even as angry at Dagon as I was, watching his nearly lifeless body tied to a cart hurt. The three of us were forced into the cart while Dagon lay motionless next to the wheels. "Aren't you going to bring him in?"

The man only chortled and closed the hatch. Three other men jumped into the cart with us, swords at the ready if we did something to displease them. The other two men mounted the horses pulling the cart. It started rolling along, dragging Dagon's naked body with it. I flinched every time we hit a bump in the road, and I could almost hear his skull crack on stones. A trail of black demon blood followed behind him.

It didn't take long before we entered a strange old building. It was tall and oval-shaped, with dead vines almost completely covering it. I had never seen an ancient building so large before.

"Impressive, isn't it?" one of the men asked when he noticed my gawking. "They say the ancients used to play a sport called 'baseball' here. Now it's just a ruin, but it keeps us dry at night."

I didn't respond, though I had questions. If I found this place under any other circumstance, I would have asked them. What was baseball? What types of artifacts did they find? As it were, I wanted as little interaction with these men as possible. As we were forced inside, they still didn't bother to pick Dagon up from the ground.. they simply pulled him along with the rope. The tear in his midsection was getting wider, and I hoped the spear would eventually pry itself free. As much as I hated seeing the image in my head, I knew it was Dagon's only chance of healing quickly.

The entrance was filled with dry leaves and trash that had been discarded. The halls were lined with torches that allowed little visibility. We walked into a large open area and were forced down metal stairs with thousands of seats lined up on either side, all surrounding a circle of overgrown grass. Below were cages with several demons inside and at least five other Priestesses. As we got closer, I noticed most of the captured demons were merely imps. The only exception was one lust demon. He was large with bull-like horns and red skin. Oddly, it was handsome, with a humanlike body and an exceptionally large penis hanging between his powerful legs. Quickly, I looked away, not wanting to be mocked by the men who captured us. They seemed like the type that would find enjoyment in my humiliation.

Putting their swords to Ermek's back, a group of men forced him and Sheldon into one of the empty cages. Roughly, the group's leader pulled me to a shelter close to the stands. When I stepped down to the warped concrete, he tied my hands to a rusted pole and snatched my sword from my side.

Pulling it from its casing, he gazed at it for a moment, then sheathed it. "Nice blade," he commented, then tossed it to the other side of the enclosure.

"What do we do with the demon?

Jose walked out of the shelter and went to Dagon. "Leave him.. he's not going anywhere. I'll be back in a little while."

The man left with two of their comrades, leaving two remaining guards. I watched as one of the men opened a cage that a Priestess was locked in.. she screamed and fought as he pulled her out.

"I'm gonna have a bit of fun with this one. When I get back, you can pick one."

The other man turned to me, and I recoiled. "I kind of like the new girl." He leered, showing off a full grin of rotting, yellow teeth.

"The boss will have your balls if you fuck her before he does. He likes to pop their cherry first, and we get the leftovers."

The man forced the woman he had chosen through the field of tall grass and into the walls of the building. I watched, horrified, as the other man picked his prize. It wouldn't be long before one tried to get to me, and I couldn't have that happen.

Since I couldn't reach my sword with my hands, I turned around and stretched my legs as far as they could go. I felt the tip of my toe hit the blade, and it clanked loudly. I reached again and was able to get my toe behind the scabbard. Every time I hit it, it slowly nudged its way toward me. When I had it about halfway to me, I heard footsteps.

"And what exactly do you plan to do with that?" It was the group's leader, and he led a diminutive, red-headed Priestess bound in chains.

I stood up and glared at him.. I would show him no fear. This man was no Priest I had to submit to.. he was nothing more than a predator. An evil man bound for Hell.. I would be damned if I gave him any satisfaction.

"I hear Priestesses of your strength are taught how to fight. You could be very valuable to us. You could join us, and no harm will come to you and your friends."

My eyes narrowed hatefully. "And what about Dagon?"

The man glanced over his shoulder. "I can't let you keep the demon. Evalyn would have my head if I let a Demon Lord slip through her fingers. If you

145

had the power to capture him, you could easily capture another strong demon." He picked up my sword. "So, I need you to transfer your demon to this Priestess."

I looked at the girl he was referring to. She had a tiny mark, barely large enough to catch an imp. "She's not strong enough to hold Dagon."

"She doesn't have to be. That spear will keep the demon in check until she can transfer him to Evalyn."

"I won't," I declared stubbornly. "If you're this cruel to him, I can only imagine what this Evalyn would do."

He cracked a grin and untied my hands. Then he escorted me over to where Dagon still lay motionless. "So, this is Dagon. The fish god. My grandfather used to tell me stories of the ancient gods, and I remember them well. His priests used to worship him while wearing fish hats, and, now look at him, lying naked with a spear through his chest. Oh, how the mighty have fallen."

"Take the spear out, then tell me how hard he fell."

He shifted back to me. "Have you gained feelings for this creature?"

"Dagon and I are a team. If you let me keep him, we can close the Gates of Hell, and, all these demons will return to Hell, where they belong."

He laughed. "A demon will help you close the Gates of Hell? That's funny, Priestess." He tossed me my sword. "But I'll make a deal with you. If you can kill me, you, your demon, and your friends are free to go, but if you can't, you will fight for Evalyn in the Heathen army."

I looked at my sword, clenching it tightly in my hands. I had never fought a human to the death in a battle.. I had only ever sparred. The demons I fought didn't have their own weapons. But they were crafty nonetheless and not very easy to take down. If I could take them on, I could take him on. After all, Dagon did say I was a badass.

I tossed the sheath to the ground and took my stance. The man pushed the young girl away and reached for his own sword. "I'll try not to maim you."

He struck first with his sword high in the air, and I dodged it easily, spinning around to face him. He came at me again.. this time, I deflected it with a loud clang. He advanced at me repeatedly, and I managed to deflect his blows each time.

"You are good," he admitted as he took a step back and readied his stance again. He came at me, and I dodged once more. He thrust at me from above, and I used my sword as a shield. He pushed down hard, and I could feel my feet digging into the dirt, my knees buckling. He was strong, perhaps too strong for me. I pushed back with all my strength, then kicked him in the midsection. He staggered, and I advanced on him, slicing down with my sword. He dodged it, but barely. I could feel my blade slash into his forearm and see blood dripping from his wound.

"You don't play around," he panted and came at me again.

Our swords clanged together several more times until I found an opening. I slashed him again, connecting with his hip and flaying it open. He cried out in pain and staggered to the ground. I held my sword above my head to finish him off but paused. I could accept killing a man as he was coming at me, but I couldn't justify killing him while he was on the ground. It would no longer be self-defense.. it would be murder.

Grunting with agony, the man tried to force himself up from the ground. As I readied myself for another attack, three long prongs plunged through his chest, and blood dribbled from his mouth. My heart fluttered. The man fell to the ground.. a long, black trident stuck up from his back. Dagon's trident. He was half sitting up with black blood pouring from his mouth.

"The mighty just fucked him up, is what it did," he groused, then fell backward again.

Dropping my sword, I rushed over to him and cradled his head in my arms. "Dagon?"

"Get this fucking thing out of my chest so I can eat these mother fuckers."

The intense shock attacked my hands as I yanked at the spear, but this time, I forced myself to endure it. However, I wasn't sure if Dagon could. With every tug I gave, he let out a shriek of pain. With all my strength, I yanked until the spear fell out and lay bloodied beside Dagon. It was no wonder I had a hard time pulling it out. There were jagged hooks carved into the blade that undoubtedly tore at his insides with every tug.

"That was so fucking amazing. Let's do it again!"

"Really?" I almost wanted to slap him. Clearly, he had lost too much blood.

"No, I don't want to do it again. That sucked."

"What can I do?"

He grinned at me. "You can suck my dick.. it's the only way to save me."

Slapping him hard, I remarked, "You're a pig."

148

"And you just slapped a wounded man. You're a bitch." He chuckled, then winced. "I'm fine. It'll take me a moment to heal, but I can stand." He got to his feet but shook with every movement he made. His clothing slowly manifested onto his skin, covering his naked body.

"Let's get our people, and then I'm going to sleep for a while."

JAZZERA

CHAPTER 21

A s I helped him limp over to the cage where Ermek and Sheldon were being kept, I heard a voice echo throughout the field. "Dagon, why is this human still alive?"

The voice manifested in the same fashion Dagon's did when he was in animal form. There was no source to it. Bewildered, I looked around until a form appeared roughly one hundred feet away. It was a woman with long, black hair tied into a ponytail. Her skin was a light brown, her eyes painted with golden eyeshadow, and her lips were painted black. She wore what looked like a golden bra and a wrap skirt around her waist.

"Leave her be, Mother," muttered Dagon.

So, this was Lilith, Dagon's demon mother, and the creature that strangled infants while they were still in the womb.

"I don't murder babies, mortal. That was a story made up by a pissed-off angel."

I flinched, realizing she could read my mind.

150

She can only read your fears, Jazzera. Don't let her scare you. It was Dagon's voice in my head.

"Release my son."

I didn't know how to reply. I couldn't expect Dagon to fight his own mother, especially while he was severely wounded. Standing up straight, I narrowed my eyes at her. "If I could take down one Demon Lord, I can take down another."

Lilith's eyebrows rose, and the buds of her lips curled into an amused smile. "I am much older than Dagon. He is merely thousands of years old, and I am billions. Older than the world itself. Do you think him my equal? He is part of me, yes, but I am stronger."

The smile stretched across her beautiful face as she manifested a sword into her hands. I recognized the blade from the armory, though my temple only had a replica. The sword she held was a Khopesh, which was used in the days of Ancient Egypt.

In response, Dagon produced his trident. The strength it must have taken for him to call upon it must be greater than I could imagine since it made him wince. I couldn't let him fight her.. she was stronger, and her aura was much more powerful than his. His aura was only slightly more substantial than the lust demon while he was still bleeding.

If only I could have gotten Ermek out of the cage, I could have had some backup, but even if I could let him out, his weapons were left behind in the field. He was very skilled at hand-to-hand combat, but I couldn't ask him to face a Demon Lord with his bare hands. It looked like I would have to fight this beast on my own.

Backing up, I slowly reached down for my sword and readied my stance. Dagon tried to take a fighting stance as well but faltered. Shifting to him, I commanded, "I forbid you from interfering.. you will stay out of this."

"Jazzera, she will kill you! Let me fight her!" His words verged on panic.

"Sweet little Dagon, always rebellious." Before the words completely left her lips, she was on me. I barely had enough time to bring my sword up in defense. As our swords collided, I was thrown back, sliding on my feet, and nearly fell to the ground. She rushed at me again, her sword slicing toward my side, and I could barely deflect it. She was fast, too fast. I couldn't defeat this demon, and, the smirk on her face told me that she knew it. She was simply toying with me, humoring me.

She kept advancing, her sword slamming against mine. She pressed her body against me, trying to push me over. I felt her skin, and a surge of energy snaked through my body. My angelic mark lit up. Focusing as hard as I could, I willed the surging energy to collect into my hand, pushing against the demon. I screamed as a burst of white light sent Lilith soaring through the air.. she landed several feet away. As she got to her feet, I saw that her face and several body parts were severely burned. Rushing at her, I swiped my sword toward her neck but missed and only nicked her shoulder.

Losing my balance, I staggered and felt her blade rake across my back. Pain seared through my body, but luckily, I could still stand upright. Twisting around, I saw Dagon trying to fight my command. The invisible collar around his neck lit up brightly, burning him.

Stay out of this, I said in my mind, not knowing if he could hear me. My attention returned to Lilith, whose burns were slowly beginning to heal.

She rushed at me again, slicing her blade up through the air.. I caught it, but not before she managed to cut my upper arm. My blade suddenly felt like it weighed ten times as much as it was supposed to, and I could no longer use my left arm to hold it. Lilith struck again, I tried to block, but she knocked my blade from my grasp. Terror raced through my body as she lifted her sword for the killing blow. I closed my eyes, not wanting to witness my own demise.

I was shoved to the ground, and a blood-curdling scream filled the air. My eyes shot open. Dagon fell to the ground in front of me. Somehow, he fought my command and came to my aid even though I told him not to. I got to my knees, trying to get to him, but Lilith dropped and scooped him up in her arms. It was she who had screamed.

His head was limp, lying across her arms, and a new gaping wound stretched along his neck. He had nearly been decapitated. Lilith's mournful cries sent panic through my body. Did she manage to kill him? Was he wrong about how a Demon Lord could be killed?

As he lay in her arms, he looked utterly lifeless. I couldn't tell if he was breathing or not.

Lilith's face was streaked with tears, but these were no tears of a mortal.. she was crying blood, red blood. Grabbing her sword again, she thrust it at me, and the blade penetrated just above my right breast. She pulled it out, and it vanished. Not being able to move, I could only watch as she brushed the hair out of his face and began rocking him.

"My love. My precious son." As she rocked, she began singing a gentle tune in a language I couldn't understand. I realized that she was singing him a lullaby. This was my chance to strike her down, my only opportunity, but the lullaby was making me want to sleep, and I didn't have the strength to move from my spot.

She lifted her hand and pointed toward the center of the grass field. Her dark brown eyes began to glow red, and I could feel heat pulsating through the air. Flames began to dance up from the ground, but it wasn't a normal fire. Normal fire was orange, not blood red.

As the fire grew, she got to her feet and cradled Dagon in her arms as if he weighed nothing. Ignoring me, she walked toward the fire and gently laid him in the center of the flames.

"No!" I cried, wincing in pain and almost falling forward.

She twisted toward me. "Do you wish him to heal or not?" My jaw clamped shut. "He was struck down by a celestial blade, much stronger than anything you pathetic half-breeds use.. the Fires of Hell will heal him."

I swallowed and looked up at her, ready to accept my fate.

She sneered at me. "Don't worry, girl. I'm not going to kill you. I have a feeling my son would never forgive me, and, all a mother really wants to do is protect her children. His suffering drew me here.. I can feel all of my children's pain." She headed to the cages, and I watched in amazement as the locks melted away. She walked toward the gate we had been escorted through.

"You're just going to leave him?" My voice was barely a whisper.

She stopped and turned. "Dagon will rise on his own when he is healed, but I am hungry. Heart of rapist sounds particularly delicious right now."

I knew better than to try and talk her out of it. If I were completely honest, I didn't want to stop her. I knew those men were evil, and, they deserved everything that was coming to them.

Pushing myself up, I felt my body shake, and my vision became blurry. Before Ermek could catch me, I fell to the ground.

DAGON

CHAPTER 22

I woke to the Fires of Hell burning around me. For a moment, I thought I was actually home, but as I stepped out of the flames, I realized I was still in the stadium. Calming the fire to a smolder, I looked around, trying to recall exactly what had happened. I spotted Jazzera lying on the ground and rushed to her side. Ermek cradled her in his arms, and I felt her head with my hand.. she was going cold.

"She's losing too much blood," I observed, inspecting her arm. The gash was large, showing muscles and tendons. Her back had also been slashed, but I couldn't see the extent of the damage. The wound in her chest worried me the most, and I didn't have the power to heal her. But I knew who did.

Getting to my feet, I clasped my hands together, focusing hard. It had been millennia since I prayed to Heaven, and I hoped the being I was looking for would hear me. The longer it took, the more panicked I became. If Jazzera died, she would go to

Heaven, and, I would never see her again. Even if she closed the Gates of Hell, I could still watch over her in my spirit form.

"Come on, Enlil," I whispered.

After what felt like an eternity, a bright light appeared, and I smiled warmly as the figure took form. I scrutinized Enlil up and down and embraced him.

"It has been so long," I gently kissed his forehead.

Enlil stepped back and nodded to me. "It has been centuries. The Gates of Hell have been opened for two hundred years, and you only now call me?"

I frowned, knowing that he was right, but my explanation would have to wait until later. Gripping him by the shoulder, I led him over to Jazzera. He cocked his head to the side, and his dark eyes lingered on her wounds.

"I can't help her," he sighed heavily.

"Yes, you can. You may not be able to heal her, but I know who can. I need you to find him and bring him here. I need you to find Caim."

"Why don't you bring her to him?"

I shook my head. "I can't bring a mortal through a portal I create.. I'd have to bring her to an open gate, but you can bring Caim to me. Just think about him, focus on him, and you'll find him." I reached out and rubbed the scruff of his chin gently. "Please."

He stared down at Jazzera. "She's in bad shape. What do I do if he won't come?"

"He'll come. Tell him his daughter needs his help."

Enlil nodded and vanished. I paced, agitated. He was right.. Caim may not come, even if it was to

157

save the life of his only living heir. It would be especially unlikely if he knew what saving his child's life would cost him.

As time passed, I heard the screams of the would-be Demon Hunters as Lilith finished them off one by one. The Priestesses would be safe.. my mother hardly ever harmed a human woman. After that incident with Adam, she gained a sour taste in her mouth regarding men.

"I can't stop the bleeding," worried Ermek as he pressed his hand firmly on one of Jazzera's wounds.

"Enlil will be back soon," I stated, crossing my arms impatiently.

"Former lover?"

I may have laughed if it hadn't been for the current circumstances. "God, no. He's my son."

His eyes widened. "Sorry. It's just you two look nothing alike."

I smiled gently. "It's an angel, demon thing. Beings like my mother, who were created, don't have a human form. They are simply energy and light. When a human first looks upon them, the human gives them their form. They become whatever the human imagines they look like. After several humans, they eventually just pick and choose a form. Whichever one they like best, but beings like me, born instead of created, take on the form of our parents and how they looked at the time. My parents were in Europe when I was created in the womb. So, I have natural European features. My son was also born, obviously. He was born in Ancient Sumer. So, he looks like the native population from there. Their race became known as 'Middle Eastern.'"

Ermek looked confused, and I didn't blame him. Since the Rapture, most knowledge of the outside world was lost. Nobody dared to cross the ocean since the Leviathan had been set loose. It was mind-blowing that Jazzera's mother had crossed the sea to make it here, but then, there was little left of Japan, so there weren't too many choices. When the world went to Hell, entire cultures were destroyed, and, even though Ermek wore braids in his hair, I highly doubted he knew why his ancestors wore them.

Enlil returned moments later, to my relief, and, in tow, he had brought with him the only person who could save Jazzera's life. It had been centuries since I laid eyes on Caim, but he hadn't changed. Like my mother, he was created and not born.. thus, he would take the form of what humans thought he should look like. Upon discovering Japan, he refused to leave, falling in love with their customs. It was said that he even helped mold some of them. When the Gates of Heaven and Hell closed, Caim refused to leave Earth, turning him into what was known as a 'Fallen Angel.'

Caim looked down at Jazzera, who appeared weak in Ermek's arms. "You do know what you ask of me." His gaze moved to me.

"Yes. I'm asking you to save your daughter's life."

"At the cost of my own."

"You will live on through her. Your daughter is on a quest to save the human race. What are you on a quest for? To find more women to knock up? To create more Nephilim, and for what? Why have you and the other Fallen kept breeding her kind? If not for this exact purpose."

"To give humans a chance against your kind," he sneered.

"And if Legion has their way, the Gates of Hell will never close. Think about it this way, this would be self-sacrifice, and, God loves self-sacrifice. You may just be re-created and get your wings back."

He glared at me. We both knew that was very unlikely. "You will die for her?"

I nodded.

"I want to hear you say the words, Dagon. Will you die for her? Will you become part of Legion if you have to?"

"Yes. I will die for her."

I felt another presence. Typically, an angel's presence was calming.. however, this one felt like doom.. death was near.

"Don't you dare, Azrael." There was no answer. "Don't fuck with me, Azrael! Show yourself!" The form of a man materialized only inches from Jazzera. She was still alive, so he hadn't reaped her soul yet. "Don't take her. Not yet." I stared at the Angel of Death in his dark, almost purple eyes, begging him. Pleading with him.

"She is calling to me, Dagon," he murmured flatly.

"Don't you have a million other people to kill right now? Can't you just give it a bit?"

He tilted his head slightly. "I don't kill people, Dagon. You know this. I don't take a soul without their permission. They call to me. Your mother killed her, not I."

I wanted to cut his head off. "But she's not going to die because you aren't taking her soul."

"Her body is broken, Dagon. There are no doctors in this era with the ability to heal her, and, you remember the last time I didn't collect a soul.. I can't afford for that to happen again."

"That's not going to happen again, Azrael!" I pointed to Caim. "Because he is going to fix it."

"I never said I would do this, Dagon," replied Caim.

I gave a mean, icy glare. "Either you give her your life force. Or I will kill you."

He scoffed. "You can't kill me. I may not have the power I once had, but I'm just as immortal as you are."

I manifested my trident. Like my body, I could alter it, though only slightly. The three prongs developed a knife-like edge, strong and sharp enough to cut through bone. Then before either angel could react, I swiped my trident at Azrael, cutting off his hand and causing him to drop his scythe. Keeping the momentum, I spun around and swung my weapon high, connecting with his neck. Golden blood and bright, white light poured out of both wounds. The angel's mortal form fell to the ground.

I screamed, "Pick up the scythe! Now! We have no time!" I pulled Jazzera from Ermek's arms, and he dove to the ground, snatching up the weapon.

I felt the warm glow surround his body. *Don't let go of the scythe. When Azrael returns, don't fear him. He can't kill you without his weapon, and, both of them know that his blade is the only thing that can kill them.. they won't attack you. Right now, you are Death. Play along if you want to save Jazzera.*

He nodded at me, and I turned to Caim. "Now, let's see how immortal you really are."

Caim backed up. Azriel's body disappeared, but it didn't last long. Moments later, Azrael fell, practically putting a crater into the ground. I had to resist the urge to chuckle. "Azrael's back, and, just as sexy as ever."

He grunted and pushed himself to his feet. "You said this wouldn't be like last time."

"And it's not, but I wouldn't try anything if I were you. The significant difference between this mortal and the last one is that he's a Demon Slayer and will fuck your world up." I turned my attention back to Caim. "You have two choices.. either save your daughter or be erased from existence. Either way, you don't walk away from this."

"You can't just force people to sacrifice themselves, Dagon," voiced Azrael.

"I can. A life for a life. Isn't that right, Caim? I'm asking you to save your daughter as retribution for killing mine."

Caim became deathly still. He knew of what I spoke, the death of an unborn child in her mortal mother's womb. It was Caim who had given the mother the potion to create a miscarriage.

It had succeeded, though the infant was never expelled from her mother's body.. she later died of infection. At the time, I had felt very little. I was a god then, and the woman wished for a child.. I simply answered her prayer. The woman was happy until Caim told her that I was no god but a demon.

In the long run, Caim killed her and the infant. Even though I wasn't the type to hold that kind of a grudge, he didn't know that. The infant hadn't been born, so I had little attachment to it.

But I needed Caim to fully believe I expected an eye for an eye.

Defeated, Caim walked over to Jazzera, placed his hand on her head, and closed his eyes.

His body began to glow a soft light that grew until it was nearly blinding. His form exploded into millions of tiny, flittering lights that danced around until they fell to the ground. Jazzera opened her eyes.

JAZZERA

CHAPTER 23

When I opened my eyes, all I saw were specks of white light, like fairies dancing around my head. The lights seemed to take form for a moment, almost like a human with wings. Then it was gone. At first, I thought I was dead and that this was Heaven, but with Dagon kneeling over me, I knew I was either alive or in Hell. I sat up, amazed that not a single bone in my body throbbed. In fact, I had never felt better in my entire life.

I about jumped when I noticed that we weren't alone. Two handsome men stood nearby. One had pale white skin and dark brown hair.. the other had light brown skin and big brown eyes.

"What happened?"

"You almost took a walk with this motherfucker." Dagon pointed to the paler man. "This is Azrael, and, this handsome young fellow is Enlil."

"More demons?"

The one called Azrael scoffed. "That's insulting."

Dagon chuckled. "Yeah, he's much worse.. he's Death itself...actually, Ermek is technically Death right now."

"Something that needs to be remedied," groused Azrael, holding out his hand.

Dagon frowned and looked over to Ermek. "Let Daddy Death have his toy back." He smiled at Azrael. "As further thank you, we could get a room, and I could call you Daddy there. We'd have a good time."

"Dagon, nothing would make me happier than not seeing you again for another thousand years."

"The offer still stands." He shrugged. "I've been trying to get a piece of that ass for centuries, but he is so painfully heterosexual."

Ermek returned the scythe to Azrael, who nodded and vanished.

"You're such a pig," I said to Dagon.

The younger man snickered. "He's been like this for as long as I can remember.. you should ask my mother."

"Mother?"

Dagon's eyes went wide. "Jazzera, I would like you to meet my son, Enlil. His mother and I have been broken up for a long, long, long, long, long time."

Enlil smirked and commented, "She hates him."

"Still?" asked Dagon.

"Yes. Very much so."

"Well, you can tell her I hate her too. She's a bitch." Dagon hugged his son. "Since I may not be around for much longer, we should meet up the next time Hell's Gates open.. we can have a drink and watch humanity freak out again. Those were good times."

"I'll look forward to that," replied Enlil as he embraced his father. A moment after they let each other go, he was gone, as if he was never there.

Dagon pulled me aside and explained the events that had unfolded. Lilith nearly killed me, but my father gave his life up for mine. I was also no ordinary woman.. I was, in fact, a Nephilim.

"Any Priestess that has a mark has angel blood flowing through their veins. The larger the mark, the more closely related the offspring is. Yours is so large because your father was an angel." He softly ran his fingers over my angelic mark. "Priestesses were never meant to be oppressed.. they were meant to protect humankind and lead them to the light. You were meant to be a leader." Placing his hand gently under my chin, he smiled softly at me. We stood there, staring at each other for a few seconds before I went to retrieve my sword. "And your sword is now activated, Priestess."

I studied it briefly. I didn't know what he meant by activated.. it still looked the same. "What do you mean?"

"When your father gave you his life force, he gave you the full ability to wield his weapon. Celestial beings can't touch each other's weapons. That's why Ermek had to pick up Azrael's scythe. Once he did, he was given some of Azrael's power. Not a single person in the world could have died unless Ermek said so, but it would have thrown off the balance of the world. Ermek wouldn't be able to hear the dying call to him or be in a billion places at once. Because he's mortal, he only got a shred of Azrael's power. Because you are half-mortal, you could pick up your father's sword, but the angel in you wouldn't be able to use its power. Now that your father gave you his life force, your sword will be much more powerful."

I stared at the blade, which shimmered in the setting sunlight. As much as I wanted to curl up in Dagon's arms and forget all of the world's problems, I knew that wasn't possible. I still had a mission to do, no matter how horrible it was. I didn't have time to mourn a father I didn't remember, and, if what Dagon had told me was true, I had a responsibility to close the gates to save the human race, which meant I would eventually have to say goodbye. That thought hurt much worse than any wound Lilith could have dealt me.

I sheathed my sword and called out, "We should start moving.. we still have a long way to go."

"Not exactly, Priestess," interrupted Dagon. I gave him a questioning look. He had made the journey sound like it could take years to accomplish. "We can't continue on the way we were going."

"Why can't we?"

"Evalyn will be hunting you."

There was that name again. Some woman I had never heard of until today. "You know of this woman?"

"I met her once, and she didn't have a clue who I was at the time. When we were looking for the Priestess who held the key, we thought it may be her."

"She is a Nephilim like me?"

He nodded. "Yes, her mother is a Fallen Angel." Pausing, Dagon scratched at his chin hair as if contemplating the meaning of life. "Her mother kept her out of Follower territory and raised her in

Heathen lands. Eventually, she rose to power and now leads the Heathen army. If, by some small chance, word gets out that we were here and got away, she won't stop hunting you."

I considered this for a moment. Why would anyone bother with me? I was surely not worth hunting, and, even if I was, it didn't change anything. I still had a responsibility to close the Gates of Hell. Even if I risked capture, I still had to try.

"We have no choice."

"But we do," he admitted. "I can take you through Hell itself."

The thought of it brought chills down my spine. Everything I had ever been told declared Hell as the worst place imaginable. Even according to my demon, it was a place I never wanted to visit. How could going through Hell be any safer than going through Heathen territory?

As if reading my mind, Ermek asked, "How would going into Hell itself be any safer?"

"Well, for one, you're all mortal. Even if the Priestess here is a little more angel than she started with, she is still mortal. The demons down there shouldn't pay us too much mind. Most will follow my command. I'm a Demon Lord, remember? And it will be faster. When the Rapture happened, several gateways to Hell opened in every large city worldwide. The bigger the population meant more sinners. The closest one is in a city that was known as St. Louis. It's not too far into Follower territory, but first, we have to make it through the city itself. It will be crawling with demons and angry spirits. If we can reach the core, there will be a portal that will take us into Hell. Once there, I can find the correct gateway to take us straight to the Babylon gate."

We unanimously agreed that it would be best not to have Dagon return to his dragon form. At least, not until we had traveled for a full day. We wanted to be as far away from the stadium as possible before he transformed again. Unfortunately, no matter how long we waited, it would still be a risk. We didn't know how far the Demon Hunter territory was, but the journey to the gate would take weeks if we continued on foot.

We traveled about an hour into the dark of night, veered off the road, and camped deep in the woods. We didn't want to make a fire, but it was too cold to go without one, especially since none of us knew exactly where we were or how to get back to where we had left our gear. Our supplies and tents lay in a wheat field behind us.

Luckily, the hellfire burned hot and warmed the ground enough for us to lie down without freezing to death. I laid down close to a tall oak tree, trying to gather some of its leaves to create a type of bed. Dagon sat beside me when I settled in, stroking my hair for a bit. I felt myself starting to drift off until I sensed Ermek's eyes on us.

Dagon glanced up before smiling down at me. "I'll keep watch for the night. You mortals need your beauty sleep." He took his raven form and flew off.

When Dagon was no longer in sight, Ermek took his spot. "You care for Dagon."

I stared at him, not knowing how to respond. Do I tell him the truth? What would he do if he found out? What would he say?

"If I tell you something, do you promise not to get angry with him?"

I wasn't sure I could keep that promise, but I nodded anyway.

169

"Your father didn't give his life up willingly. Dagon forced him."

I almost got to my feet. "He what?!"

"He cut off the Angel of Death's head for you. Your father wasn't going to help you, and he did that to save you."

"It doesn't matter.. you don't force someone to sacrifice themselves."

Ermek grabbed my hand. "I never said Dagon was perfect. He's a lustful pig who is often indifferent to morals. My point is that he was willing to do whatever he could to save you, and, that wasn't your binding spell forcing him to do it. He fought your command to fight Lilith, and, he beheaded the Angel of Death to keep him from reaping your soul." He kept my hand in his as he stared at the dark forest. "What if Dagon is right? What if everything we had been led to believe was a lie? Or at least not full truths?"

"What do you mean?"

"Angels and demons are supposed to be mortal enemies. Yet they didn't hate each other. At least not Azrael and Enlil. Sure, Azrael seemed a bit annoyed by Dagon, but he didn't hate him, and, why would God care if we mix fabrics? Why would any god be so petty? What if Dagon has been telling the truth all along, that God doesn't care who you love?"

I kept my eyes locked on his for a long while, contemplating his words. The mixed fabric rule seemed a bit silly now that I truly thought about it. Very silly, actually. Would God really hate me if I fell in love with a demon? Would he turn his back on me if I made love to a demon? A demon who has been kind to me. A demon who was nearly decapitated by his own mother to protect me. A man who faced the Angel of Death himself to make sure I lived. A demon who possibly loved me back.

"What are you getting at?"

"Maybe we don't close the gates."

I stiffened. Out of all the people in this world, I couldn't believe those words came from Ermek's lips. Closing the Gates of Hell would mean the demons would go away. Children could sleep soundly at night. People could walk through the woods without fear of being eaten. Why would anyone throw that chance away? To live happily ever after with their demon lover? A man who had never touched me outside of a dream, except for a kiss?

"We have to close the gates, Ermek, for humanity's sake. I can't be selfish. No matter what I may feel, this isn't about me."

He frowned and looked away, releasing my hand. "I hate to admit it, but I'm starting to be fond of that ill-mannered demon." He gazed into the forest for a moment. "I won't return to the Followers afterward, and I'd like it if you came with me."

"To Heathen country?"

He nodded.

Before I could answer him, he got to his feet and walked to the other side of the campfire.

I stared into space for quite some time before I laid down in the little pile of leaves I mashed together. I wanted nothing more than to stop this quest, to run into Dagon's arms and never leave.

It broke my heart to think I would never see his face again if I went through with this quest. I would miss his long, dark locks, sneaky grin, and even his pitch-black eyes, as unsettling as they could be. Even when he hinted that he enjoyed other men's company, I didn't care. I just wanted to be with him.

I clenched my eyes closed to keep the tears from falling. I felt a hand on my shoulder, and I rolled over.. Dagon lay beside me, softly stroking my arm. I sat up, dried my eyes, and ran my hand through his soft, black hair.

"Why are you crying, Priestess?" His finger ran along the trail of my tear.

Instead of answering, I lunged at him, pressing my lips firmly against his.. he returned the kiss eagerly. Before I could control myself, I began yanking the jacket from his body.

He pulled back and gripped my hands in his. "Not tonight, Priestess."

"Why?"

"Because I don't want to torture you or myself anymore."

I felt my body shake. What was he saying?

"Before I am cast back to Hell, I would like to feel you just once in the real world. If I keep giving your body what it wants in here, then I can't see that happening. If you want me, Priestess, you will have to come to me."

Dagon vanished, and I was left alone with only the fire to keep me company. I was dreaming. His presence here wasn't real, only an illusion. It wasn't until the scenery suddenly changed that I knew, beyond a doubt, that it was a dream. At first, I was in a beautiful meadow.

Getting to my feet, I walked through the tall grass, gently touching the tips of the taller flowers. As I headed to the tree line, everything around me burst into flames. I was left in a barren wasteland of falling ash. In the center of it all stood a giant red door, and next to it was Dagon with another figure. This figure wore all white from head to toe.. even its hair was pure white, hanging freely until it reached the being's calves. The creature thrust its hand forward, wrapping around Dagon's throat. It shifted to me, its glowing green eyes feeling like daggers that pierced my heart.

"Stay away," it whispered with an echo of multiple voices. It looked back at Dagon, and I watched helplessly as his body turned to ash, absorbed into the creature.

JAZZERA

CHAPTER 24

I woke with a start. The sun was rising to the east of us, casting shadows through the trees. The fire died down quite a bit, and I felt my body shiver from the cold. I could see my own breath as I sighed, thankful that what I had experienced was only a dream. Or was it? The shiver returned while I pondered whether that was merely a dream or if it was something more. Dagon could slip into my dreams, and, based on Lady Ester's description, that being in my nightmare was Legion. Legion ate souls. What other abilities did they have? Did they have the ability to show the future? Would Dagon perish forever in the battle? Or was it my own paranoia?

The sound of a bird flapping its wings caught my attention, and a dead rabbit fell at my feet. Had I not known that the creature was Dagon, I would have been amazed at the sight of the proud bald eagle as it took to the sky once more. I supposed the rabbit was meant to be our breakfast, and he was most likely flying off to try and find more. After all, this scrawny little creature would barely be enough for two grown men and a woman, and, that was without adding Dagon into the mix. He barely ate, and when he did, I felt like he preferred raw meat.

Drawing my sword, I made an attempt at skinning the creature. It was much harder than I expected, especially with such a long blade, but since we lost practically everything, I had no choice.

By the time I was finished, Dagon had dropped another rabbit. This one was only slightly larger than the other. He didn't fly off like I expected him to. Instead, he took his human form and headed into the woods. As I began working on the second creature, he returned moments later with a small pile of timber and dropped it onto the fire.

The clatter of wood caused Ermek to stir, and he was soon up and off to take care of some personal business.

"I'm sure glad I never have to worry about doing that," mentioned Dagon as he worked on skewering one of the rabbits.

"You never have to relieve yourself?"

He shook his head. "Demons don't have to eat or drink. Any time we do, it's because we actually like the taste, but after that, I have no idea what happens to it. It never comes back in the form of shit." He chuckled, and I couldn't help but smile despite how gross his little joke was.

Sheldon was the next to wake. He got up to relieve himself but didn't bother going too far into the woods. It seemed Heathens weren't as concerned with modesty as us Followers were. When he was finished, he moved quickly over to the fire and began rubbing his hands. "So, this quest you're all on. I'm still not invited, am I?"

I shook my head. "It's too dangerous for someone with little combat experience."

"Good. Because you're right, I don't have any combat experience, and I'm a lover, not a fighter. You should drop me off at the nearest Heathen city.. I think I'm far enough away from River Bed."

I placed the skewers over the fire. "I thought you wanted to go to Follower country and be absolved of your sins."

He scowled at me. "I only said that to get you two to take me with you. I always planned to stay in Heathen territory. I like having sex with men. I'm not sorry for that, and I don't believe I should be."

Everything I had ever been taught suddenly came rushing into my head.. sodomites were some of the worst people in the world and were predators that would hurt small children if ever given a chance. God hated them and demanded their death. They were a disgusting plague on humanity, and they sold their soul to Lucifer.

I almost let those words leave my lips until I looked at Dagon. He had never been shy about the fact that he also enjoyed sleeping with other men and women. Did the rules not apply because he was a demon? God would hate him no matter what he did. Wouldn't that be correct?

That's what the Followers had always taught me, but then there were so many other things that felt so wrong. Why did God care so much about mixed fabrics? Why did a woman have to cry while being beaten to prove she wasn't a witch? Why were women treated as no more than livestock to be bred, yet I was denied the right to have a husband and children?

If Dagon was pure evil, why would he risk himself for me against my own will? Was it because he knew he couldn't die? Not by Lilith's hand, anyway. Lilith was supposed to be jealous of human women, so why did she spare the Priestesses? She went after the men because they were rapists. Angels stood side by side with Dagon, and they didn't fight. One even embraced Dagon, and Dagon called him his son. So, if a demon could have an angel for a son, why couldn't a man love another man?

"You will have to get new clothing anyway, Priestess. A few more days in that top, and your boobs are going to plop out." Dagon grinned. "Not that I would mind. I love boobs.. boobs are wonderful things that shouldn't be hidden."

"You're one of them," said Sheldon before I could call Dagon a pig again.

"And what would that be?" asked Dagon.

"One of those confused souls who can't decide which type you wish to be with. You're one of those selfish men who like it both ways."

Dagon laughed. "I am tens of thousands of years old. Do you really believe I am confused? And I don't just like it both ways…." His grin widened. "I love it all ways. In fact, you humans even coined a term for it. Pansexual, I believe, is what you called it."

"I've never heard of it," I admitted.

"Of course, you haven't. Your righteous leaders made anything but the term "sodomite" forbidden. Like I said, you humans were much more fun before you went all super religious. I tried to keep the fun going once I had mortal form again, but that didn't quite work out how I wished it would. Your kind clung to your Bible as if God was suddenly going to stop what was happening. As if he ever stopped anything."

I focused on the rabbit. This entire conversation had me so confused. I was taught very specific, strict rules since I was a small child. After spending a couple of months with Dagon, suddenly, I'm questioning everything. Even Ermek was starting to question the things we had been taught. Out of everyone I had known before leaving the temple, Ermek would have been the last person to have doubt.

After we ate, Dagon pulled me to my feet and walked me into the woods.

"Where are we going?"

He didn't respond, only continued to tug me along. When we reached a small pond, he led me to a large bolder and instructed me to take a seat. He sat next to me and took both of my hands in his. "I'm going to take you on a journey, Jazzera, and I need you to trust me."

"I trust you." I didn't know why, but my words were true.

He smiled. "Then close your eyes and let me in."

I did as instructed, and everything was pitch black, and it was much darker than when I closed my eyes in the daylight. Eventually, Dagon's form appeared, and he still had his hands in mine.

"What you are going to see are my memories. The world before yours. Don't be frightened. Nothing there can hurt you, and they won't realize you are there. Those times have already long passed."

I nodded, eager to see where he would take me. I felt a slight breeze hit my body. Then sand crept in around my feet until light struck me, and I could see that we were standing in a desert. Around us were gigantic stone buildings. People rushed about, pushing and pulling giant rectangles of stone. Men high up on scaffolding shouted orders in a language I didn't recognize. Other men were holding whips, slashing men and women alike when they slowed their pace.

"This is Ancient Egypt," explained Dagon as he walked along the base of the giant pyramid. "These people are the Pharaoh's slaves."

We walked toward the river, and I spotted men pushing dead bodies into the water, giant lizard-like creatures started feasting on their flesh. Two more men were pulling a tiny infant from its mother's arms, and she begged to have her child returned, but the men slit the babe's throat.

I covered my mouth and shut my eyes.. the darkness returned. When I opened them, we were in a new place. We were on a field of swords that clanked together in continuous battle.

Men fell to their deaths, and blood covered the desert sand. Some rode horses, holding crosses and wearing metal armor, much like what the Holy Knights of the Followers wore.

"These were the Crusades. A king and religious leaders decided they needed to force their beliefs on others. They burned many people and slaughtered thousands of innocents, all in the name of God."

The world went dark again. We were on a ship bobbing around on the ocean. Men were chaining several other people together. Men, women, and even children. The people in chains were naked, their dark skin covered in filth. I screamed as I watched one of the sailors push a metal ball off the ship's edge, dragging the chained people along with it, all of them forced into a watery grave.

"These people were captured for slavery. There wasn't enough food for them, so they were tossed into the ocean. I was here as a witness to the crimes of these men. Their crimes of not only murder but enslavement. Yet your Bible will say that slavery was the will of God."

The world faded.. we were standing in a crowd at the edge of makeshift gallows where three women and two men were standing with nooses tied around their necks. They were filthy and looked sickly and starved. A crowd was gathered.. all of them were dressed in black and white. The men wore funny hats, and the women wore bonnets. One man stood off to the side. I couldn't hear his words.. however, it seemed like he was preaching. Then a wagon was pulled out from under the prisoners, and they dropped to their deaths. Their legs kicked as they struggled to find air.

"These were some of the more famous Salem Witch Trials. Many more came before these, and many followed. Yet every person who died was innocent.. their only crimes were being enemies of more prominent families."

We were in a small village made of large cone-shaped tents. Men, women, and children were running for their lives as uniformed men on horseback rushed through the village, blasting their weapons at the people.

"When these men decided they wanted this land, they slaughtered thousands of native people and almost caused the extinction of an entire race."

I didn't know how much more of this I could handle. I could almost feel the pain and sorrow of every person who had fallen before my eyes, but before I could ask Dagon to stop, he pulled me into another world. This one was surrounded by fences. People within the barriers looked sickly and starving. They wore stripes and had golden stars stitched to their sleeves. A group was pushed toward a small concrete building in the center of the yard.

"These people were imprisoned, tortured, and murdered because of their religious beliefs."

"Dagon, I can't do this anymore," I begged, grabbing his hand tightly.

He squeezed. "Only a couple more."

We were pulled into another scene. This one looked even stranger. Buildings surrounded us, the largest buildings I had ever seen. The streets were made of flat stone, and motorized carriages pulled people around. In my time, there were shells of these contraptions, rusted remnants of the past. The roads were crowded with people walking around, going about their daily lives.

Then suddenly, two contraptions slammed into the top of two buildings. I was paralyzed as smoke wafted from the structures. Time seemed to speed up. People ran in every direction, twice the speed of any normal human, and abruptly the buildings collapsed.

"Three thousand people died in this attack. All because a small group decided their God demanded the death of 'non-believers.'"

The scene shifted, and this time, we were inside a building. People were dancing, and I noticed each of them was paired with a member of the same gender.

Some held hands, while others kissed. There were several loud popping sounds, and people fell to

181

the ground in pools of blood as a man with a strange weapon attacked. There were screams and cries of terror from people who must have known they would die.

"This man killed people because they fell in love with someone of the same sex as theirs because his God demanded they die."

Again, the scene morphed until we found ourselves in a large room. The chamber had a long table with several men sitting around it. At one end of the table, a man spoke to the others in a strange language.

"This is where the Bible was constructed. The man at the end of the table is Emperor Constantine. Rome was torn apart by a religious war between the new Christians and the Pagans. This is the Council of Nicaea. This group of men decided what would go into the Bible and what would be taken out. They even added a few things, such as render, onto Cesar. His old pagan faith wasn't too good at controlling people, but this new faith was much harsher and stricter. If the rich wished to be absolved of their sins, they only needed to pay the Church. The poor, who couldn't afford penance, would risk going to Hell if they misbehaved. It was a very effective tool. It struck fear into the hearts of the peasants and kept them in line."

The blackness returned a final time, and we were in the woods where we had begun. I blinked my eyes several times and realized tears were running down my face, and I wiped them away with my hands. "That was so awful."

"That was only a tiny fraction of the things I have witnessed. A small portion of the evilness of mankind." Getting to his feet, he reached out his hand and pulled me to my feet. "The Rapture didn't happen because men loved each other or because humans created flying contraptions. The Rapture happened because of centuries of evil. Those who were behind those atrocities became putrid souls, and putrid souls count for a thousand sinners in Hell. God only wants humans to live their best lives on Earth before going to Paradise. He doesn't care if you believe in him or worship another god. He only cares about whether or not you are a good person." Squeezing my hand, he let go and began walking back to camp.

DAGON

CHAPTER 25

After the fire had been put out, we resumed our journey. I had to admit that the closer we got to our goal, the more anxious I became. My reasons were many. If I didn't execute the plan precisely, it could all fall apart. I risked losing Jazzera no matter how I played my cards.. either she'd get killed or end up hating me. The last mortal I dared to care for betrayed me. Why would Jazzera be any different? Like Jade, Jazzera cared far too much for the lives of others. In the end, she would make the same choice Jade did. In the pit of my stomach, I just knew the results would be the same.

I shuddered at the thought of my long-lost lover. We were never actual lovers.. I was bound to spirit form, only able to make love to her in dreams. When I finally did get to feel her flesh, she was dying in my arms. Her soul fluttered off to Heaven while I remained behind, never to look upon her face ever again.

Clenching my fists, I snuck a glance over at Jazzera. Deep down, I wondered if she truly felt the same about me as I did for her. I knew she cared for me but was it because she had been denied love for so long? I surely wasn't her ideal mate. I was a horny asshole who enjoyed orgies, and, the very idea of marriage made my dick soft. Maybe it was better if she ended up hating me. After all, most women do, eventually. With time, I learn to hate them back, but Jazzera was so very hard to hate.

When dusk began to settle, we decided it would be safe for me to take dragon form. It would be next to impossible for any Demon Hunter to shoot me down in the dead of night.. they would need night vision for that, a technology that was long gone.

Once the humans were safely mounted, I took flight. Even though I knew I should fly high in the sky in case a Demon Hunter decided to try their luck, the bitter cold in the air made me stay slightly above the treetops. I told the humans to stay close to my skin to avoid hypothermia because demons naturally run warm. I flew as fast as possible.. a journey that would take us weeks on foot would take us only hours by air.

I spotted a cozy little village and landed in a small field roughly a mile away. What remained of Ermek's money would suffice to buy us a room for the night and more modest clothing for the Priestess. Once the humans dismounted, I noticed they were shivering violently, and I offered my jacket to Jazzera.

The small village was surrounded by a tall stone wall with a guard. We told him we were simply passing through, and he opened the gate without further questions, even pointing out an inn where we could stay.

The village reminded me of the Medieval Ages, tiny stone homes with thatched roofs and mud roads lit by candle lamp posts. Though electricity was a rare sight, a few human cities embraced it, using the power of wind and water to light up their communities. Sadly, this town wasn't one of them.

Thunder rumbled in the distance, and I rushed the humans along the path to where the guard had pointed. At the end of the road, right next to the wall, stood a cozy two-story building made of wood and stone. A wooden sign hung above the door that said, 'Ducky's Bar and Inn.'

The sight inside was comical. It looked like the twenty-first century and Medieval Times had a drunken fuck session, resulting in this twisted baby. The tabletops were made of old plastic party tables with wooden legs screwed into the corners to make them stand. The seats were plastic, two-hundred-year-old lawn chairs, and, the cups, all of different shapes and sizes, were also plastic, but the funniest part was all the rubber duckies seated on top of each table and the bar. The rest of the inn looked like a remastered version of a medieval tavern.. I had never been able to enjoy them but had seen them plenty of times in spirit form.

A short, plump woman greeted us with a crooked smile. In a squeaky voice, she asked, "Stayin' the night?"

"Two rooms, please," Ermek requested as he pushed between Jazzera and me.

He held out some paper credits for her to take. Luckily, many Heathen towns accepted Follower money since it was in paper form and easier to carry. Heathen money was nothing more than old United

States change that could weigh a person down. After handing us our keys, we went upstairs to the rooms.

Our rooms weren't next to each other, but they were close enough. Ermek and Sheldon took a room two doors down from Jazzera's and mine. Upon entering the room, Jazzera quickly laid down on the bed, a mattress made of grey material stuffed with straw. I doubted it was comfortable, but the Priestess nuzzled in and covered up anyway.

After a moment of me standing close to the door, she pulled the blanket back and patted the bed. "Come keep me warm," she invited with a small smile.

Returning her smile, my tunic and boots vanished, but I kept my pants intact. I slid between the covers and wrapped my arms around her. She shivered and nuzzled her face up against my neck. She pulled back a few moments later and gazed at me. She was so beautiful.

Her full, pink lips were curled upward, her cheeks flushed pink from the cold, and her dark, nearly black eyes were sleepy from the journey. I caught her midnight hair in my fingers and took in her smell, autumn leaves, and campfire smoke. I loved it.

Letting go of her hair, I traced my fingers down her cheek and onto her chest, drawing an invisible outline of her collarbone, then moved down to the ties of her corset. Her eyes dilated, and she clasped my hand, pushing it away from the strings. I was disappointed until she began toying with the loops and loosening the front. She giggled slightly, seeming to get stuck.

Eagerly, I reached over to help slacken the rest. Once it was loose enough, she sat up and pulled it from her body, tossing it to the floor. Jazzera covered herself before I could get a proper look. She was shy, even though I had seen her perfect breasts in numerous dreams. Clasping her wrist, I pulled it away from her chest and pinned it to the bed. Her cheeks flushed brighter.

"Why are you trying to hide such perfection?" I whispered, sitting upright. I caressed her curves with my free hand before rubbing her small, tan nipples.

"No man was ever meant to touch me this way."

I leaned down and gave one of her nipples a suckle. "I am no man, Jazzera. I am a demon of the male gender." Taking her free hand, I pressed it gently to my chest. "And you control this demon. Just tell me what you desire.. your wish is my command."

"I want you to make me feel like a woman."

"But you *are* a woman, Jazz. A strong, beautiful woman, and you don't need sex to tell you that. What you desire is to know what it's like to connect to another."

Pulling her wrist away, she sat up, cupped my face in hands, and looked me in the eyes. My black eyes were typically terrifying to humans. Yet, she held my gaze for several moments before declaring, "I desire for you to make love to me."

Those words almost made me pull away, and the look in her eyes made me shudder. I knew by the tone of her voice that those were not empty words.. they were like daggers thrust into my soul. She was saying that she loved me, yet she forced me on a journey that would send me back to Hell. Pulling her hands from my face, I twisted to sit on the edge of the bed. She embraced me from behind and pressed her cheek against my neck.

"What's wrong?"

I didn't respond because I didn't know what to say. Her quest was noble, and I couldn't fault her for pursuing it. The damned souls, twisted into demons, were not like Demon Lords. Those creatures were pure evil and destroyed everything they touched. I turned my head to gaze into her eyes. Jazzera was the type of human who would sacrifice herself for the greater good. She would jump into the Lake of Fire if she knew that would save her kind.

I ran my thumb gently over her lips. Jade had never said the word love out loud. Indirectly, Jazzera had just said it. I was torn between pure lust and the love slowly churning in my black heart. It didn't matter if she hated me at the end of this quest. Tonight, I would show her that she was loved. That she was worthy of herself and of others.

Pushing her back down on the bed, I straddled her body, leaned down, and pressed my lips to hers. She hungrily kissed me back, our tongues curling together.

Our hearts raced. I gripped her wrists, pinned them above her head, and ran my tongue down her neck. I stopped at her left breast and took her nipple into my mouth, then gently pulled, grazing my teeth along the hardened nub. Her back arched, and I kissed the valley between her breasts, moving to the other nipple and lashing it with my tongue before pinching it between my teeth. Her breath caught in her throat, and I slowly kissed and sucked my way down to her navel, licking the warm skin at her waist.

Letting go of her wrists, I tugged at her white pants, fighting with them until they rested on the floor. She lay in front of me, completely naked, and looked the same as she did in the dream world. Her skin was smooth and inviting, and her breasts were perfectly shaped as if they were meant for my hands alone. Her stomach was flat yet soft with the cutest belly button, and, then there was the crown jewel, her pussy, a triangle of thick black hair. With a snap of my fingers, my pants disappeared.

Sitting up slightly, Jazzera looked down between my legs and turned scarlet. "I've seen you naked before, but I've never touched it in the real world."

I couldn't help but beam at how innocent she was. Reaching up, I took her hand and placed it over my throbbing cock. She giggled as she gripped it in her tiny hand. "What's so funny?"

"I don't know. I thought it would be squishy."

Chuckling, I held her hand and ran it along my shaft, making her form a tight fist around it. "Now you stroke it."

I let go of her hand when she managed to gain a rhythm and laid back on the bed. I gripped her perky ass and slid her body close to mine.

"You could give it a kiss," I suggested, sliding my fingers between the folds of her soaking cunt.

She looked at me briefly, then back down at my cock. Unbelievably, she kissed the tip and then took it into her warm, wet mouth. My muscles tensed as she bobbed her head up and down in a steady rhythm. Her tongue licked up the underside of my cock to the tip, suckling the engorged head. Finding her clit, I circled it with my thumb. She gasped, parted her lips slightly, and moved her head rapidly along my shaft. If I hadn't known any better, I would have assumed she had done this before. Tangling my fingers in her hair, I had to force myself not to pull.

She had never known a man, let alone a demon. If I were to do what I pictured in my mind, I would terrify her. Maybe one day that'll be exciting, but tonight was all about her. My hips started thrusting uncontrollably, and I pushed her from my shaft, rolling her over. Pulling her legs apart, I brought my face down to her drenched little pussy and ran my tongue roughly up her slit, consuming her honey-sweet fluid. I sucked her clit, swirling my tongue around it vigorously.. the harder the suction, the more her juices dribbled down my chin. I pressed my face into her, drowning myself in her.

Her back arched, and she let out a long, pleasured moan, soaking the sheets beneath her.

Her hands clutched my back, nails digging deep into my skin. Arching, I indulged in the ecstasy of the pain it caused me. I slid a finger deep inside her. Her pussy was tight, fitting perfectly onto my finger as if it were a glove. She let out another loud moan, and I could feel her walls pulsate around my finger. One down, many more to go. Meeting her eyes, I pulled my finger out and sucked it, relishing her taste.

She panted, and her legs shook as she fell back onto the bed. I pulled her body close to me. "No, no, Priestess. You don't get to fall asleep after just one orgasm." Positioning myself between her legs, I pressed the head of my cock up against her entrance. "This might hurt a bit, but only for a moment."

She nodded timidly, and I slowly pushed myself inside of her inch by agonizing inch.

The slick walls of her sheath spasmed around me, the sensation making my cock twitch and swell in lust. She winced, and I backed off, allowing her time to regain her confidence. She nodded again when she was ready for more, and I slowly moved back in. Her face pinched, but she took in half of my cock. Leaning back, I stared between us and spread her lower lips, wanting to watch while she took it all. The walls of her slippery pussy grasped me, begging me not to leave. Pushing deeper, I kept my eyes focused on where we connected and marveled at the sight of her pussy swallowing every last, thick inch until it rested on my base.

I pulled out halfway and pushed back in. After a few more gentle thrusts, her face shifted from a look of pain to pleasure. Once I knew she was enjoying herself, I picked up the pace, forcing myself in deeper and deeper each time until I hit her cervix. She moaned loudly with every slam of my cock. I leaned back and rubbed my thumb over her clit as I moved. Her warm, wet walls pulsed tightly around my cock, nearly bringing me to my climax.

Sliding out, I pressed my lips against hers. "Roll over," I whispered.

Hesitantly, she did as I asked and rolled to her stomach. I propped her up on her knees and ran my hand over her firm ass. My cock twitched, begging for the warmth of her wet center. Gripping her hips, I pulled her onto me. Her pussy swallowed me up, and I groaned with delight.

After a few deep plunges, her moan of pleasure filled the room, and the walls of her pussy began to clench violently. I couldn't hold back and let loose, cumming deep inside her. I didn't let go of her hips until my dick went soft, and we both collapsed on the bed, trembling.

JAZZERA

CHAPTER 26

My entire body quivered as I lay face down on the bed, trying to catch my breath. Everything Dagon had said was true. Sex was amazing.. it did hurt briefly, but afterward, it was pure bliss. I looked over at my angelic mark, which gave off a soft, blue glow.

"She glows when she cums. That's awesome," noted Dagon with a chuckle.

Sitting up, I ran my hand along my mark. It was still there. Nothing had changed aside from the glow that was slowly fading. The Followers lied to me my entire life. I was denied a husband and family because they swore my mark would disappear, making me useless. I didn't know how to feel. I wanted to feel joy from the intense pleasure I had just felt, but I was also angry that I was denied that pleasure for so long.

Had I not met Dagon, I may have never felt the touch of a man. Deciding to be celibate should have been my choice and mine alone. It was my body, and I should have been able to do with it as I pleased.

Dagon slid from the bed, and his clothes returned with a snap of a finger. He gripped my hand and pulled me from the bed, sliding his jacket over my shoulders.

"What are you doing?"

"I want to make sure you remember me for the rest of your life, Jazzera. What kind of demon would I be if I only let you cum twice?" Dagon swooped me off my feet and carried me to the door. As he opened it, I almost panicked and fell out of his arms. "We can't go out there.. people will see us."

"So let them see. This won't be the wildest thing the barkeep has seen.. I can promise you that."

Gently biting my tongue, I was determined to stay quiet. I had to push the teachings of the Followers out of my mind. I needed to stop thinking of myself as a harlot and a whore, condemning myself as a lustful sinner. At this moment, I was simply a woman in the arms of a man.

Somehow, we managed to make it down the stairs and out of the building without the barkeep knowing. The wind whistled, sending a slight chill down my spine. As if sensing my discomfort, the jacket suddenly heated up, making me warm and content. The streets were empty, and the candle lamp posts were snuffed out. As we walked to the gate, soft rolls of thunder boomed in the distance.

The guard was up in his little tower, fast asleep from the looks of it, and the gate was wide open. Dagon walked on past and continued down the road. I had no idea where we were going. Had Dagon been any other man, I may have feared for my life, thinking he was about to murder me and drop my body off in a ditch. Instead, I nuzzled close to him, taking in his warmth.

We veered off the road, detouring into an open field, and headed toward the woods.

Within minutes, we were at the shore of a beautiful lake surrounded by trees slowly losing their leaves, only stubborn speckles of yellow dangled from sporadic branches. The grass was long but dying as winter approached, and it crunched under Dagon's feet. The path began to narrow as it sloped into the water. To the right was a small cliff with a single tree hanging over the lake. Most of the leaves were gone, giving the tree a slightly creepy look as it loomed overhead. Dagon put me down and walked to the water.

"Are you crazy? The water must be freezing!"

He grinned, and his clothing vanished, revealing his perfect frame. He stepped into the water and waded until it was up to his waist. Arms outstretched, he held them inches from the surface, and steam began to billow up. Bubbles began to flow to the top, like the liquid around him was now boiling. He stood there like it didn't affect him.

The bubbles slowly stopped. "Feels like a hot spring to me. Come on in Jazz, don't be shy."

I crept closer to the lake and hesitated, looking out at him. The water should have been freezing, but he controlled Hell's fire. If he could warm the cold, hard ground while we camped, why couldn't he warm up a lake? Forcing my decision, Dagon's jacket tore away from me and fluttered over the lake, where it hung above its master's head.

"It must be cold up on the shore.. why not come in?"

I rolled my eyes. As if you gave me a choice.

Taking a steadying breath, I went to the water's edge, stuck my toe in carefully, and then my entire

195

foot. He was right.. the water was amazingly warm. Rushing in, I tried not to slip on the mud but nearly fell face-first into the dark water. He caught me and pulled me toward the muddy cliff with the overhanging tree.

My eyebrow rose incredulously as his jacket began to change its form, turning into a rope. "What do you plan on doing with that?"

He smirked as the rope abruptly tied around my wrists, binding me to the tree. I tried to protest, but Dagon covered my mouth. With his free hand, he lifted my body out of the water and cradled me to him. Moving his hand from my mouth, he spread my legs, and I wrapped them tightly around his waist, moaning as he pushed himself inside. With incredible force, Dagon slammed me up against the bank. Mud slid from the cliffside onto my body, but I didn't care. I just wanted to feel him deeper and harder.

After several strong thrusts, he pulled back, taking me with him and laying me on my back, arms still tied to the tree. My lower half floated in the water. He continued wildly thrusting, dragging his thumb along my bud, which made me twitch uncontrollably. I bit and clawed at the air, not fully understanding why but knowing I wanted to sexually maul him. The ropes around my wrists vanished, and I fell into the water.. Dagon's strong arms pulled me against him as he impaled me on the gigantic monster between his legs. He sucked on my right breast till the nipple hardened and moved to my neck, gently nibbling it.

Grabbing his hair roughly, I forced his head up to look at me and bit his lower lip, drawing it into my mouth. He pulled back abruptly and savagely tugged my hair in turn. The pain forced out another needy moan, and my fingers dug into his flesh as I felt his teeth clench onto my neck. With his hand still tangled in my hair, he forced my body to take as much of his monster as possible, plunging deeper with each thrust. Heat rose in my belly, and my body began to tense.. Dagon moved faster, making my inner walls spasm with delight. I screamed in pleasure as my orgasm came with a loud thunder crash.

Bringing his lips to my ear, he whispered, "We should get out of the water. I'd survive a lightning strike, but you..." He trailed off. "Well, it might be fun with all the wiggling you would do."

Smacking him gently across the face, I pulled myself off him and swam to the shore. The rain began to pour, and my body shivered violently. Lifting me into his arms, Dagon jogged toward the trees, still naked. In the field, we tumbled to the cold and wet ground. I was momentarily confused about why we fell until he dug his hands into the dirt, warming it. Pushing my legs apart, he pulled me to him, making me straddle him. Flames began to erupt from the ground, surrounding us with a ring of hot fire.

He pressed me onto his cock, thrusting up into me. I wrapped my legs around his waist and dug my fingers into his arms. He hissed and pressed his lips roughly against mine. He pulled out and forcefully rolled me over onto my stomach.

"Get on your knees." I complied, and he ordered, "Lift your ass."

I was hesitant at first but did as I was told. My vagina pulsated in need, clenching Dagon's cock tightly when he slid into me again. I wanted to feel every sensation, every inch, every thrust, and every ripple. He hissed, driving through my spasming grip, and pushed himself deeper. I rocked with his motion as best as I could. The rain poured down, yet the fire remained strong, heating up the water as it hit my skin. I gasped as I felt something enter my other hole.

There was a burning sensation, but I didn't dare tell him to stop, not when his manhood felt so good inside me.

I couldn't believe that I felt so dirty yet so good at the same time. With his next thrust, I felt another finger slide into my back hole and held my breath. After several more thrusts, I exhaled and allowed myself to breathe again.

"Relax, Jazzera. Just enjoy it," he coaxed. It took a while, but I gradually relaxed, and, I did enjoy it.

I wanted to whimper when he pulled out until I felt him remove his fingers. The head of his penis replaced them, pressing up against my puckered star.

"What are you doing?" I cried in near panic.

"Just relax. I can't leave this Earth without feeling every hole you have. No human can fuck you like I can and make it this enjoyable. No human man has the stamina of a demon. I could fuck you for weeks straight without ever getting tired, but I'll back off if you don't want it. My dick is just as happy inside your wet little pussy."

My mind was racing, trying to find the best answer to give him. I had always been taught only sodomites had sex this way. That since having a cock up your ass didn't result in a baby, it was nothing more than a sin of the flesh. Pain welled up in my stomach as I considered his words.. he was leaving this Earth, and it hit me that it would be within a matter of days. I had very little time left with my demon. How dare I deny him this pleasure when I was condemning him to the numbness of Hell?

"Do with me as you please."

He hesitated slightly, going slow at first, very slowly. With every inch he pushed in, the more I wanted to crawl away.

"Relax, Jazz. Clenching doesn't help."

I did as he requested and took a calming breath, working against my basic instincts to relax my body, but this part was worse than when he first penetrated me. After a few moments of pain, his shaft felt good as it entered my vagina, but with this, there was an odd, slight burning sensation. I felt his body press against mine, his thick beast deep inside me.

He pulled out a bit and slowly pushed himself back in. With each thrust, I became more relaxed, and he moved faster. I moaned loudly with every push, clenching my teeth as I felt his finger rub circles over my nub. He rubbed vigorously, reigniting the burning sensation in my stomach, and the walls of my vagina pulsated. I let out a loud cry of pure pleasure, and Dagon groaned, releasing a deep, demonic growl as he went soft inside me. He must have finished.

He rolled me over, pressed his lips to mine, and smiled at me. "Give me a second, and I can be hard again."

I kind of panicked. "No! No. I don't think I can take anymore."

He chuckled and rolled onto his back. "Mortals are so weak."

Sighing, I shook my head and scooted closer to him, gently rubbing the tiny patch of hair on his chest.

"We should get you inside."

The fire around us died out. Dagon scooped me up in his arms, his clothing returned, and his jacket covered me. We walked in silence through the pouring rain until we reached the town.

There was a new guard in the small tower, but they didn't even startle when we entered. The same happened with the barkeep when we returned to the inn. Dagon once said that mortals only saw what he wanted them to. I wondered what other types of powers he possessed. I knew he could shapeshift, manipulate hellfire, and control whether or not a person could see him.

When we entered our room, the jacket vanished from my body, and Dagon ran his hands just above my skin. I watched, amazed, as the water dripping from me evaporated. He even dried my hair.. it was as if I hadn't just been outside in the pouring rain. Or in a lake...

Kissing him lightly, I made my way over to the bed and pat it. "Come keep me warm."

"Isn't that how this all started to begin with?"

I grinned and felt my legs shake as I crawled onto the bed. As much as I wanted to feel more of him, I couldn't take another round. "I just want to go to sleep."

"You know I only sleep when I'm bored, right?"

"Then come be bored with me."

JAZZERA

CHAPTER 27

When I awoke, I expected to see Dagon next to me, only to find his side of the bed empty. On the bedside table lay an article of clothing. I got to my feet and winced.. my body was still trembling from all the exercise. Every muscle in my body ached, but the pain was well worth it.

Picking up the garment, I realized it was a Priestess robe, and my breath caught in my throat. How Dagon acquired one was beyond me. As much as I hated to admit it, the robes were a practical choice. After all, we would be in Follower territory in less than an hour. The realization made my heart sink, and I slumped back onto the bed.

How could I go through with this? All I ever wanted was to be loved by another person. Even as a small child, I fantasized about my future family, a handsome husband, four children. I wanted two girls and two boys.. Luke, Amdin, Reyla, and Keena. Those were the names I had chosen. Luke, from the Bible. Amdin was a unique name I created. Reyla was the name of an orphan baby that stayed at the temple for a short while, and, Keena was the name I would have chosen for myself if I had the option.

I had many imaginary husbands throughout the years, even after I was told that I would never be able to marry. George, Max, and Keith, to name a few. They had several different careers. George was a blacksmith, Max was a baker, and Keith was a wealthy traveling merchant who would take me away to far-off lands. But those men were only ever in my mind. Dagon was flesh and blood. Granted, it may be black blood, but he was still very much *real*. I could touch him and feel him. If I kept on this path, in only a day or so, Dagon would be just as transparent as those imaginary men were.

Would he visit me when he was in spirit form? Would I be able to sense his presence? Or would he forget all about me? Or worse, grow to hate me?

Getting back up, I put the robes on and examined myself in the full-length mirror. Looking back at me was the same trapped girl I had seen in the mirror countless times. Humble, modest, timid, submissive Jazzera. Ashamed of her naked body and the need for physical touch.

What would one more day hurt? One more day to decide if I wanted to follow the path of a holy Priestess or a kindhearted demon. Taking a deep breath, I turned from the mirror and left the room. The smell of cooked meat made my mouth water, and I hurried downstairs as quickly as my sore legs would take me.

Ermek, Sheldon, and Dagon were all sitting at a table. Dagon was seated between the two, but he got to his feet when he saw me.

"You didn't have to get up," I said with a smile.

"I'd rather sit next to you. At least I know you had a bath last night." He winked, and I blushed.

"What is that amazing smell?" I asked as he pulled out a seat for me. Nodding my thanks, I sat down and pulled myself to the table, unable to hide the joy on my face. No man had ever pulled a seat out for me before.

"Well, since you two are officially going to be Heathens soon, I ordered bacon."

I gasped. "As in pork? A pig?"

He nodded. "I don't know why you are so worked up. You two had no issues with eating rabbit or squirrel." My look of confusion must have given me away because he continued, "Oh yeah, that's a sin, according to the Book. Rabbit and squirrel are unclean. Pretty much anything that's not goat, cow, chicken, or some fish is a big no-no."

"I had no idea."

"Of course, you didn't. The Priests don't allow you to read, but if you could read it, you'd realize it's almost a sin for a man to shake his dick after taking a piss."

Ermek laughed. "He isn't wrong."

Two plates were brought to our table.. one filled with strips of crispy meat and the other with eggs, fried over easy. Dagon didn't hesitate to fill both of our plates up. As he devoured his food, I picked up one of the strips of meat and sniffed it.. it did smell glorious.

Looking up from my plate, I glanced over at Sheldon. The bacon was the first thing he began stuffing his mouth with. However, I could see the hesitation in Ermek's eyes. Did we take the plunge and indulge ourselves? Or did we do what our faith had always demanded and forgo temptation?

According to our beliefs, even touching a plate that bore cooked pork was a sin. Well, that was a silly sin, indeed.

Biting the meat in half, I chewed for a second and beamed. It was just as delicious as Dagon said it would be. Looking over to Ermek, I popped the rest into my mouth.

"It's delicious," I declared before I even finished swallowing.

Ermek brushed his long braids off his shoulder, picked up a piece of meat, and popped the entire thing in his mouth. He chewed slowly, then swallowed. He grabbed at least five more strips and put them on his plate.

"This is so delicious.. it has to be a sin." He took another bite.

"Oh, look at my two glorious little sinners. There is a special place in Hell near the Lake of Fire for pig eaters," teased Dagon.

Ermek and I stared at each other.

Dagon swallowed the piece that was in his mouth. "I'm kidding.. that was sarcasm. You two should learn it."

When both large plates were wiped clean, I ran a napkin along my lips and stated, "We should stay one more day." Both Ermek and Dagon gave me a questioning look. I shrugged. "I'm tired, and I need a bed. We have been sleeping on the ground for weeks."

"It will take us that much longer to close the gates." Ermek looked as if he were trying to avoid Dagon's gaze.

"And we have been living with demons in this world our entire life. One more day isn't going to change anything, and, how do we even know if that

Legion character will be there? Why would they be?"

"Because they are waiting for us," replied Dagon as he leaned back in his chair. I raised an eyebrow. "They know you are coming for them and think they can defeat you. If they kill you, it's one less threat. Nobody will know that they possess the key."

I really wished that weren't the case. I almost hoped that this would be a never-ending search, that we could stay on the road together and engage in battle only when necessary, but if Legion was waiting for us, I had very few options. Either close the gates or tell Legion to run away with the key if they promise to leave us alone.

I got up and headed to the inn's front door. "Coming?" I asked, looking over my shoulder.

All three men stood up, and the barkeep hurried to clean the table.

"Where are we going?"

"I want some new clothes. You still have money left, don't you?" Ermek nodded. "When we finish this, I no longer wish to be confined in these robes.. I want something different to change into."

***

Only one place in the village sold clothing, but it was not impressive. I eventually settled for a dress dyed yellow at the top with orange at the bottom. It was loose-fitting and landed just below my knees. Ermek found himself a pair of black pants and a brown tunic.

"If we stay the night here, this will be the last of our money. If we don't go back to the Followers, I don't know how we will make a living."

Dagon shrugged. "Well, I'd say there is good money in ridding villages of demons, but that won't work. You could both be mercenaries, and the Heathens don't discriminate." He looked pointedly at me, and I knew he was referring to the fact that I was a woman. The Followers would never have women in their ranks, while the Heathens didn't care who fought for them.

I contemplated my future. Aside from being a Priestess and knowing how to wield a sword, I had no real skills like other women had. I've never had to sew before because that task was always given to the servants. Cooking was the same.. aside from laying a piece of meat on a fire, I had limited knowledge of the skill. I couldn't bake either. So, what good would I be if I weren't a Priestess?

After purchasing our garments, we decided to walk around the village. It was a tiny little farm town from the looks of it. There were numerous stone homes with thatched roofs and wooden fencing. Bales of hay sat in each yard, and I spotted pigs and cows feasting every now and then. The gardens were bare, having yielded their latest harvest weeks ago. Toward the center of town was a small marketplace. A woman with a dark red tunic sold animal hides, while another, clad in leather, sold small knives and arrow tips. As the nursery rhyme said, there was a butcher, a baker, and a candlestick maker, but one building at the edge of the market drew my attention. On a little chair outside, a woman in yellow sat reading a book.

The sight made me want to shield my eyes. I almost felt the dull blade of a knife slicing through my finger as I dared sneak a peek. Behind her, on the porch, was a stand filled with books, and I could see a stack of them resting on the windowsill inside. The sign on the front had a giant book painted on it. Had I been able to read, I would have been able to tell if it were a library or a bookshop. I was determined to learn how to read when this was all over.

After a few laps around the village, I needed a quick nap. As I undressed in my room, my eyes wandered to the mirror. I saw Dagon's reflection, and my heart nearly jumped out of my chest as I spun around. He was barely inches from me, and his unsettling black eyes bore into mine as if trying to consume my soul.

I pressed my lips to Dagon's, and he returned the kiss hungrily. Heat pulsed through me as he gently picked me up and laid me on the bed. He got on top of me, fighting with my clothing to free my body from its bindings. When I was finally naked, he rolled over, pulling me on top of him. His clothing disappeared, and our bare flesh pressed together.. his body warm and firm against mine. I could snuggle against his solid frame for hours and never tire of it.

Gripping my hips, he lifted me slightly, rubbing his cock along my vagina. I shook my head when I thought the word cock. Had I really been with Dagon so long that it now seemed like second nature to speak like that? I suppose next, I'll be calling my lady bits pussy. He pushed me onto it, breaking me from my train of though and I gasped.. it went deeper from this angle. He guided my movements, rocking my hips.

I gained confidence, planting my knees on the bed, and moved slowly up and down his slick cock. A smile crossed my lips as I thought the word again. If I was going to be dirty, I may as well let go completely. Cock and pussy were now going to be two new words in my vocabulary. Biting my lip I looked down at the demon I was straddling. Dagon's strong arms helped me remain steady and keep a good rhythm while he pushed up into me.

Leaning forward, I gripped the grey sheets tightly till my knuckles went white. With gritted teeth, I moaned with each deep downward slide. My eyes remained locked on Dagon's. I didn't want to miss a single reaction, the slight winces of pleasure, his lips trembling, or his flaring nostrils as he breathed. His hands reached up to my breasts, squeezing them tightly. He buried the back of his head into the pillow, neck stretched out, emphasizing his Adam's apple that bobbed with every swallow.

I sat back, running my hand gently along his scruff, then tugging at the end of his chin hair. He cracked a grin and rolled over again, still deep inside me. He set a wild rhythm, thrusting into me with abandon, bringing me closer to the edge of climax. I squirmed beneath him, my legs twitching uncontrollably, and my vagina clenched around his length. With a flick of his fingers across my clit, I ignited, nearly screaming my release as he continued to thrust.

Pushing in as far as he could, he released his seed with a deep groan that sounded almost monstrous. He kissed me on the top of my head and rolled off me. I yawned, pulling the soft, wooly covers over me.

"Nap time?"

I nodded. "Yes. I'm exhausted."

Kissing me softly, he tucked the blankets around me and crawled out of bed. "First thing in the morning, Ermek is going to take a carriage to a nearby Followers' temple to see if he can get some weapons from them."

"There is a Followers' temple nearby?"

"Less than an hour from here and just past the border. After that, it's only a few hours walk until we reach Hell's Gate."

I swallowed hard and rolled myself deeper into the blanket. I didn't want Dagon to leave this room.. I wanted him to stay with me forever, forget this entire quest, and live out the rest of my life as a woman in love with a demon.

JAZZERA

CHAPTER 28

The world around me was dead and desolate.. large cracks were carved into the soil, dead plants were everywhere, and black lightning flashed across the blood-red sky. In front of me stood Dagon. I walked up to him and placed my hand on his shoulder.. he smiled and pressed his lips to mine.

"Welcome home, Priestess."

Pulling away, I stepped backward, tripping on an old, dead root. Something caught me before I hit the ground. The large root wrapped tightly around my wrist, holding me in place. I struggled as it transformed into a tree, branches binding my other limbs and pulling me into the air.

Dagon began to transform. Long, black horns grew from his forehead, his pale skin turned a dark red, and the lower half of his body took the shape of a goat. His cock stood erect, long, hard, and twice the width it usually was.

"You will stay here with me forever, Priestess. Eternally bound to this tree so that I may fuck you whenever I desire. This is my true form." Bat-like wings emerged from his back and extended to their full length. They blocked everything but him from view. Dagon stepped closer to me, his hoofed feet echoing with each step. He gripped my legs tightly, and I whimpered as his long, black claws dug into my skin.

"Dagon, stop!" I begged.

"I will never stop. I will fuck you for all eternity. Here in Hell, my little sinner. For this is the fate of every little whore who gives herself to a demon." His voice deepened into a sound I didn't recognize.

Without any amount of gentleness, he thrust his cock deep inside me. I screamed as I felt the pain of my vagina being torn with every violent jab. His eyes turned a bright scarlet, and his leer was full of long, sharp teeth.

I was startled awake. My heart beat so fast I feared it would pound out of my chest. Panicked, I jumped from the bed and scratched my body, trying to get the dirty feeling off my skin. Eventually, I calmed down. It was a nightmare, only a nightmare. I glanced at the mirror across from me. Was I now the Devil's whore? Was that truly Dagon in my dreams, or was it the guilt I felt in my stomach for going against everything I had ever been taught?

Reluctantly, I pulled on the dress I had purchased earlier that day. I didn't want to leave the safety of the bed covers, but I had to get moving to clear my head. I had nightmares before,

so this was no different. It didn't mean that Dagon or any demon was creeping around in my subconscious. That dream was built from my fears and guilt for letting go of the teachings that the Followers drilled into my head.

I went downstairs, a bit shocked that my companions weren't sitting at any of the tables, and I wondered where they were. The room was practically empty, with only a few people sitting at the tables, talking amongst themselves. As the barkeep stepped behind the counter, I waved to get her attention.

"What will it be for you, dear?" she inquired sweetly.

"Have you seen my three companions?"

She nodded, picking up a plastic cup from the countertop. "I remember hearing that pale, dark-haired fellow say they were heading to the lake."

I thanked her, headed out the door, and marched down the dirt street. Looking up at the sky, I guessed there would be about four hours of sunlight left. Why Dagon took the other men to the lake was beyond me, but I felt uncomfortable spending too much time at this inn alone.

Children played in the street, and a group of men laughed and conversed at the edge of a small farmhouse. As I walked past, I paused and looked up at an older gentleman sitting on a mule-driven cart.

"Do you take people into Follower territory?"

He nodded. "The temple is as far as I go. There are too many demons running around past that point. I get good trade from the temple, though. Do you need a ride, miss?"

I shook my head. "Not at the moment. Perhaps tomorrow."

He bowed his head slightly and smiled. I returned the gesture and continued on my way.

It took a bit to recognize the way to the lake. It was dark the last time I had been there, but I knew that if I reached the hay crops, I had gone too far and would have to turn around. I spotted a small, beaten path that cut through a field and into a tree line.. I figured that must be the direction of the lake.

Walking through the field, I hesitated. The dress didn't have a belt to hold my sword, so I didn't bring it. What if this was the wrong path, and I found myself in front of a demon that wasn't Dagon? Would he get to me in time if I needed help?

Stop being so paranoid. This was the way to the lake, and I would find my boys at the end of this path.

Sounds of laughter echoed from ahead, and I beamed, picking up the pace until I saw Ermek and Dagon. The sight hurt my heart, and it seemed to freeze in my chest. I darted off the path and hid behind a thick tree, peeking around it while staying hidden.

Ermek was shirtless, with his arms wrapped around Dagon, his nose nuzzled deep into his neck. One of his hands slowly reached down into Dagon's pants. Sheldon walked up and began rubbing Dagon's chest. I swallowed hard, feeling like my knees were going to give out. I had just shared my entire being with the demon, and here he was, giving himself to Ermek.

Unable to watch any longer, I ran down the beaten path as fast as possible. How could this be? I knew Sheldon was a sodomite but Ermek? Ermek couldn't be. He wouldn't. I stopped running when I reached the end of the field and thought back to my nightmare. It wasn't Ermek.. it was Dagon. My dream had been trying to warn me. Demons lie. Demons tempt. Demons betray, and, Demons trick. Dagon wanted me to fall in love with him so that I wouldn't close the gate and he could be free to torture

213

souls on Earth. He must have tempted Ermek, too, turning him against his true nature. Wasn't it Ermek that stated that we shouldn't close the gate? He must be Dagon's backup plan. If he couldn't convince me to keep the gates open, he could get Ermek to talk me into it.

Well, the Devil wouldn't win this round. I would go to the temple and get a new Demon Slayer to accompany me. The Priests at the temple would understand once I had explained my mission to them. I could tell them that Ermek was injured and that I had to leave him behind, and, whether he liked it or not, Dagon would help me close the gates. He had no choice in the matter. I was his master, and he was my slave.

Determined to set my plan in motion, I returned to the inn as quickly as possible. I stripped out of my Heathen clothing, pulled on my Priestess robes, and grabbed my sword before racing down the road. In my rush, I pushed past the group of men until I found the old man with the cart.

"Are you leaving for Follower territory any time soon?" I panted.

"What's the rush?" He questioned with a smile.

"I have to get to the temple. It's important.. so much is at stake."

He tilted his head and pointed to the back of the cart. "Get in. I wasn't supposed to deliver their barrels of wine until the morning, but I suppose I can get an early start."

I thanked him, climbed into the cart's bed, and pressed my back against one of the barrels.

The frame jolted as the mule began to pull. I slunk down behind the barrier planks and prayed softly that Dagon and the others wouldn't see me as I left.

The long, bumpy road made my butt numb, and I shifted around most of the ride, trying to stretch and stay limber. The grey sky and dying surroundings didn't help the ride much. Without something nice to occupy my mind, my thoughts continued straying to the sight I witnessed near the lake.

The old man whistled, and I looked around curiously. We were coming up on a far more impressive temple than the one I had come from. The stone it was built from was white and towered proudly over every tree surrounding the stone gates. On top of the walls stood several men, all armed with the strange contraptions I had seen in Dagon's visions of the past, lethal weapons that made loud popping sounds.

One of the guards shouted as we approached the gates, and the cart stopped. Two men walked up to the older gentleman and spoke for a moment before coming to the back of the cart.

The young blond-haired guard shouted at me, "Get out of the cart!"

I sucked in a shocked breath, wishing for the kinder guards from my temple. My legs were numb, so it took me a moment to comply with their orders. Unfortunately, patience was not their virtue. The darker-skinned guard climbed into the cart, grabbed my arm, and yanked me to my feet. Jolts of electricity surged through my body as the blood began to flow. My legs weren't fully working when he pulled me harder, causing me to fall from the back of the cart. The wind was knocked from my lungs, and I grunted through clenched teeth.

I tried to take a proper breath, but the darker-skinned guard yanked me up violently by my hair. "Are you smuggling in whores, old man?" he accused.

I tried to twist my body so the pain wouldn't overwhelm me. "I'm a Priestess," I stated, trying to hide the fact that I wanted to cry.

He released my hair, and I flung it out of my face. "I need to see the Head Priestess of this temple."

Both men looked at each other and chuckled. "And what are you doing without your Demon Slayer?" pressed the blond.

I thought for a moment, what if Ermek came to look for me? No doubt that lying, cheating snake Dagon could locate me. If I lied, they could punish me for it. So, did I tell them the truth? That Ermek was a sodomite fornicating with a demon? I bit my tongue before the words escaped me.

"Speak up, bitch! Where is your Demon Slayer?"

My eyes narrowed at the name-calling. I had had enough of these men and their superiority complex. Standing up straight, I looked the blond in the eye. "I am not a bitch. I am a Priestess of the Followers of the Horsemen."

I felt the pain before I saw his fist. The force of it caused me to fall, and I tasted a small trickle of blood on my tongue. My lip stung as I pressed my fingers to it, and I glared hatefully at the man. What was I doing? Why was I here? Why would I ever willingly come back to this place?

I stood there, glowering at him, when I felt a form of clarity. Ermek and Dagon had never harmed me. Neither had Sheldon, for that matter. God

216

doesn't care who you sleep with as long as it's consensual. That's what Dagon had said, and, for the first time in my entire life, I truly believed it. If anyone was the sinner right now, it was me. My sin was envy.. I was jealous of Ermek, and, because of that, I almost turned him in to these insane people. The same people who forced me to remain silent while I bleed monthly and threatened to cut off my finger if I dared read a book! These people said God would strike you down for wearing mixed fabrics or eating a pig. Dagon spoke of a God who only cared that you were a good person, and, that was the God I wanted to believe in.

"Go to Hell."

His fist swung at me again, and I dodged it, only to be struck in the stomach by the other man. Falling to my knees, I was roughly pulled up by my hair again. "I'll show you, you little whore!"

"Wait, Inan. She really is a Priestess.. she has the mark," said the darker-skinned guard.

Inan released my hair and gripped my arm. "Then we will take her to the Head Priest and see what he wishes to do to her."

I didn't bother to struggle as they escorted me through the gate. There was no getting out of this. Yes, I could skewer them both with my sword, but the men on the wall would kill me shortly after. I could only hope that Dagon could sense what was going on.

My former home only had a large temple, two one-story buildings that served as sleeping quarters and mess halls, a small bathhouse, a barn, and stables. This place was vastly different from my own.. it was almost like an entire city within the stone walls. It was built like a grid with structures made of stone and wood crammed tightly together. Halfway down the cobblestone path was a fork in the road, which led to even more buildings. There were more than just Demon Slayers and Priestesses roaming about. There were ordinary people. Men, women, and children, all of whom were clad in the appropriate color of their status. This place was packed with life but less beauty. It almost felt too crowded.

The glorious temple had grand stairs, tall white pillars, and a golden dome. On the inside, it became even more apparent that it was much larger than the temple I called home. The foyer was spacious, with statues of all four Horsemen of the Apocalypse resting in the center of the large room.. War, Famine, Pestilence, and Death. Shelves carved into the stone walls held urns of fallen Priests and Priestesses of the past. A large altar took up part of the space with a tall, golden cross affixed to the wall. On both sides of the room, winding stairs led to the upper floor of the building.

At least four Priests walked about, each wearing the brown robes of their position. On the top of one of the staircases stood the High Priest, given away only by his brown headdress.

"I hope you have good reason to come into this temple during prayer hour," admonished the Priest as he moved to the lower level. Prayer hour was when the temple shut down for the Priests to pray in silence.

Both men bowed, as did I. "This woman claims to be a Priestess.. she has the mark but no Demon Slayer."

I had no good explanation or excuse.. no matter what I said, there was a chance I could end up branded or worse. I couldn't tell them about Ermek because they would stone him to death if he showed up, and, I would be beaten if I lied about him being injured or killed and he showed up unharmed.

The Priest leered at me. "What a marvelous mark it is." I pulled back as he ran his hand through my hair, exposing my mark. "And ever so beautiful."

I knew one thing for sure, I didn't want this Priest touching me.

"Bring the young lady to my chambers. We shall find out her business there."

My lips parted. Why would the Head Priest be taking me to his chambers? And why did these guards seem okay with that idea? Without questioning him, they violently forced me up the stairs and escorted me to a smaller room at the end of the loft. They pushed me over to a large stained-glass window and waited for the old man to join us. The Priest closed the door and walked up to me, running his pale, wrinkled hand along my face.

"So very beautiful."

"Please, your Grace. I am on a mission, and I only came here to ask if we could use some weapons."

He chuckled. "And why would a woman need a weapon?" His eyes landed on my sword.

"It looks like you already have one." Cautiously, he reached for my sword and pulled it from its sheath. He placed it down on his dresser and moved closer to me. "Now I know that some temples will teach exceptional women how to fight. Those with large marks. Are you one of those women?" I nodded. "Let me see." I squinted, not knowing what he was asking. "Let me see your entire mark."

My eyes went wide. "For a Priestess to undress in front of a man is a sin, your Grace."

"But not in front of me, dear child, for I am a man of God. I shall bless you with my seed, my girl, and you will be stronger with it in your belly."

Horrified, I fought the two men that were holding me, but the harder I fought, the tighter their grip became. The Priest ran his hand gently down my face.

"This is the will of God, Priestess. He brought you here for a purpose. He has been talking to me in my dreams, telling me that I must place a child in the belly of a strong Priestess. Our son shall be the Savior for humankind, and he will rid the world of these demons."

I didn't understand what was going on. Every Follower knew that a Priestess was to remain pure and untouched. Yet this Priest was demanding that I lay with him, and, what was worse, the two young men holding me didn't seem to be bothered by it, as if it were normal.

They even paraded me here as if I were a gift to the old man. How many Priestesses did this man have in his bed chambers? How often did these guards collect victims for him?

Knowing I could do nothing while I was bound, I lowered my head. "If God wills it, your Grace."

The Priest raised his hands in the air. "Release her and come, my child. Lay down. It will only hurt for a moment."

The two men complied, and I inched toward the bed. It was now or never. I lunged for my sword, gripped it tightly, and spun toward the men. The first raised his weapon, but I swung at him, severing his arm from his body.

I pivoted and thrust it into the midsection of the other man, his eyes bulged, and he fell to his knees. The first assailant screamed, holding up his nub while blood gushed from the wound. To ease his pain, I severed his head from his body. I shifted to the old man next, and his face turned a ghostly white. I could see pure fear in his glassy blue eyes. I raised my sword to attack but stopped, looking down at the dead and dying men. I had just become a murderer.

DAGON

CHAPTER 29

Earlier that day.

When the Priestess fell asleep, I crept silently out of her room, closing the door softly behind me. Heading out of the inn, I went to a small shop I had seen earlier. Inside was an older man with brown, wrinkled skin and a much younger woman filling the shelves. The flowery smell of the room was a bit overpowering, but I forced myself to endure it.

There were wooden barrels all around, each filled with a different soap. They were mostly made of lard mixed with dried flowers and other herbs. Though I enjoyed our sexual encounters, I didn't know how much longer I could handle the stench of Ermek and Sheldon.

Between the barrels were small bins set on shelves filled with perfumed oils. Picking one up, I popped the cork and took a sniff. This one smelled of roses.

"May I help you find anything?" inquired the woman as she approached me with a sweet smile.

SHENEMEN

I set the oil down. "My companions stink."

The girl giggled. "Well, we have soaps and bath oils in many scents and fragrances."

Smiling, I walked closer to her and whispered in her ear. "I seem to be short on cash as well." Taking her hand in my own, I added, "But I could owe you a favor. Would you make a deal with the Devil?"

"At the cost of my immortal soul?" she asked, amused.

I looked up at the ceiling. "No, just the cost of some soap."

The girl laughed again, clearly not knowing how to respond to me. Looking into her eyes, I searched her soul, trying to find something she desired that I could get her. "How about a mule for your father? You haven't been able to trade the soaps you make to other towns since your last animal passed. I could get you a mule. All I ask for is a bar of lemongrass soap and some of this fine rose oil."

She backed away from me. "How did you know we needed a mule?"

"Give me the items I request, and you shall have a new mule within a week. You have my word."

Reluctantly, the woman picked up a bottle of rose oil and got lemon grass soap from one of the barrels. She handed them to me without saying anything.

"Thank you."

Not wanting to stay in that awkward situation anymore, I hastily left with my items safely in my pocket. Undoubtedly, the woman was wondering how I planned to get her this mule. All I had to do was send a small prayer to Heaven, and some angel would fetch it for me, and, if they refused, I would get some lesser demon to procure one. They would send the mule to the woman, and I would be debt free. My way of making deals was much better than Legion's. They would create an illusion of a human's desire. They may make a human famous, only for them to be overwhelmed later when the magic collapses around them. One way or another, their deals always ended in catastrophe, with the humans losing their souls.

I wandered around the town, mingling with the humans for about an hour or two before I decided to find Ermek and Sheldon. They were sitting outside of the inn, conversing with each other.

"I have someplace I want to take you."

They got to their feet. "Should we wake Jazzera?"

I shook my head. "No, there is no need. I'll bring her by later. Let her sleep."

Without hesitation, both men followed me out of town and toward the lake where I had taken Jazzera the night before. They stopped abruptly when we reached the water's edge and waited silently as if asking me what we were doing there.

"You two need a bath."

"I'm not going in there. There's ice on top," whined Sheldon, wrapping his arms around himself.

"He's right.. it's nearly winter, and we are mortals," Ermek agreed.

Rolling my eyes, I strolled to the water and placed my hands above the surface. After a moment, steam bellowed from it, and bubbles began to appear. When it was warm enough, I gestured to the water. "There. Nice and toasty. Courtesy of Hell's fire."

Curious, Ermek walked over to the water and stuck his hand in. His jaw dropped. "It's warm.. maybe a little too warm, but it isn't freezing."

Ermek sauntered to me, wrapped his arms around my waist, and pressed his face to my neck. I froze. This bath thing wasn't an invitation for sex. As much as I enjoyed plowing the Demon Slayer and his little friend, I decided the night before that I would no longer touch them. I no longer wished to toy with him or Jazzera. As much as he sometimes annoyed me, I was growing rather fond of the Slayer. Like Jazzera, I wanted what was best for him. This Sheldon character was a nuisance, but he would be a better fit for the Demon Slayer than I was.

As his hand slid down my pants, I willed my cock not to get hard. I would have a more challenging time saying no if I were sporting wood. When his little friend walked up and started rubbing my chest, it made it all the more difficult to remain unaffected.

A noise from the woods drew the humans' attention, and they let go. I took this as an opportunity to get back on track. "Don't worry, it's not a demon.. it's most likely a deer or something." Reaching into my pocket, I pulled the soap bar out and handed it to Ermek. "And I wasn't kidding when I said you two stink. Demons don't have a better sense of smell than humans do. So if I'm telling you that you stink, every human in that town thinks it too."

Looking defeated, Ermek and Sheldon began to strip. Even though I was trying to keep my dick under control, I still couldn't help but sneak a peek. Sheldon still wasn't much to look at, but Ermek was delicious looking. I did prefer my men to be buff and chiseled rather than scrawny like Sheldon, and I also liked my men to look more mature. Ermek looked his age, while Sheldon barely looked older than eighteen. In reality, he was older than Ermek, but it didn't help matters. I chuckled to myself. I was worried about their looks of maturity when I was older than them by eons.

"Are you sure you won't join us, Dagon?" Ermek called as he lathered his body.

"I'm good. I took a bath last night." Grinning, I thought back to the water sports I had played with the Priestess. Perhaps I could convince her to do it with me again tonight. This time I would bring soap.

The men stayed in the water until it began to cool off. Without me in the water with them, the heat wouldn't last much longer than they needed it to. They drip-dried for a bit, then pulled their clothing on. A cool breeze caused them to shudder, so I ushered them through the woods before they got sick.

We had just got to the clearing when an overwhelming sensation of pain struck my head, and I was pulled into a vision—Jazzera, held by two men in front of a white stone gate. One of them hit her, causing rage to boil in the pit of my stomach, but it wasn't her pain that had called me.. it was her guilt. A demon was drawn to a human's guilt, and with Jazzera and I connected, I could sense hers no matter how far away she was. I tried to burrow deeper into her mind to figure out what she felt guilty about. "We have to go!"

"What's wrong?" demanded Ermek with alarm.

"Jazzera is in trouble."

His body stiffened. "Where is she?"

"She went to the temple without us. Come on, we don't have time to sit here." I didn't wait for questions and transformed into a black horse.

Kissing Sheldon hard on the lips, Ermek gripped his arms tightly. "Stay here. I will return for you when we have completed our quest."

Ermek jumped on my back and gripped my mane tightly. I formed a saddle under his body so he wouldn't slide off. "Hold on," I ordered. "I'll run faster than any horse you have ever ridden."

He gripped my hair tighter, and I took off. The wind almost ripped Ermek off a few times, but I dared not slow down. I didn't know what those men were doing to Jazz, but I could feel her fear from here.

When we were nearly at the temple, I almost had to run off the road to avoid a cart being pulled by a mule. My first instinct was to ignore the old man until I felt the aura of his guilt float by me. Digging my hooves into the ground, I instructed the Demon Slayer to climb off my back. I transformed and ran up to the old man in the cart.

"Oh good, a mule." I willed my trident to solidify in my hand and thrust it into the man's back.. he slumped over. I burned the harness off the mule and whispered into its ear, "Go to the woman in the soap shop.. you are hers now."

"What the hell was that all about?" cried Ermek as he rushed up to the man.

"I owed someone a mule," I stated, pulling my trident from the dead man.

Ermek glared at me. "So you killed an innocent man?"

My trident disappeared, and I took my horse form once more. "This man was far from innocent. For years, he had been gathering young women to trade to the temple's Priests, which was why he gave Jazzera a free ride."

"Why would the Priests need young women?"

"Think about it, Ermek. How often have I told you that most of these Priests are not as righteous as you believe they are? They rape these women, then sell them off into slavery."

He was speechless, but I could feel his guilt floating over to me. He felt guilty for believing the preachings of the Followers, and, he felt guilty for leaving Jazzera alone.

We were nearly at the temple when I crashed into something on the road. I couldn't see it, but the impact of whatever I struck had caused Ermek to fly off my back and tumble onto the roadway. Retaking my human form, I tried to rush up to him but was blocked by an invisible force. I reached forward, feeling energy prickling at my fingertips. A demon barrier surrounded the temple. I forced my body through, enduring an electric shock that coursed through my body until I was on the other side.

I knelt down near Ermek. "Don't be dead."

Slowly, Ermek sat up and groaned. "What happened?"

"Those assholes set up a demon barrier around this place. A prayer circle."

"How did you get through?" he asked, rubbing the back of his head.

"When will you realize that I am not an ordinary demon?" Getting to my feet, I helped the Demon Slayer up. "I wasn't lying when I said Jazzera only caught me because I wanted to be captured. It only worked because I submitted.. she isn't the first Priestess with an angel parent to try and trap me. However, once I submitted to Jazzera, I couldn't and still can't break free of the damned thing."

"Well, perhaps she will free you when we rescue her."

Ermek tried to walk toward the temple, but I stopped him. "I need you to stay here."

"I'm not staying here. I have to help you save Jazz."

"She knows, Ermek. She saw us by the lake, and she thought we had sex. I don't know if she told them, but she felt guilty for coming here to turn you in.. it's how I knew she was here."

The look of pain and betrayal on his face made me wince. "She wouldn't do that. Jazzera is like a sister to me."

I grimaced. "She didn't see you as a brother, Ermek."

"But we were friends."

I could almost see tears welling up in his eyes. Placing a hand on his arm, I squeezed it gently. "All Demon Lords have the power to see a human's guilt, sins, and desires. When I first met you, she was infatuated with you, practically in love, and I think seeing us together broke her heart, and, Hell hath no fury like a woman scorned."

"I still can't believe she would do that."

"Ermek, you two have been brainwashed since you were children. You have grown up believing there was no worse sin than being gay. Even you don't fully believe me when I tell you God doesn't hate you. I don't sense any more guilt past the point when she planned to tell them. Considering how guilty she felt for even thinking about it, I don't think she went through with it.. I would have felt it."

He seemed satisfied. "I'm still going with you. I still love Jazz like a sister, regardless of how she feels about me."

I shook my head. "I saw guns through her eyes. Guns are ancient weapons that are faster and stronger than any arrow. I can take the bullets, but you can't, and, you have no weapons anyway. I have a feeling I'll need to fight my way in."

Giving in, Ermek walked over to the grass and sat down. "Bring her back safely."

DAGON

CHAPTER 30

When I was sure Ermek wouldn't follow, I strode to the temple's walls as quickly as possible. A few guards rushed from their posts, going deeper into the walled-off city. One man noticed me, and I called upon Hell's fire to burn him from the inside out.. he only screamed for a second before burning to ash.

A barrage of fully automatic gunfire ripped through me.. it stung like wasp stings but did nothing more than make me angry. That was good. The angrier I got, the more powerful my hellfire would become, and, right now, the pathetic little mortals were pissing me off. I grinned maniacally and raised my hands, focusing on the men on the wall. The flames raged, literally lighting a fire under their asses. The pained screams were almost musical. Being away from Hell for so long almost made me forget how much fun this was.

I followed the path toward the temple. Every interfering human was coated in hellfire, and only the truly innocent were spared from the flames. For

231

those special cases, I knocked them on their ass and told them not to be heroes. This city reeked of guilt. Behind these walls were murderers, rapists, and child abusers. Some of these men had sold their daughters to the Priests for wealth and power in neighboring villages.

As I got closer to the temple edifice, I realized where those Demon Hunters got those Priestesses. They had been requesting temples to send Priestesses to them.. the Priests here would rape them and sell them to the Heathens. I wondered if they thought the Heathens would spare them once their army was strong enough to attack.

Casually, I walked up the temple steps. People were screaming and running in every direction.. it was glorious. I missed these times.. I hadn't had a good reckoning in centuries.. I hadn't needed to. It was my nature to let humans die of natural causes and torture them for eternity. Hearing their screams made me remember how amusing it was.

Another guard pulled out his rifle and began firing at me. I tilted my head to the side, held up my hand, burned him to a crisp. Picking up his weapon, I toyed with it for a moment, trying to remember how one of these things worked. When I fired off a single round, I smirked and walked through the doors.

Brown robes ran in every direction, and, as a tune started to play in my head, I began to sing. A song from the twenty-first century, Pumped Up Kicks, if I remember correctly. I only knew the song's chorus, but it seemed fitting.

I didn't bother to aim as I pulled the trigger, releasing a wave of bullets as I rotated in a half circle. I only managed to strike down three Priests before the weapon jammed up. I fidgeted with it, gave up, and tossed it to the ground. One of the surviving Priests stepped toward me, holding out a golden cross.

"In the name of God, I command you to go back to Hell where you belong, demon!"

Gripping my chest, I fell to one knee. "Oh no! It burns! It burns me! Make it stop! I yield!" I stopped yelling and smirked. "I'm just kidding." With a cackle, I got to my feet. The Priest backed away, still gripping the golden cross in his hands. Focusing on it, I heated it until he dropped it. "Look around, Priest. God isn't here. Pray all you want.. God doesn't protect rapists, and God doesn't save murderers. No Priest, God sends them—to *me*."

I was about to pull his tiny little head from his shoulders when I felt Jazzera in my head. I felt her guilt slithering through my body. Through her eyes, I saw the bodies of two men. One was decapitated, and the other was bleeding out. Then I saw the Head Priest standing in front of her.

Ignoring the tormented Priest before me, I rushed up the stairs. Pausing briefly to gauge my surroundings, I noticed that he was running for his life. I would get him later. There was no way I would allow him to live, thinking that God had spared him.

She's in here, Dagon. I smiled slightly at the voice in my head. I could not believe that son of a bitch Azrael was helping me out. More often than not, he tried staying out of other beings' affairs.

"Are you reconsidering that room?" I teased as I walked to the back of the loft.

I'm not.

"Damn." I pushed the door open, and my eyes fell on Jazzera. She was standing next to two bodies on the ground.. the one she disemboweled had just taken his last breath. "May as well stick around, Azrael. I'm burning this place to the ground."

Jazzera took a step toward me, but I ignored her, going straight for the Head Priest. I looked deep into his eyes and took in his stench. The closer I got, the more of his sinful memories I could see. Ever since he was a young man, he prayed on women, forcing them into his bed. If they refused, he would have them burned as a witch. He would have their tongues cut out and stoned to death if he got them pregnant. He only recently started selling the girls he raped, realizing how much money he could make.

A rage filled my body, but instead of calling Hell's fire, I punched my hand through his chest, pulling out his still-beating heart. "Don't reap him just yet, Azrael. I want him to watch this. When I'm done, you can have him."

The man's eyes filled with fear as I lifted his heart in my hands so that it was only inches from his eyes. I bit into the muscle, causing the man to scream in fear and pain. Slowly, I consumed his heart until there was nothing more than a bloody mess on my lips. Dismissively, I wiped my hand on his shirt and used some loose fabric to clean my lips.

"Now you may have him." The man dropped seconds later. Unluckily for the Priest, Azrael wasn't fond of rapists and murderers any more than I was. After ensuring my face was completely clean, I turned to Jazzera. "Are you alright?"

Her skin was as pale as mine, and her face looked slightly green. I stepped back, giving her room to vomit without getting anything on my shoes. It felt like an eternity had passed before she spoke.

"I killed them." Tears began to run down her cheeks. "I'm a murderer."

Shaking my head, I went to her and cupped her face. "This was self-defense. They were going to rape you. The Priest first, and then these two men would have had their turn. This was self-preservation and nothing more."

Sniffling, she ran her robe across her eyes and took a deep breath. "How did you know where I was?"

"We are connected, Jazz. I can always find you."

She wrapped her arms tightly around me and buried her face into my chest. Stroking her long hair, I kissed the top of her head. "We have to go," I whispered.

Pulling back, she gripped my hand tightly, and I escorted her out of the room and down the stairs. When I got to the bottom, I glared at the tapestries on the wall and sent out a blast of hellfire to set them aflame. This whole damned city would burn if I had anything to do with it.

Every being who dared look at her cross-eyed would be destroyed. Close to the front door, I paused when I heard whimpering. Looking around, I maniacally smiled when I spotted the Priest from earlier trying to hide under a dead body. His plan may have worked if he weren't so utterly terrified.

"I spy with my little eye a terrified Priest pissing himself underneath one of my victims." The man looked up, and I winked. "Found you."

Shoving the body away, the man got to his knees and crawled over to Jazzera. "Please, Priestess. Please spare me. Have mercy on an old man! Please!"

"You will not be spared this night, Priest!" I bellowed as I held my hand up to call the fire.

"Dagon, no."

The flame sputtered, and I turned to her. "He's an evil man, Jazz. He deserves everything he is about to get. If you spare him, he is going to think God interfered."

"But if you kill him after he begged me to spare him, that makes me a murderer."

I frowned. "Well, an accessory anyway."

The fact that she was right made my blood boil. It would seem that this Priest would once again live to see another day and escape the pit of Hell. I was about to leave him be when a thought crossed my mind, and a wicked grin stretched across my face.

"Just give me a second, my Lady," I implored and then pressed my hands together.

"What is he doing?" blubbered the Priest.

I looked down at him. "I'm telling my mommy on you."

"Dagon!" Jazzera yelled before a portal opened on the other side of the room. One thing that could be said about Lilith was that she loved every one of her children deeply. If one of us called, she would rush to them within seconds. I could have spared Jazzera a lot of pain had I called Lilith when the Demon Hunters speared me.

My mother stepped out of the portal, her sword hanging at her side. Her eyes narrowed at the sight of Jazzera, and she quickened her pace toward us. "What have you done to my son?"

"Not her, Mother," I said, stopping her before she cut Jazzera's head from her shoulders.

Glancing down at the Priest, I sneered. "This little asshole found a loophole, and he thought he could get away with his life." I pointed to myself.

"And this bigger asshole also found a loophole that won't mark Jazzera as a murderer."

Lilith beamed and cupped my face in her hands. "You are such a clever boy."

"I know. I'm brilliant."

Lilith winked, then turned to the Priest, who defecated in his robes. I might have cringed if I hadn't been so used to the smell of dead bodies shitting themselves. Gripping the man's head in her hand, I heard her nails tear his flesh and dig into the bone. She twisted her wrist sharply, and the top came off with a sick cracking sound. She held it up for a moment, gazing at the flesh of his face that was still attached. Cackling, she kicked his body, sending him into a violent seizure for several moments until his body stilled.

"I'm going to get the Priestess to safety. Burn it to the ground." Cradling Jazzera in my arms, I twisted to Lilith. "And please spare the innocents the best you can."

My mother nodded. "Tell your little toy that if she does not set you free soon, I will eat her heart."

"Don't worry about her," I whispered to Jazzera when I felt her body tense. "She's just overly dramatic."

JAZZERA

CHAPTER 31

I couldn't bear the sight that greeted me outside. Everything was burning.. people were running and crying in the streets. A child cried for their mother, and I had to bury myself in Dagon's chest. All of this death was because of me, all because Dagon needed to rescue me.

These children suffered because I was jealous enough to betray my dearest friend. I deserved this Hell on Earth just as much as the men I killed did, and, when I die, I deserve to burn for all of eternity. I was in a daze, unsure how long it took us to get a safe distance away from the flames. But when Dagon put me down, I couldn't look him in the eye. So many mixed emotions bombarded me all at once. Did he betray me? Was he trying to stop me from shutting Hell's Gates? Did he genuinely feel anything for me?

I let my eyes flicker from the ground to the burning city for a brief second. This man burned an entire city down for me. I gazed at him, trying to figure out what I was looking at. A monster? Or a man? He ran his hand gently down my cheek, and I timidly smiled. I was looking at a demon, neither monster nor man. A being that was only doing what was in his nature, punishing the wicked as he rescued the woman he loved.

The expression on his face and his gentle touch told me that. Pulling his face to mine, I pressed my lips firmly to his. He kissed me back, and we stayed locked in that dance of passion for several moments before he pulled away.

Running his hand gently through my hair, Dagon whispered, "You need to talk to Ermek." I cocked my head to the side, waiting patiently for an explanation. "He knows."

Dagon must have seen everything that happened with his demon gaze. Ermek knew that I had come here to betray him. My mouth opened, but no words came out. What was I supposed to say? That I was jealous and wanted to cause him pain? Because that is precisely what happened.

I had felt betrayed and lied to. My heart was shattering, and all I could think to do was cause pain. To make one of them feel as much pain as I had when I saw the throuple by the lake.

"I didn't—"

Dagon cut off my words before I could utter an excuse. "I know you didn't."

"I didn't tell them."

"What you saw wasn't what you thought it was." He shrugged. "Well, not really. Did Ermek and I have sex? Yes, a few times, and, I liked it, and so did he. It was a good ol' time, but I know you can be a prude."

I scoffed, unsure if he was apologizing or what. It was starting to feel more like a Dagon-style lecture.

He rambled, "Sorry. Not really.. you are a prude. Humans and their monogamy. Fun fact, monogamy was just a way for men to control who a woman slept with." He looked at me for a moment as if expecting me to have an epiphany. When that wasn't going to happen, he brushed the hair off his shoulders and continued, "I know you believe in monogamy, so I turned them down. Ermek doesn't know how I feel about you. So he tried to get me to have sex, and I turned him down, and, not just because they stank."

I turned to survey the burning city, absorbing his words. The screams had died down, and several people fled through the gate, either trying to escape Lilith or the fire. I wanted to distance myself from all of it.

"I believe you, and, I shouldn't have acted that way. I need to talk to Ermek."

Dagon and I walked down the old road that led away from the city, hand in hand.

"I told Ermek that the Followers' teachings made you react like that. Mix rage with a dogma taught since childhood, and it becomes hard to shake free from." Releasing my hand, he paused for a moment and looked at me. "I need you to know, deep down in your heart, that I have been telling you the truth. Nothing Ermek did was sinful.. he really doesn't have a choice because nobody can choose who they are attracted to. Why would anyone risk such a horrible death if they could choose it?"

Mulling it over, I realized what Dagon said made sense, and, who was I to judge, anyway? I would be alongside Ermek if the Followers found out I had slept with a demon. In fact, my punishment may have been worse. Instead of outright killing me, they would've tortured me first.

Ermek sat below a naked elm tree. The last leaf had fallen, bathing the ground in a yellow blanket. He got to his feet when he spotted me, and an awkward silence passed between us. I could see in his eyes that he was happy to see me alive, but I could feel his uncertainty. He felt betrayed, and rightfully so. I took the initiative and wrapped my arms tightly around him.

He hesitated momentarily, then hugged me back. Placing his head gently on the top of mine, we stayed locked in our embrace for a long while before I eventually pulled away.

"I'm sorry." Looking directly into his golden eyes, I started to sob. "I'm so sorry!" I buried my face into his chest.

Kissing the top of my head softly, Ermek pulled away and smiled. "Can I honestly say I wouldn't have done the same? If I were in love for the first time and saw what you did, I can't promise I wouldn't have turned you in for sleeping with a demon."

I rubbed my arms, desperately needing something to do with my hands. "I didn't say anything. You can say that the guard knocked some sense into me. After that, it was like my eyes finally opened. Why would God favor such cruel men over us? Why would he shun love yet embrace hatred?"

"For what it's worth, I'm sorry for my behavior as well. At times, I treated you as if you were beneath me, and, I shunned you while you were suffering through Eve's curse."

"Not Eve's Curse!" shouted Dagon.

241

Ermek chuckled. "This entire time, Dagon has been trying to tell us that all God cares about is if you're a decent human being, and, I think the only one who has been decent is the damned demon."

"I went on a homicidal rampage and ate a man's heart," commented Dagon, stroking his chin hair. "So, I'm sorry too." He laughed. "I tried to keep a straight face while saying that. I'm not sorry. All that fear just pumps right through the heart. It was so good."

Ermek's eyes widened as he looked to me for confirmation. "He ate a man's heart?"

I sheepishly nodded. "I'm trying to pretend that didn't happen."

Dagon shrugged. "I'm a demon. It's not cannibalism."

"Can we forget the heart thing?" I begged, trying desperately to get the image out of my head.

Again, Dagon shrugged and clasped his hands together. "Alright, let's forget the heart thing and get back to the Hell thing. We can be at the gates before dark if we leave now."

"I'm not going to the Hell's Gates.. those doors can stay open for eternity for all I care."

Ermek placed his hand on my shoulder. "Are you sure?"

I nodded. "I deserve this Hell on Earth. I killed two men, and humans keep killing each other. It's a never-ending loop. So let the demons have them."

Nearly shoving Ermek away from me, Dagon gripped my face. "You don't deserve anything to do with Hell. You killed those men in self-defense.. they were going to hurt you, and, you spared a Priest who is in Hell right now. You were confronted by an evil man, and you spared him. Hell is not in your forecast. Except to close the gates."

I pulled away. "If I close them, I will never see you again!"

"And maybe that is a good thing!" He nearly yelled the words at me, causing me to flinch. "I'm a demon, Jazzera. I belong in Hell. Hell is my home. This entire thing happened mainly because angels and demons couldn't mind their own damned business. Eden wasn't a garden. Eden is an angel that had a garden. A garden where she kept a human child tucked away from other humans. She helped create a little narcist who truly believed he was the first man. The Moses versus Pharaoh thing started because Moses got his hands on my son's staff! The concept "man shall not lay with a man" was because a Priest was mad that my brother was banging his son. Even that ended up getting screwed up along the lines. Originally it was something like don't fuck you uncle, or aunt, or whatever." He paused then shook his head as if his mind was being overwhelmed. "And don't get me started on Sodom and Gomorrah. It was all us the entire time. It's why God made us leave, and, even after we left, we still managed to fuck shit up. Ask Azrael. That was so bad that a group of angels had to erase the collective of human memory so they'd forget the divine existed. Before the Rapture, things were getting better. Unfortunately, racism and homophobia were still alive and well, but it was getting better. People were letting go of the hateful beliefs of the Church. If you keep demons around, people will cling to the one thing they think will keep them safe, like the teachings of the Followers. So, you are closing Hell's

Gates." He turned to Ermek. "But first, you need weapons."

Ermek and I were stunned into silence, blankly watching as Dagon set off into a full sprint back to the city. I could have ordered him to come back and demanded that we settle down in a quaint little cottage and live a quiet life, but I knew Dagon wasn't the silent type. He would fight me every chance he got, and, how long would he put up with being my captive? How long until he decided he needed his freedom, and that need turned into resentment? And if I did free him, how long until he decided to take up the mission by himself? How long until he eventually succumbed, becoming just another soul in the demon that was Legion?

I wanted to resent him, to hate that he was taking this choice away from me. The very thought of losing him made me want to fall apart. I didn't want anyone else.. I just wanted my demon. I looked over at Ermek and knew he felt the same. He may not love Dagon as I did, but it was apparent that he cared for Dagon's well-being. Ermek hated this idea too.

Dagon came back bearing gifts. He handed Ermek a new longbow with a quiver of arrows and a couple of blades should he need to fight in hand-to-hand combat. Ermek felt the bow in his hand, weighing it, and nodded with approval, securing it in place. Testing the blades, he slashed them quickly through the air.

"These will do," he said appreciatively.

Dagon shifted to me. "You know when you use your angelic mark to conjure up a burst of energy? Like how you burned Lilith? Channel that into your sword. It will cut straight through any demon you meet. It will amplify your angelic powers, and Legion won't know what hit them."

I pulled my sword from its sheath. It was still the same sword I had before I fought Lilith and almost died.. nothing about it had changed. Focusing hard, I tried to conjure up my angelic power. Most of the time, I could only use it when feeling strong emotions.. fear or anger was its main trigger.

I felt energy surge through my body and race down my arm, making my mark glow brightly. It flowed into my blade, imbuing it with power and matching angelic symbols. I stood with newfound confidence.

"Let's close that gate."

JAZZERA

CHAPTER 32

We walked for hours, trudging through a tall, dry grass field and following a rushing river until we found a suitable bridge. It was ancient and crumbling, with gigantic holes throughout the pavement. Most of the metalwork was rusting and weak, groaning with each passing rush of wind. Dagon insisted this was the safest place to cross before the gates. I suggested flying across the giant river, but he dismissed it, saying it would only attract other flying demons.

I felt the gates' aura before I saw it.. a massive orange cylinder of light forcing its way up from the ground and into the clouds as if to penetrate Heaven itself. I felt nothing but despair, almost like my entire body was beaten down by sorrow, anger, loneliness, and pain. It made me want to stop and lie on the ground in defeat. It made me feel like nothing was worth taking another step or exhaling another breath. Dagon must have sensed my turmoil because he squeezed my hand gently in reassurance.

"You haven't felt anything yet. Hell gives all mortals a feeling of despair. Keep hope in your heart. The hope that you can make it through this is the only thing that will help you survive."

I returned the gentle squeeze. The problem was that I had no real hope because I didn't want to go through with this anymore. The only hope I could hold onto was that Dagon wouldn't leave me, but according to him, he was about to vanish from my life forever.

The closer we got, the louder the portal became.. it was like the rumble of a million roaring fires burning simultaneously. Demons were everywhere, mainly imps and shadow dwellers, but none approached us.

As if sensing my confusion, Dagon explained, "They are staying away from me. I'm a warden of Hell, and they don't want me to drag them back."

Closer up, the gates looked more like a wall than just a beam of light. Aside from the orange hue, there were swirls of greens, purples, reds, and yellows.. it looked like oil on water.

"The Demon Lords were the only ones that were supposed to exit Hell. This barrier was meant to keep the lesser demons inside, but several smuggled their way out. Regardless, it still holds the majority of them back. If it weren't here, the world would have been overrun with demons, causing the extinction of the human race. Once we pass the barrier, we will be confronted by more demons than you have ever encountered in your entire life. There will also be souls of the damned that have managed to escape Hell." Dagon looked intently at us. "Only attack if you are attacked. Some demons are wardens, trying to keep the damned from leaving. You are alive, so they won't bother with you." With a sigh, Dagon turned to the wall. "Just push your way through."

Hand outstretched, Dagon walked through the orange wall with Ermek close behind him. I took a deep breath and followed suit. On the other side, I almost dropped immediately. The negative feelings were overwhelming, gradually becoming worse until I gave in. They pushed down on my very soul like a heavy weight on my chest, causing me to collapse onto my knees.

How could anyone keep hope alive while facing this? It was no wonder God made the Demon Lords numb. This much despair would cause any soul to be ripped apart.

Ermek's body was stiff, and he seemed to struggle just as much as I did. A tear slid down his cheek and seeing such a strong man shed tears gave me strength. Ermek would be my hope. We had to survive this for him.. he deserved to live outside of the Followers. Even though I may lose the man I love, Ermek deserved to be reunited with the man he loved.

Getting to my feet, I pulled my sword out, and it glowed with power. My angelic mark shined with an intensity I'd never seen before. We could do this.. we could close the gates and banish the monsters to Hell for the sake of humanity. *For Ermek.*

We barely had time to acclimate before the first demon attacked, a bright red, winged monstrosity with a long tail. Ermek dispatched it with a well-placed shot, and it flopped around for a moment before finally lying still. That first kill triggered a feeding frenzy.. demons rushed at us, some viciously attacking while others devoured the corpses of their fallen comrades.

Ermek latched his bow to his back and pulled out his Katars. A gruesome fate ended each new attack as he slashed and stabbed with grace and accuracy. He fought with such skill that even Dagon seemed to pause, admiring Ermek's dance of destruction.

Endless waves of demons bore down on us, and I was getting winded. My body ached as I decapitated yet another demon, leaving its body in a puddle of green ooze. If this kept up, they would wear us down, and ultimately, we would meet our demise. Dagon was the only one who didn't seem to be battling both demons and fatigue. He wielded his trident with such expert precision that he could take out several demons in a matter of seconds.

We slowly battled our way into the ruined city. The orange glow of the wall gradually gave way to dark grey light, leaching every building of its natural color. Though severely damaged, the ancient structures weren't piles of rubble.. many still stood proudly as if two hundred years had never passed. My jaw dropped at the sight of a gigantic arch near the river, the largest structure I had ever seen, standing tall without a hint of damage.

"We aren't far," murmured Dagon as he started to take my hand.

A nearby roar rent through the air, and I spotted a look of fear on Dagon's face for a split second. Ermek must have seen it, too, for he got back into his fighting stance and frantically looked around for whatever creature had made that noise. My biggest concern was, what type of demon could make a Demon Lord flinch?

A red glow came from around the corner of a nearby building. The demon was tall and muscular, standing at least twelve feet in the air. It wore a long, black robe that emanated the red light, and fire danced at the hem with every menacing step. The creature had giant bat wings stuck out from its back like two massive sentinels protecting the creature from behind. On its shoulders, it wore armor with jagged spikes and a metal mask in the shape of a skull. Behind the mask was nothing but fire. There was no neck or head structure, only two long red horns that seemed to float within the flames.

"It's a wrath demon!" bellowed Dagon.

My body went cold. I had never seen a wrath demon before, but I had heard the stories, and, not a single one of them ended in a happy ending. Every Demon Slayer who faced such a beast lost their life in the battle.

The demon raised its arms, and flames engulfed them, forming a giant ball of fire. The creature threw it in our direction, and Dagon darted in front of it, pointing his trident at the beast.

"You two are on your own!" he shouted. "I have to focus on controlling his fire! If I slip up, he will turn you into ash!"

The demon drew forth more fire, aiming it straight at us. Ermek sheathed his bladed weapons and pulled out his longbow. He loosed an arrow toward the creature's skull, but it pinged off the metal mask and fell to the ground. I darted toward the beast and slashed at the lower part of its body. The demon faltered, raised its hand, tried to bathe me in Hell's fire. Dagon pulled the fire back toward him while Ermek planted an arrow in the creature's chest. It staggered back, roaring. Another arrow flew, hitting the chest a second time.

We tag-teamed the demon, Ermek releasing arrow after arrow while I dashed up and sliced it with my blade. We were holding it back, but this couldn't go on forever. I could feel my body slowing down, and Ermek would soon be out of arrows. I looked down at my blade.. it wasn't glowing! I had to remember to channel my power through it.. it was the only way to defeat this monster.

Taking a step back, I focused on calling upon my power. I used every emotion I felt. fear, sorrow, despair, love, hate, and anger. My blade shone, and as Ermek let loose another arrow, I jumped toward the creature. I sliced at the demon, pushing all my power from my mark into my weapon. The blade cut clean through. The top half of the demon slid sidewise from its body. The moment it struck the ground, it turned into smoldering ash.

DAGON

CHAPTER 33

The relief I felt when the demon finally hit the ground was indescribable. Thinking over the fight, I realized I had made a grave mistake. I had forgotten about Hell's fire. Lesser demons could use it, but it took more energy than the smaller demons were willing to use in battle.

Demons that resembled their greatest sins could call upon it almost as much as a Demon Lord. I was stronger than the wrath demon, so I could restrain its fire, but when I came face-to-face with Legion, that would be a different story. I couldn't control another Demon Lord's fire.

With a single thought, Legion could turn Jazzera and Ermek into embers the moment they left the gate. Lilith didn't use hellfire because she was cocky and enjoyed the battle, teasing her victims with a false hope for victory, but Legion wasn't like my mother... they would want to dispatch the humans as soon as possible if things didn't go according to plan. They would rid themselves of the only humans who knew exactly who possessed the Key of Babylon.

"We're almost at the portal and need to run for it."

Jazzera and Ermek didn't hesitate to run, dispatching a few lesser demons while avoiding the bigger ones. The humans would have to conserve their energy for the battle with Legion, but hopefully, there would be no battle.

I stopped our progression when we neared the portal that would take me home. "I need you both to hold my hands."

"What are we getting into?" asked Ermek as he gazed ahead.

I glanced at the portal. There wasn't anything particularly terrifying about it. It looked like a giant, orange tear drop that ripped a hole between time and space, but I knew what was on the other end, possibly the most terrifying part of Hell.

"Beyond that gate is the first ring of Hell. You will be confronted with your worst fear. You won't see me, and you won't see each other. If you do, remember that what you are seeing is not real. Nothing there can hurt you because you are mortal. This ring doesn't affect me, so I will pull you through it. You will be able to feel my hand and hear my voice. Just don't let go, and I will get you out."

With looks of concern plastered on their faces, they grasped my hands. I pulled Jazzera close to me and pressed my lips against hers. I wanted her to know that whatever she saw in there, she would make it out if she trusted me.

When we broke from the kiss, I looked at Ermek. "I'd kiss you too, but she might get mad at me." He smiled in response, which was the only reassurance I needed to know that he trusted me.

I pulled us into the portal, entering a void of nothingness. No sky, no ground, no walls. It wasn't long before the humans started to see their visions. Ermek reacted first, and even though I couldn't see the background, I could understand the gist of what he was seeing. A few figures appeared.. one was Lazlo, the previous love of his life, and the other was Jazzera. Jazzera stood there for a moment glaring at Ermek. It was hard to hear, but it sounded like she was blaming him for something. Several Priests marched toward them, grabbing both roughly by the arms. Jazzera and Lazlo fought against the restraining holds, but it wasn't enough. The Priests succeeded in tying Jazzera and Lazlo to a pole and setting them ablaze. Their screeches were so real that I grimaced in horror, almost having to remind myself that my hand was holding the real Jazzera. As they burned, demons clawed at Ermek, making him scream and pull away from me.

Gripping his hand tighter, I tried to keep my voice calm. "It isn't real, Ermek. Just keep walking."

I turned to Jazzera, hoping her greatest fear was spiders or mice. Instead, I saw a perfect copy of myself, morphing slowly in front of her. I grew horns, wings, and goat legs. Why humans always pictured demons with goat legs was beyond me. My skin turned red, and a long tail wrapped tightly around her body. The false me used its elongated tongue to lick her face. Its sharp claws ripped at her clothing and whispered in her ear, "I never loved you. I was only ever using you."

I winced and squeezed her hand. "It's not real, Jazz. I have you.. the real me has you."

We were almost at the core of Hell.. I could feel it. If they let go, they'd be trapped, forever tortured by their fears. The closer we got to the barrier, the more they fought me. The visions had grown more intense, and their fear was more potent. I ignored their struggles, pulling them hard, and continued forward.

I hit the wall and pressed my body against it until it gave way. We were on a free fall to the floor of Hell.

JAZZERA

CHAPTER 34

He was here, in his demon form, with long, black horns, red skin, and furry goat legs. His monstrous tail coiled around me, and I flinched.

This isn't real, and this isn't Dagon. The real Dagon is holding my hand.

The monster pushed its body against mine, and I couldn't contain my whimper. I fought the urge to wretch as it rubbed its elongated, sandpaper-like tongue against my face.

"This isn't real!" I shouted.

The beast didn't seem to believe me. He laughed in my face, then used his talons to tear at my robes, reducing the fabric to ribbons. The sharp tips tore into my skin, leaving deep, bloody gashes. He wrenched my thighs apart.

This isn't real. This isn't happening to me. This is like that dream, and it's not real! The more I tried to convince myself, the more unsure I became as his claws dug deep gouges into my legs. Warm blood dripped from my wounds, and the demon bent over to lap it up.

"Dagon!" I screeched, praying the real one could hear me.

"I love it when you call my name," the demon said smugly.

I scowled at him. "You aren't the real Dagon!"

The creature grinned, showing off double rows of serrated teeth. "I never loved you. I was only ever using you. You know it in your heart. I was never going to allow you to close those gates.. I was going to fuck you and then kill you." It paused as if contemplating something. "And then fuck you again, in every hole I can find. The eye socket is especially tight."

I yanked away, but something tugged me in the opposite direction, the *real Dagon*. He was holding my hand and pulling me through this nightmare. Even though I couldn't see him, he was there. That gave me a small fraction of hope that I wouldn't have to deal with this too much longer. The demon backed off, and a long appendage protruded between the beast's legs. It was at least the size of my arm and had thorns covering it. My eyes watered, but I fought back the tears and tried again to pull myself free.

"It's not real, Jazz. I have you.. the real me has you." That was Dagon's voice.

I swallowed hard as the demon mounted me and forced himself between my legs.

Hearing the real Dagon's voice calmed me.. this wasn't real. I could feel the claws digging into my skin and the thorns pricking my inner thighs, and I knew it wasn't real.

Looking up at the imposter, I scowled at it. "Do your worst, demon."

Suddenly, I was falling, as were Ermek and Dagon. I twisted around, trying to see my surroundings. A giant black cliff loomed above as the ground rushed upward to meet us. We were too high up! We would never survive this. In a panic, I looked to Dagon, who managed to twist his body so that he would land feet first. I hoped he would transform into a flying animal and catch us, but the descent was too fast. My body slammed onto the ground, and everything went black for a second. I groaned. Every single part of my body hurt. One would think that was an indication of life, but even souls could feel pain in Hell. Dagon was already on his feet.

Ermek was balled up on the floor, and from the sound of it, he was crying. I forced myself to stand and surveyed my body.. nothing was broken. I looked up at the cliff. *How* was nothing broken? That was going to have to be a question for later. I went to Ermek and pulled him up into a sitting position.

His eyes were dilated from fear, and he wrapped his arms tightly around me. "You're okay. Thank God you're okay."

I patted the back of his head reassuringly and twirled my fingers in his braids. "Everything is fine."

He pulled back, wiping his nose on the back of his arm. "As fine as it can be in Hell, I guess."

I felt a hand on my shoulder and yanked away before realizing it was Dagon. I felt a small ounce of relief.

"It's really me, Jazz. I would never take that form.. it's too cliché."

I wanted to roll my eyes at his joke but knew the entire experience had bothered him. He must have seen what I did. "I know it wasn't you, and I don't see you like that."

Biting his lower lip, he murmured, "Yes, you do. Or Hell wouldn't have used it. You may not know it, but I am your worst fear deep down."

"No, Dagon, that's not true," I assured, wrapping my arms around him.

He pulled away. "It is, and, that's fine. It's perfect, really. It gives me the incentive I need to finish our quest. Soon, we'll be done with this, and you won't have to be afraid anymore." He began walking away.

Tears streamed down my cheeks. "No, Dagon, I'm not afraid of you. I love you."

He didn't look back at me and began walking to only God knows where. "Let's get going.. we still have a long way to go."

My heart was breaking. How could I have done that to him? How could I let my fears get the best of me? I knew that, eventually, I was going to lose him, but after that vision, I would lose him sooner than expected. I didn't want to lose him at all, but I definitely didn't want to lose him like this. Before this was over, I had to make amends. He couldn't return to this horrible place, thinking I was afraid of him. Somehow, I had to fix this.

"What is that?" Ermek was staring upward.

It looked like balls of fire were falling from the sky.

"Souls," answered Dagon. "People die practically every second, and, many of them come here. Once they manage to get away from the first circle, they make it to the core of Hell as a blazing fireball."

I scanned the scenery around us.. I had always been taught that Hell was engulfed with flames, but there was no fire here. What lay before us was a barren wasteland. The ground beneath our feet was dry and cracked. Off in the distance, old dried-out trees and bones lay about.

"What circle of Hell is this?"

Dagon looked back at me. "There really aren't any "circles." Hell isn't like how it's described in Dante's Inferno. The outer ring we had to pass through is like a planet's atmosphere, and Hell is like an ever-changing planet. When souls fall, Hell guides them to their most suitable punishment. You two are alive, so Hell didn't know what to do with you. So it dropped you here, where souls wander around dying of thirst. Only, they never die." He pointed over to a dead tree. "And when they fall, they become part of the landscape."

I stumbled back in horror and revulsion. The tree wasn't a tree at all.. it was two dehydrated human bodies fused together and molded to resemble a tree. The bodies began to groan in agony, and I flinched, turning away from the gruesome sight. Their moans were still audible, and Dagon kicked them.

"Shut up," he commanded, and they did as they were told.

"You don't have to be cruel to them," said Ermek with an empathetic look.

"They are in Hell, and I'm a demon. It's my job. One of them locked their child up in a closet until they died of thirst. The other stopped giving water to their bedridden mother so she would die quicker. That's why they landed in the desert. If you deny the innocent water, you will be denied a drink for all eternity." He looked at Ermek. "Do you still want me to stop being cruel?"

Ermek didn't respond, and I didn't blame him. Seeing these souls suffer was hard, but if what Dagon said was true, I had to admit that this was justice. How a person could kill their own family member in such a way was disgusting. As much as I hated to admit it, they deserved this fate.

It felt like hours before the scenery finally changed. Far off in the distance, I could almost make out what looked like a town nestled in a dead forest. "Is that what I think it is?"

Dagon looked up, and his expression changed from somber to almost giddy. "Oh, we have to go there. Towns are so much fun."

"There are towns in Hell?" Ermek asked.

Dagon nodded. "Yes, and they are one of the best torture spots. A town sprouts up when a bunch of wicked people die around the same time from the same place. Maybe a sickness hit their town or something like that. They end up in a town that looks almost exactly like the one they left, only creepy, and, Then, we fuck with them." He chuckled. "You see, when a town shows up, the people inside don't realize they are dead. They just go about their lives as normal until demons turn up and create chaos. It's almost like every hour. We do give them a fighting chance. Every town has a church, and they are safe from torture if they can make it inside. No lesser demon can go into the church. We thought it was ironic and funny, so we gave it to them, but a Demon Lord can go into the church. So they get this false sense of security until someone like me shows up."

Raising an eyebrow, I glanced over to the town. "If this happens every hour or so, how do they not realize they are dead?"

"They forget that some of their people were torn apart. The people who don't make it to the church sort of re-spawn. Like a video game." He cracked a grin when we had no idea what he was talking about. "Right, video games were before your time. They just re-appear. Everyone forgets that they were destroyed. However, occasionally, we will reap a soul. After tearing them apart, we take them to another part of Hell. The people of the town remember that. They remember that demons came to their village, which keeps them in constant fear."

"This truly is a horrible place," muttered Ermek.

Dagon practically skipped in the direction of the town. I didn't want to follow him, but I also didn't want to wander around Hell without him.

"What about the other demons? Won't they attack us?"

Dagon considered that for a moment. "No. At least, they better not. For one, in Hell, I am at full power, and, unlike me, lesser demons can feel pain. Even the demons of the deadly sins. Also, Lucifer made it a rule that no living soul is to be harmed in Hell. Or they face his wrath."

I shuddered at the name. Even though I was literally in Hell, I had forgotten that the actual Prince of Darkness called this place home.

"There isn't a chance we would run into Satan, is there?"

Dagon stroked his chin hair. "Doubtful. Satan won't go out of his way to bother us, and I don't think we will run into Lucifer, either. Unless I fuck up somehow."

I stopped in my tracks. "Aren't they one and the same?"

Dagon shook his head. "No. Common mistake. Satan was once like God's prosecutor. He absolutely hates humans and believes every one of them is rotten to the core. He's obsessive about it and will try to get humans to do evil because he believes, deep down, they all want to be murderous asshats. Lucifer is a pretty cool guy, though. He doesn't try to get anyone to sin. He just punishes those who do."

I had always been taught that they were the same entity. As I continued this journey, I gradually realized how much of what I was raised to believe was false. Lucifer can't be pure evil if he doesn't allow living souls to be harmed. On the other hand, Satan seemed to be exactly like the Bible depicted. someone who wanted to tempt humans from the light.

As Dagon got closer to the small, wooden town, the gates began to smolder until they caught ablaze. Demons materialized. Children swarmed into town, tiny beings with decaying bodies and gaping holes for eyes, crying tears of blood. Their movements were rigid and jerky until they spotted an unsuspecting victim. Their jaws pulled apart at the hinges, showing sharp rows of teeth with long, forked tongues. Screeching, they pounced on a woman who had dashed out of a small hut after it caught on fire. She screamed and tried to run away but was overwhelmed by the horde of demon children.

More demons clawed out from the ground. Their bodies looked like women, but their skin was so charred I couldn't make out any features. Blackened skin cracked, and bright red flames burst from the fissures as they moved. Inhuman screams tore from scorched throats and shook me to my very core. Like the children, they moved in jerky and sharp motions. They didn't charge victims but marched steadily toward them, reaching out and wailing their mournful cry.

As the wooden homes burned, more victims rushed onto the dusty street. They were all pale-skinned and wearing outfits of black and white. They looked just like the folk who had hanged innocent individuals for witchcraft. It was primarily men that fled for their lives, with a few women speckled in between. Their ages ranged from just above my own to elderly. The burned women snagged two men, and their charred touch began to melt the victims' flesh. The pained screams made me bolt to Dagon and wrap my arms around him. Thankfully, he returned the gesture, pulling me closer to him.

I spotted four more people, only a stone's throw away from the safety of the church, cornered by more demons. They were large, at least eight feet tall, and completely naked. Their excessive rolls of fat drooped low to the ground with infected pockmarks that oozed yellow pus. The very sight of them made me sick to my stomach.

The demons lunged at their victims, latching on with gaping mouths before tearing flesh from bone. Screams and cries for mercy filled the air, but no clemency would be gifted. Burying my face in Dagon's side, I walked blindly next to him, unwilling to witness any more gore. Could anyone actually be evil enough to deserve a place like this?

When we reached the church's door, Dagon turned around. Pulling away from his warmth, I saw Ermek standing as still as a statue on the bottom step.

"If you're going to go in there just to torture these poor souls, I can't go in.. I can't watch this anymore." Ermek gestured toward the people who were literally being torn apart. "Nothing these people have done could be worth this much torment."

"Ask their victims," remarked Dagon in a calm tone. "Every being here was involved with the torture and murder of eight innocent women. Those women were burned, pulled apart, and some were even eaten by pigs while still alive. Do you still want mercy for them, Demon Slayer?"

Ermek looked Dagon in the eyes. "Yes, I still want mercy for them."

Dagon scoffed, then ran his hand through his thick, raven hair. "Fine, but only because I like you, but remember, Demon Slayer, this is my domain. My world. I am a demon, and never once did I pretend to be anything else. Humans are always trying to figure out the will of God. Well, here it is. God created Hell. God gave me a job to do, and my job is to give these souls what they deserve. In a way, I am God's hand. At least a fingernail, anyway."

I shivered at Dagon's answer. I had seen his dark side when he ate the Priest's heart, and, when he refused to show mercy to the man who begged me for his life. He may not have killed the man himself, but he made sure the deed was done. Being in this place, the place he called home, seemed to draw the darkness out of him more. I recalled Dagon telling me that he volunteered to come to Hell and turned down the chance to be an angel. He could have been in Heaven.. instead, he was in the bowels of Hell and having the time of his life by scaring the shit out of souls. I didn't want to believe my fear was well-founded, that Dagon could be evil. No, there was good in him. I had to keep that hope alive. He was just a demon doing his job and nothing more. Dagon could still be a good person.

Pulling me back into his body, Dagon focused on the carnage. "Times up," he hollered, and the demons retreated slowly, returning to whatever shadow conjured them. The bodies of the tortured souls gradually vanished, and I looked over to Dagon for answers. "Their souls won't return until I leave the town. Once I do, they will come back, and the cycle starts anew."

JAZZERA

CHAPTER 35

We left the town and followed a beaten path toward the woods. The forest was packed with trees of the damned. They were enormous, comprised of at least a few hundred souls per tree. As we passed them, the souls groaned and moaned, creating a cacophony of misery. Every so often, I saw creatures resembling demonic lumberjacks striking the trees with wickedly sharp axes. The creatures were various colors.. red, green, and white seemed to be the standard. Most had horns of varying shapes and sizes, and a few had wings. The one thing they all had in common was how terrifying they looked. Piles of wooden souls, stacked high in wagons, were dragged off to some unknown place. Just past the tree-line was a crimson river of blood with a bridge constructed of human bones.

"What did these poor souls do to deserve this fate?"

Dagon glared up at the moaning trees. "The one thing these people have in common is greed. They caused suffering to other people, either by taking their homes or possessions, all for financial gain. Deny your fellow human a place to dwell, and you will find yourself here. Your soul will become wood to build the towns like the one you just left."

Every petrified body was twisted in pure agony, begging for a release that would never come. Demonic bird-like creatures with bright red feathers and horrifyingly long, black beaks pecked at the trees. Blood seeped from the ragged wounds, and I averted my eyes from the gory sight. I would be lucky if I ever had a proper night's sleep after this journey.

After about an hour more of traveling, Dagon finally let us rest in a clearing. The logger demons still went about their business, ignoring us for the most part. Occasionally they would pause, and one sharp look from Dagon had them rushing about again.

"How much longer do we have to travel?" I asked, trying my best not to lean on a damned soul.

"We still have to go past the Lustful Lagoon and the Freak Show that is pride," yawned Dagon as he slumped against a tree. "You two should try to get a little bit of sleep."

"And how do you suppose we get any sleep in Hell?" Ermek wondered in bewilderment.

"The end of this journey is still a long way off, Demon Slayer. I'd try and get some rest if I were you."

Ermek swung his arms wide, gesturing to our surroundings and the open sky. "Why can't you just turn into a dragon? Fly us across this wretched land."

Dagon chuckled. "For one, I don't want to constantly dodge fireballs, and, two, I don't want to draw the wrong attention."

"I thought you said demons wouldn't harm us!" Ermek groused.

"They won't, but humans aren't supposed to be here, and I don't need any other Demon Lord finding out you're here. Or why you're here, for that matter. If Beelzebub, Satan, or Lucifer find out you are here, that is no good for me. Beelzebub will just tattle, but Satan and Lucifer can make me feel pain worse than any soul here will ever endure."

I stood, walked over to Dagon, and pulled him up. "Let's go for a walk and relieve some of this tension." Dagon raised an eyebrow but didn't argue with me.

"You're just going to leave me alone?" demanded Ermek incredulously as he, too, got to his feet.

I sighed heavily and went to Ermek, placing my hand gently on his shoulder. "I need to be with him alone. Please. Just stay here."

Ermek narrowed his eyes and crossed his arms over his chest. He kicked the ground and huffed, "Be quick. I don't like being here any more than you do."

I stood on my toes and kissed his cheek gently. "I promise to be fast."

I grabbed Dagon's hand and led him through the tangled foliage. When Ermek was out of sight, I pressed my lips against Dagon's. He kissed me back tenderly, running his hand through my hair. I reached down to his groin and gave it a gentle squeeze. Instead of enthusiastically being on board, he groaned, pulled my hand away, and broke the kiss.

"What's wrong?"

"I'm in Hell and can't feel any of it. So pardon me if I don't feel like fornicating at this moment."

Swallowing hard, I nodded dejectedly before staring up at Dagon. "I'm sorry. I didn't mean to hurt you. I'm not afraid of you. Really, I'm not."

I hated how his eyes made it almost impossible to tell if he was rolling them. At this moment, it felt like he was.

"I'm not mad at you. We're on a quest, and I don't feel like getting distracted anymore. I just want this over with." He turned his back on me and started to leave.

My blood boiled, and I angrily searched the ground for something to throw at him. Finding nothing, I slipped one of my boots off and threw it as hard as possible, hitting him in the middle of his back.

"Can't feel pain, remember?"

"I don't care!" I shouted. "I don't want to complete this quest! You shouldn't either! You're a demon, for Christ's sake. Start acting like it!"

He twisted around. "You don't want me to start acting like a demon, Priestess."

"And what is with this 'Priestess' thing?' Ever since we got here, you haven't called Ermek or me by our real names."

"Because you are afraid of me, Jazzera! I saw it! I am your worst fear!" He was shouting now. He balled his hands into fists. "And you should be. I am a creature of nightmares. I am the shadow on a dark street. The monster under your bed. The bump in the night. I ate a man's heart right in front of you, and I'm not sorry. I'd do it again. I liked it. Fear makes my dick hard."

He backed up and raised his hands in the air. His body began to shift into the creature of my nightmare. The false Dagon- hairy goat legs, red skin, and all. "This is what you see me as.. this is your worst fear."

I stalked toward him, balled up my fist, and swung with all my might, punching him in the face. He staggered. "Didn't feel that."

"Well, I did, you dick. It hurt!" I swung my fist harder, hitting him directly on the nose.

He felt around his face for a moment. "I think you broke my nose! Bitch!"

Putting my hands on my hips, I sneered, "Good! Now turn back! Get out of this *cliché* form."

His eyes narrowed, but eventually, he did as I asked. The nose was crooked. "You did break it!" he exclaimed.

"I thought you said you couldn't feel it," I taunted, crossing my arms.

There was a popping sound, and his nose was back to being perfectly straight. "I can't. But you broke my fucking nose."

"Take me up there again." He cocked his head at me. "Take me up to the atmosphere. Let me see my worst fear again, and I promise you, it won't be you. It will be me losing you."

Exhaling heavily, he crossed his arms. "Forget about me, Jazzera. When this is over, find yourself a human man and make lots of babies just like you always wanted. Hold your first child in your arms, and you will forget I ever existed."

I wanted to argue more, but he walked away. Frustrated, I shouted, "I command you to come back!"

He staggered for a moment, then held his middle finger in the air. "Doesn't work as well down here. Try harder, *Priestess*."

JAZZERA

CHAPTER 36

When we returned to the clearing, Ermek was asleep under one of the moaning trees. I settled next to him and eventually fell asleep too. When I awoke, I realized I hadn't dreamed.

That was a relief. It was bad enough that being down here would most likely trigger horrible nightmares when I returned to Earth, and I didn't need them while fighting my way through the pits of Hell. Stretching, I stood and looked around for Dagon. He was lying on one of the limbs of a nearby tree, arms behind his head and one leg kicking freely.

"Wake the Demon Slayer."

I hated that he regressed to calling Ermek and me by our titles instead of our names, but I didn't feel like arguing with him about it again. Instead, I went over to my sleeping friend and nudged him slightly. He yawned and blinked his eyes open, sitting for a moment as if confused about where he was.

"We're still here," he stated flatly.

273

"Sadly, yes," I lamented.

When Ermek and I were mobile, Dagon dropped to the ground and began walking through the trees. His pace was quick, so Ermek and I had to add more pep to our step to keep up. The walk through the forest was long, and the scenery stayed the same. Twisted trees of dammed souls, waiting to be chopped down or pecked at, stretched as far as the eye could see. I was actually excited when I finally spotted another clearing. Hastening my steps, I caught up to Dagon, eager to leave the forest.

Our new surroundings were strangely beautiful. Two large 'lavafalls' cascaded into a lake that branched into a winding river. Next to the lake sat small trees with red fire dancing on their branches, giving them a beautiful glow. Had the lava been water instead, this would have been a beautiful and peaceful oasis. The ground and the rocks shined with a purple hue that gleamed brightly with the molten rock's light.

"What is this place?"

"The Lustful Lagoon," Dagon replied as he shoved his hands deep into his pockets. "You should know a few people here, Priestess."

"So, the seven deadly sins are real," Ermek concluded. It wasn't a question.. We had both heard of the deadly sins demons.. They resembled God's greatest crimes.

"In a way, any sin committed to send you here must be bad." Dagon gestured to the lagoon. "Like this place, this isn't the only area that tortures people for lust, but not all lust is a sin. Like I've said over and over, God doesn't care who you fuck. He cares when you hurt someone while doing it. The people you will find in this particular spot are those who used their power to force someone to have sex with them. They may not have physically harmed them, but their victims didn't want to fornicate. Let's say a landlord wants to evict a tenant because that tenant doesn't have rent. The landlord says they will take sex instead, but the victim didn't want to and only did it to survive. Or let's say a Priest tells a Priestess that God demanded she lay with him to provide a holy heir—"

I shivered at the memory his words conjured, then thought back to my temple and realized that I should have known what was happening around me. Often, a young woman at my temple would be hand-picked by the Head Priest to go into a private prayer ceremony. When the girl emerged, she'd look ashamed and almost humiliated. I felt so stupid for not realizing what had been happening. The Priests covered it up by sending the Priestesses away. The prayer ceremony was supposed to be for those who were about to leave for their duty, to become "pure." Those young girls were being raped and shipped off so they wouldn't tell anyone the truth. I almost couldn't believe how naive I was.

In the middle of the lava lake were islands with more fire trees. Cages dangled from the branches with crying people confined inside them. Every once in a while, lava demons would crawl their way up from the lake and choose a soul to torment. Once the cages opened, the screaming and pleading started. I deliberately kept my eyes away from the islands, not willing to stomach the sight. Instead, I focused on Dagon, who crouched next to the lake. The heat kept me away, but I was curious as he manipulated the lava. After a few minutes, he returned carrying something in his hands.

"Made you two a gift." He handed us both a piece of jewelry.

I studied it in the lava's glowing light.. it was stunning—a necklace of black metal holding a glass teardrop encased in a spider web of metal tendrils. Nestled inside the glass was a tiny burning flame.

"It's beautiful," I murmured as I marveled at it.

"How did you manage this?" inquired Ermek as he gazed transfixed at the tiny flame.

"The landscape in Hell is mine to command. Any Demon Lord can shape it to their will. These talismans contain a tiny bit of Hell's fire. Wear them, and hellfire won't harm you."

"Thank you, Dagon," I said as I put it on.

He smiled. "I didn't think of it until we battled the wrath demon. I never worried about Hell's fire because I couldeasily control it, and, I can control the fire of any lesser demon or deadly sins demon." He sighed, exasperated. "But I can't control the fire of another Demon Lord. Lilith could have killed you in an instant. She didn't because she enjoys hand-to-hand combat. It's like a sport to her, but Legion is nothing like my mother. They are going to try and kill you as quickly as possible. If I had to guess, I'd say hellfire would be their first move. Without this necklace, you two would be ash within seconds."

"And you're sure this will work?" Ermek clasped the chain around his neck, still studying the teardrop.

"Yes. Demon Lords who grew fond of humans would make these, just in case some other demon decided to attack. I've made them before."

Dagon's words stung more than I thought they should. He was thousands of years old.. it would be stupid of me to believe he hadn't had a lover or two within those years, and, knowing Dagon's personality, I was almost positive he had a few demon enemies who may want to harm those he cares about.

Dagon began walking again, and I had to quicken my pace to follow. He walked along the shoreline to where more souls were being tortured, most of whom were men. The souls were stuck in the ground with lava crashing against them like waves, burning their flesh to charcoal. I passed what looked like an old stump that sat just out of reach of the waves. I would have paid it no mind, but it spoke my name! Freezing, I turned to the stump, which wasn't a stump at all. It was a man, charred beyond recognition, but I knew his voice.

"Lady Jazzera. Please free me," pleaded the soul.

I recognized that voice because I had heard it so many times throughout my life. It belonged to none other than the High Priest of my temple, Priest Brocklen. Shaking my head, I took a step back.

"I can't help you." My words were small and weak, and I hated myself for feeling intimidated by this man. Even stuck in the soil of Hell, his voice still caused my body to stiffen.

"You can. You are an angel," he begged weakly. "You can set me free."

Dagon stood next to me and grinned as small creatures crawled to the shore. At first glance, they looked like oversized black crabs, but when they neared the Priest, a baby's head popped out of the front. It was a monstrosity, and I couldn't help but scream. Babies were supposed to look innocent and adorable. Yet, these demon-baby creatures were perhaps the most terrifying things I had seen thus far.

The crab babies swarmed the Priest like ants, and his agonized screams sent a shiver down my spine. I walked away, trying to distance myself from those horrid demons.

When Dagon finally followed, I asked, "Is there any truth to his words?" He shrugged. "Is it because I'm a Nephilim?"

Dagon shook his head. "No. It's because you're a bit more."

"What do you mean?" My voice raised in pitch.

Running his hand through his hair, he hesitated. "When your father gave you his life force, you may have become more angel than human."

"And what's that supposed to mean?" He shrugged again. "What does that mean?!" This time I shouted it.

"Yes, you can free tortured souls. As long as they aren't putrid."

"And what is a putrid soul?" This time it was Ermek asking. He made his way to my side at some point, still gawking at the crab babies.

"Souls that are so evil they can't be redeemed. Typically, mass murderers become putrid souls, and after one thousand years, they become deadly sin demons, but this bastard isn't putrid. So, if he truly regrets his sins after one thousand years, he will be reincarnated, and, if he doesn't fuck up, he'll go to Heaven. If he does, he'll come back here, be tortured for a thousand more years, and become a lesser demon."

"So, I can send him to Heaven right now?" My body shook at the possibility.

Dagon sneered. "Yes, but do you really want to? He deserves to be here, Priestess.. they all deserve to be here. Think of his victims. Had you not been in line to be the next High Priestess, you would have been one of them. He lusted hard over you, the exotic, foreign girl. He fetishized you."

Taking in a shaky breath, I looked over to the stump that was once my Head Priest. If I were honest with myself, I hated him. I always feared that one day he would come up with an excuse to have me killed. Finding out what he thought of me made me sick to my stomach.

Looking away, I walked in the direction that Dagon was initially heading. When my companions caught up, I asked Dagon, "So, you said I was now more angel than I once was. What does that mean exactly?"

Dagon huffed. "It means you don't have to worry about getting old any time soon."

I stopped abruptly. "And what the Hell does that mean? Stop talking in riddles!"

He made a face and crossed his arms. "Angels and demons like me, who were born, stop aging when we hit our prime. In human years, we look to be in our late twenties to early thirties, and we never get any older. So, you will never look any older than thirtyish."

"You mean it made her immortal?" Ermek inquired.

"Well, she can't die from old age or illness, but she can still be killed. She still has a little thread of humanity left, just enough to make her not quite immortal."

Hot tears streaked down my face. This was so overwhelming that I couldn't contain them. Balling up my fists, I glared at Dagon. "You should have let me die! You make me immortal when you fully intend to leave me! What good is finding a husband or children if I'm going to outlive all of them?"

Dagon bowed his head and stuffed his hands into his pockets. "Plenty of fallen angels are roaming the Earth, and they have been doing it for centuries. Your father did.. he had countless families and countless children. You learn to get used to immortality."

I couldn't contain my rage. Pulling my sword from its sheath, I swung it. The blade connected with Dagon's neck, and his body collapsed. I couldn't look at the heap that lay at my feet, so I walked away. The sound of Ermek's rushing feet made me pause.

"What have you done?" cried Ermek, gripping my shoulders tightly.

Yanking away, I glanced over to Dagon's prone body. His head was nowhere to be seen, and I suddenly felt horrible at the possibility that it rolled into the lava.

Wiping tears, I scowled at Ermek. "He's an immortal demon in Hell, and I have a feeling his head will grow back." I spat the words like venom through clenched teeth.

Ermek began to shake me. "You need to get a grip!"

"He should have let me die!"

"And for what, Jazz? He saved your life! He beheaded the Angel of Death to make sure you lived!"

"And for what?!" I was still shouting. "So he could leave me? He gives me immortality so he can leave me forever? I will never see him again, Ermek!

I don't want to live a thousand years or more without ever seeing his face again!" I was sobbing now.

Everything I said was true. Whether I wanted to admit it to myself or not, I was in love with Dagon, and, I could feel my heart slowly shatter every time he pulled away from me. It was a pain I didn't want to feel for the rest of my life. I couldn't understand why he wanted to leave me. Why did he insist I close the gates so he could be locked in this prison he calls home? What had I done to make him feel that way?

Ermek wrapped his arms tightly around me. I tried to pull away, but his strong grip held firm. I gave in and wept heavily into his tunic.

"What in the fuck was that all about?" I turned to see Dagon glaring at me.

Pulling myself away from Ermek, I returned his glare. "You know very well what that was about."

"First, you break my nose, and now you cut my head off. You know damned well I can't feel it, so what the fuck?"

"Let's just get on with it," I growled through clenched teeth.

Flipping his hair off his shoulder, Dagon marched ahead without arguing. I waited for him to make a decent gap between us before I followed.

DAGON

CHAPTER 37

I couldn't believe the nerve of that woman. Punching me was one thing, but cutting my head off was an entirely different story. It was humiliating.. that's what it was. I could only imagine all the gawking that was likely going on by the other demons, witnessing a Demon Lord losing his head in his own domain. It was bad enough that her stupid spell was still attached to me.

What was worse was how ungrateful she was after I saved her life. I could have easily let her die, and, if I did, I would have been free to move on with my life. I could have banged an infinite number of women, men, and anybody in between. I could have been having the time of my life, but instead, I saved her life, and, how does she thank me? She cuts off my fucking head.

A giant bone dragon flew overhead, grabbing my attention. We were leaving the Lustful Lagoon territory and heading toward the Fire Canyon. I watched the dragons drop souls into the fire below, and the souls' squeals of fear gave me a warm, fuzzy feeling.

We had to take the rock bridge across the canyon, and after about fifteen minutes of walking, we would hit the Prideful Freak Show. Beyond that was the demon city and the infamous Black Palace. The portal to Babylon was deep in the palace bowels.

The city itself was going to be trouble because it was where the Demon Lords dwelled. Hopefully, most of them decided to go to Earth and play around with the humans, but I knew a few would go home every once in a while to unwind. Even I went home from time to time, mostly when my senses were too overwhelmed. If we could get through the city, we could spend the night in my domicile. The humans could sleep comfortably on beds and regain their strength. They would need it because the most challenging part of our journey would be getting into the palace alive.

Stopping before the bridge, I fell to my knees, hands firmly pressed to the ground. I envisioned an apple tree and a water-filled stone fountain. My desires became a reality as a lush apple tree sprouted out of the dirt, and a small fountain materialized beside it.

"You two need food and water," I stated.

The humans dashed to the fountain, seeming to lose their manners completely, as they used dirty hands to scoop water and swallow as much as their bellies could contain.

Hindsight being tewnty-tewnty, I suppose I could have fashioned glasses for them to drink from, but it was too late. They each picked a couple of apples and devoured them greedily. I had to look away for fear of getting sick. Having been punched and decapitated, the last thing I needed to do was vomit.

"These aren't poison, are they?" Ermek's mouth was still full.

I rolled my eyes. "If I was going to kill you, I'd just push you off the canyon. I don't have to eat, so I easily forget that you do."

Jazzera took a bite, swallowed, and asked, "You can just grow random apple trees?"

"I told you.. I can make anything I want in Hell."

Ermek polished off three apples by the time we were ready to leave, and Jazzera only ate two. I wanted her to eat at least one more, but I figured her lack of appetite was due to her anger. I wished I could make her understand why I was doing this. I would explain, so she wouldn't hate me, but she had already beheaded me for saving her life. I could only imagine what she would do if she found out the truth.

I wished I could make her see that, over time, we could fix everything wrong with this world, and things could go back to how they were before the Rapture. Eventually, the Followers would fall, one way or another, and people would be free again. I smiled, thinking back to when the gates had first opened. Some of the people left behind treated the world's end like a giant party. There were drugs, endless sex sessions, and all the booze a person could want. Which worked fine for me since it took several bottles to get me to feel the slightest buzz. I fucked whoever I wanted and dined on steak and lobster. Everything was glorious until the food shortage and the power blackout. When the humans stopped having fun, the lesser demons came out to crash the party. Eventually, people returned to their churches, thinking if they prayed enough, God would pull them up to Heaven to be with their loved ones.

And naturally, the Church blamed women, homosexuals, and non-Christians for all their problems. They blamed technology and literature for their rejection into Heaven. Human nature got the best of them.. instead of looking inward, they wanted to blame their sins on something or someone else.

People were afraid, and the Church used that fear to control them. That was always what religion was about. It had little to do with being a good person and loving God and everything to do with power. So-called "holy men" would con people into building mega churches instead of feeding the poor. They would blame women for being too provocative instead of punishing the attacker. They would openly preach about killing people simply because they fell in love with someone of the same sex. Those supposed "God-fearing men" were as far from God as any human could get. But now was the time of the demons' reign, the churches would fall, and the people would rise up. Jazzera could be a part of that glory. The people would follow a Priestess, and Jazzera could guide them to the truth. All she had to do was follow my lead.

Coming out of my musings, I realized that we were nearing the Prideful Freakshow, possibly one of the most gruesome places Hell had ever invented. It housed some of the worst people in human history.. Adolf Hitler was a main attraction.

The demon who had come up with the idea for the Freakshow had gotten it from the late eighteen hundreds to the early nineteen hundreds. The setup was filled with brightly colored tents containing about three souls each. The crowd of demons adopted the visage of ordinary people. They had one job and one job only, to laugh and gawk at the tortured souls.

"So, this place is for the prideful?" inquired Ermek as he finally caught up with me.

Grinning, I looked around. "Oh yes."

"It doesn't look so terrifying."

I grinned wider. "You say that now Demon Slayer, but come with me, and I'll show you the gory truth of this sideshow."

We wandered into the growing crowd, and the humans marveled at the colorful facade. The first wonder was a claw machine borrowed from the twentieth century. Inside the main compartment were heads of the damned.. the claw plucked them from their bodies and dropped them as prizes for demon children. Then there was a cotton candy stand, but this candy was made from human hair, freshly pulled from a soul's bleeding scalp. Floating human body parts were tied to strings and attached to children's wrists as they ate bloody flesh. Intestines were turned into funnel cakes, eyeballs into ice cream, and deep-fried fingers were dipped in blood.

The gore was by far the main attraction but not the only draw. At the entrance to one of the tents stood three people on display. A large audience gathered around, pointing and laughing as the souls slashed at their skin, peeling it off in strips. They would carve and cut their skin until every last bit was gone. When the last piece was removed, it would grow back, and the cycle would start anew.

"What would cause this type of torture?" Jazzera appeared no longer angry with me as she clutched my arm tightly.

"These particular humans thought themselves superior due to the color of their skin. As punishment, they will spend eternity carving it off. They can't resist the urge. When a patch grows back, they have an insatiable need to be rid of it, no matter how much pain it causes them." I pointed to a group of demons laughing at the three damned souls. "These people are not actually people. They are demons replicating the appearance of those these souls hurt. The baby clutching his mother was used as alligator bait because of his skin tone. An innocent soul could not live a full life because that man thought the child was less than human, and, now, not only will the man be forced to carve himself up, but he will be mocked and treated as subhuman."

I looked over at Ermek, who trembled in horror and rage. Ermek was naive to his heritage.. the Followers had seen to that. Most of world history was lost, leaving humanity ignorant. All cultures vanished so that Follower culture would be the only one left, the only thing people could turn to. Jazzera's mother had to let go of her Japanese culture or be labeled a witch.

Nudging Jazzera, I pointed toward the skyline. "Not much longer, and we will reach the demon city. Only Demon Lords live there.. we don't like to look at lesser demons more than we have to, so they aren't permitted access. There is no torture within the city's boundaries.., and, in the epicenter is the Lake of Fire, where the Black Palace resides."

"What's the Black Palace?" Her tone was rigid with anxiety.

"Lucifer's domain. Many Demon Lords spend their time there as members of the court. But it is Lucifer's home. The portals to the human world are in the lower levels of the Palace."

Jazzera

Chapter 38

The crowd thinned out, and I could clearly see the demon city. It wasn't what I expected, not that I was sure what to expect to begin with. I may have guessed a sprawling community of dark mansions that appeared haunted from the outside or a city like the one we had to pass through to get into Hell. Both guesses would be wrong.. the city sat along a bowl-shaped crater, its infrastructure circling the rim and spiraling down to the bottom. The buildings looked like temples instead of homes, as if they were shrines to a personal god. A drop-off was at the bottom of the crater.. I couldn't tell how far it fell. If I strained my eyes, I could almost make out the steeples of the Black Palace resting in the city center. The closer we got, the warmer it became.

The ground had gone from red clay to pitch black with cracks that gave off a soft orange glow as if fire flowed beneath the surface. Dagon was alert as he led us past the first row of buildings. A statue stood in front of each temple domicile. Each sculpture was different.. some were poised in a fighting stance, while others stood with prideful dignity, and a few looked like they were contemplating the meaning of life.

Whenever we heard a noise, Dagon practically shoved us against a wall and told us to get down. I barely stopped a surprised squeal when I spotted a group of demons. I was frightened but also really confused. They looked more like shadow dwellers rather than Demon Lords. Their humanoid-shaped bodies were nothing more than shadows, a dark void with glowing red eyes.

"I thought you said only Demon Lords live here."

Dagon hushed me and tugged my arm, motioning us to go around the temple instead of heading toward the cluster of demons. Cautiously, we made our way through the city until we were nearly at the edge of the drop-off. In front of a temple stood another statue, a perfect replica of Dagon. His hair was carved to look as if it were blowing in the wind, and he was shirtless, wearing a pair of baggy pants with a sash around his waist, the extra material hanging between his legs. He stood in a dignified stance and held his trident proudly. At the base of the statue, etched into the stone, were strange symbols.. they somehow looked different from the other monuments' hieroglyphic texts. These symbols were closer to the ones that made up my angelic mark.

"It says Dagon."

The real Dagon waved us toward the temple behind his sculpture. The building was closed off by a tall, black stone wall. Eight large pillars, with swaths of awning fabric stretched between them, lined the ebony stone pathway that led to the front door. The door was strange, made of woven metal..

it looked like spider webs but not quite. It took a moment to notice, but the metal was in the shape of venomous snakes coiled together, their open mouths displaying long fangs. When Dagon approached them, they opened automatically, slithering apart to allow entry.

The temple's interior looked a lot larger than the exterior made it seem. The ground looked like marble with an unusual color pattern, primarily black, with bright red and orange streaks splashed about. Large torches flared to life as we passed, illuminating the room just enough for us to see clearly. The furniture was odd. In the right corner sat a long, black table with a red top. Several multicolored balls were arranged in a triangle on the table's surface. Two long sticks rested in racks along the wall. Another black table, smaller than the other, had a stack of playing cards resting neatly on top.

Beyond two grand staircases sat a comfortable-looking couch and side table facing a mounted black glass box. Other objects were scattered around the room, things I could barely describe because they were so foreign, like the table device that stood on four legs making obnoxious noises and sporadically blinking with lights.

Dagon smiled proudly. "Impressed?"

"It is lovely. Though odd."

Dagon pointed to two of the gadgets I was confused about. "Those are pinball machines. The greatest thing about being a Demon Lord is making anything I desire." He then pointed to the square on the wall. "I can even play video games."

Not having the faintest idea of what he was talking about, I changed the subject. "Speaking of Demon Lords, I thought you said lesser demons couldn't enter the city. On our way in, I spotted a group of shadow dwellers."

He shook his head. "Those weren't shadow dwellers. Shadow dwellers are skeletons with black cloaks that are slightly transparent. Those figures you saw outside were Demon Lords in their true form. They are pure energy with a somewhat human shape. Because they are in Hell, they radiate dark energy, making them appear black."

"So, is that your true form?" inquired Ermek as he rolled one of the balls on the long table.

Dagon joined him and rolled the white ball toward the black ball, clacking them together.

"I already told you how this works. Demon Lords take on the appearance humans conjure up in their minds. Then they choose a form they like best. Demons like me who were born on Earth are stuck in one human form, and, our race depends on where we are born. I was born in Europe, so I look European. Had I been born in Japan, I would look more like Jazzera.. had I been born in Africa, I would look more like you. Get it? In early times, humans didn't mix too often. So, my parents took on the look of Europeans while they were visiting Europe, but before the Rapture, people of all races lived all over the world, so now the demons take on the appearance of any form they like best. My mother always adored Ancient Egypt, so she tends to stay in that form."

"Then why are they appearing as shadows now?" I asked, taking a seat at the card table.

Dagon pulled up a seat and motioned for Ermek to join us. "Because they are in Hell, and every demon knows what they are. So why not be themselves?"

"What is our next move?" I could see the relief in Ermek's eyes as he finally got off his feet.

"I figured we would stay here for a bit. Let you two bathe, eat, then get some rest before we take on Legion. We must devise a plan to get you two into the palace without being noticed." Dagon stood and walked toward the stairs. "It will take me a few minutes to set up your quarters and bathrooms. I'll be right back."

I wanted to follow him out of curiosity, but my feet weren't allowing it. I didn't realize how tired and sore I was until I sat down. I was not opposed to getting some rest and cleaning up.

Eating food also sounded nice. Those apples Dagon had given us earlier were the sweetest I had ever tasted, and, had I not been so on edge, I would have devoured a few more.

About ten minutes later, Dagon descended the stairs and leaned against the banister. "I ran you two a hot bath. If you each go up one staircase, a bathroom will be directly in front of you, and your rooms will be next to them. Let me know if you want to eat."

Hesitantly, I got to my feet and winced as I put weight on them. Limping for a bit, I finally got my legs to work and forced myself up the stairs. Ermek was suffering, too, he wasn't as slow as I was, but it was evident that he was uncomfortable.

I was impressed with the lovely bathroom, especially since it was thrown together last minute. There were two counters along the walls with candelabras dimly illuminating the room. In the center was a black clawfoot tub filled with steaming hot water. Resting on a table near the tub was a soft-looking red towel and a change of clothes.

Before undressing, I picked up the clothing Dagon had set out for me. One of the garments looked like a short nightgown made of red lace. The other outfit was strange.. the pants were soft, but the lavender top was woven from a material I had never felt before. It also had armor-like plating built into it—no doubt for my battle against Legion. The shiny purple plates encased the arms, torso, and back. I couldn't place what they were made of, but they felt just as strong as metal. I fidgeted with the garment, and the plates shifted easily, allowing the wearer to have flexibility and range of movement.

Setting it down with a heavy sigh, I tried to come to grips with everything. I still couldn't believe Dagon was making me go through with this, and, I couldn't really figure out why. Did he truly believe that banishing all the demons would suddenly change anything? We would have a better chance of fighting the Followers' mindset together rather than apart. I may not be able to age, but I could still be killed. Even if I did close the gates, what would stop the Followers from burning me at the stake?

I pulled my dirty robes from my body and heard the door creak. Dagon slipped inside, and part of me wanted to cover up, while the other part realized there was no point. He had already seen every inch of me, and there was no point in modesty anymore.

"I thought you said there was no point in fornicating in Hell," I flatly commented as I dipped my toes into the hot water.

"Look who's always got sex on the mind. One good dick down, and you're hooked." He cracked a smile and closed the door behind him.

I rolled my eyes. "Then what do you want?"

"I figured I'd wash your back for you."

294

I slid into the tub and couldn't help but let out a loud groan of relief. This was the most wonderful thing I had experienced in quite some time. As I settled in, Dagon sat on the tub's edge, manifesting a small, red sponge in his hand. He dipped it in the water, lathered it up, and rubbed my body down. The sensations dragged a deep breath from my lungs.

"Before you created these rooms, what was up here?"

Squeezing the sponge, he let the water drip over my shoulders. "My collections. A library and random stuff from the ages." He chuckled. "I had an iron maiden, and that was one of the more interesting torture devices humans had ever come up with."

"You didn't have a bedroom?"

He shook his head and ran the sponge down my chest, caressing each breast tenderly. "There is no point.. I don't sleep while I'm down here, sex is pointless, and Hell is extraordinarily boring."

I groaned softly as his arm reached lower into the water, gently using the cloth to massage my mound and lower lips. "You didn't have anything to entertain you?"

He sighed as his fingers caressed my folds, causing me to moan and close my eyes in pleasure.

"Now you understand why we torture people so much. You can only play pinball and pool so many times before it becomes redundant."

Releasing the cloth, he slid two fingers inside me, using his thumb to caress my clit. The water sloshed around as he moved faster and faster. My body tensed, poised on the edge of release. I reached up and caressed his face.

"You should join me," I gasped with a smile.

Instead of responding, he pressed hard on my clit, moving his thumb in a quick, circular movement. Heat flowed through my belly, making my walls pulsate around his fingers. A tremendous calm fell over my body as I came down from the high.

Dagon got to his feet, flipping hair out of his face. "Again, I can't feel it, but since you may die later, I felt it would be rude not to make you cum one last time." He abruptly left the room, leaving me in a bath that was quickly cooling.

DAGON

CHAPTER 39

I considered going to Ermek next but thought better of it. The Demon Slayer's honor was too great.. he wouldn't allow me to do anything with him after finding out how the Priestess felt about me. In a perfect world, I could have both of them, but this was far from a perfect world, and it was more likely that I would end up with neither.

I headed downstairs and laid down on my couch. When I finally got comfortable, one of the doors upstairs opened. Craning my head, I saw Ermek, long braids dangling over the banister, giving me a slight wave.

I nodded in acknowledgment.. as much as I hated to admit it, I had become rather fond of the Demon Slayer. I hoped he would survive the fight to come. He was a force to be reckoned with, that was to be sure, but the real question was, would he be strong enough against Legion? I hoped he was. In truth, I hoped he would stay out of it the best he could. I wanted to be the only one to face Legion head-on.

Sitting up, I manifested a recurve bow and a quiver packed to compacity with arrows. I needed to try and keep Ermek as far from the fighting as possible. It was a shame Jazzera wasn't trained with a bow because I would do the same for her. Her only saving grace was her ability to channel her angelic energy into her sword. If Legion did attack, cutting their head off would be the most effective thing she could do, buying us some time before they respawned.

Thinking back to my little mishap, I chuckled quietly to myself. I had to give Jazzera some credit. Nobody had ever gotten close enough to take my head, and I had often wondered what it was like. Come to find out, it's pure blackness, almost as if I were floating in the void of space. After a period, it felt like I was sliding down to the ground on a slide. The feeling then morphed into a free fall, and I slammed hard into the ground. I was surprised I didn't leave a crater.

I waited downstairs for hours as the humans slept.. with no clock, it felt like ages. The worst part was how pathetically bored I was. I tried pinball at first, then shot some pool. Eventually, I went to the video games. Everything in my home was a replica of things I wished I could have experienced while on Earth. Every time celestials stepped foot on Earth, the humans became primitive, losing their ability to play games or make funny dog videos.

At times like this, I envied the fallen for being able to experience everything the world had ever gone through. I got to see the change but never got a chance to feel it. I never got to ride a rollercoaster, play a real pinball game, drive a fast car, or play an online shooter game and make fun of little twelve-year-olds, telling them that I was going to fuck their moms. I had existed for thousands of years but only ever got to experience the dull stuff.

"At least I had plenty of sex," I muttered to myself. I walked to the center of the room, manifested a table, and conjured food for the humans. Everything I set out was of the vegan variety. It didn't dawn on me until that moment that I couldn't create animals. Not even animal meat or byproducts, since butter didn't want to form for me. So, I supposed I actually couldn't make everything my heart desired. Still, the spread was impressive. I had two salad bowls, mixed fruit, warm loaves of bread, and some strawberry jam to spread on top.

It was a good fifteen minutes until I heard the first door creek open and footsteps plodded to the bathroom. After a few moments, I saw Jazzera walking down the stairs. I had hoped to see her in the cute little nighty I created for her, but instead, she was outfitted in purple armor. "Well, good morning, sunshine."

"Is it morning?" she grumbled, rubbing her eyes.

"I have no idea," I replied with a shrug. "We don't really tell the time in Hell."

"What did you make?" she asked, taking a seat at the new table.

I conjured two glasses of fruit juice. Picking one of them up, I handed it to her. "I hope you like mixed berry."

She smiled pleasantly as she took it from me, sniffing it curiously before taking a sip.

After a few more swallows, she set it down and looked at the spread. "I'm almost surprised you didn't make bacon."

I roughly ran my hand through my hair. "Yeah, I just now realized I can't make animals.
So apparently, I can't make everything I want."

Shrugging, she picked up one of the plates and made herself a salad. "This is perfect.. it looks much fresher than anything I have eaten in a long time."

Ermek finally made an appearance. His clothing was fashioned like his old Demon Slayer armor.. the only difference was the color. I wasn't sure how he felt, but I no longer wished to see him garbed in the Followers' uniform. So instead of green, I made his armor orange, which went perfectly against his dark skin tone.

I sat silently while the humans ate, not wanting to ruin their appetite. As they slowed down, I decided now was a good time to share my plan. "We must follow the crater's edge until we find the path that leads down to the Lake of Fire. Once there, I can create a boat to take us to the side of the palace. It's better than crossing the bridge where everyone can see us. We'll have to figure out how to get into one of the windows."

"There isn't a side door?" inquired Ermek as he took a bite of his bread.

I shook my head. "Why would there be? It's not like Lucifer is in any danger and would need a quick way out. There isn't a single demon in Hell that can harm him, not even Legion. When God made him the King of Hell, that was that. No powers can be used against him."

"And what happens if Lucifer does catch us?"

"I have no idea. He could end us all or let us go. Or he could stick me in a wall and let you go. I honestly don't know."

"What do you mean stick you in a wall?" exclaimed Jazzera.

"He's done it before. Azazel pissed him off at one point, and he spent three thousand years as décor." I chuckled at the thought of the fellow Demon Lord stuck in the wall like Han Solo. "Lucifer made him able to feel pain, so every so often, I'd punch him in the face to ensure he was still with us. Good times."

Ermek blinked. "It's no wonder the Angel of Death wasn't so fond of you if that's how you treat your comrades."

I shrugged. "Yeah, people get annoyed with me pretty quick, but hey, I'm fun."

He rolled his eyes. "Yes, you're a true treat."

"You know, I would remind you that you seemed to really enjoy my dick up your ass, but there is a lady present."

Jazzera nearly spit out her drink. "Oookay. So, we climb through a window or, more than likely, just walk right through the front door."

I nodded. "It's really the only thing we can do.. let's hope no Demon Lords are hanging out in the front."

After their food had settled, we were off to the bridge. No Demon Lords were in sight, but I was still cautious. I couldn't feel pain, but the humans could, and, if the other Lords found out why they were here, they may ignore that little rule Lucifer made about not harming the living. Ermek had his bow out and ready, it was pointless, but I liked his enthusiasm.

The lake's lava had risen to be flush with the path, and I hoped the heat of it wouldn't affect the humans too much. At the lake's shore, I placed my hand into the fire and pictured a small, efficient boat that would fit all three of us. A small Viking-style vessel emerged from the flames, bobbing with the lava's waves. I pulled the boat onto the land and waited for the humans to climb in. I waded the boat into the molten rock until I was knee-deep and climbed inside.

"What would happen if we fell in?" Ermek was fidgeting nervously with his quiver.

My tone turned playfully. "I don't know. You won't die because Hell can't kill you, and, I gave you those necklaces, so you should be protected." I tapped on my chin. "I really don't know. How about you jump in, and we find out?" He scowled at me, and I grinned in response. "Stop being such a sissy. It's just a little lava."

Conjuring an oar, I did my best to paddle through the not-so-liquid rock. It was a good thing I didn't get tired. They made this look much easier in cartoons. I felt like I would never make it to the palace. We may have had an easier time just walking down the damned bridge. I'd much rather fight a horde of demons than force my way through this muck any longer.

After what seemed like ages, we reached the other shore. I silently cussed the moment my feet hit the solid ground. I should have just taken the bridge. I only chose this option because I didn't want a group of Demon Lords to see us coming.

"Wait here," I ordered as I jumped out of the boat and pulled it to the shore.

I kicked the molten rock from my feet and walked around the giant structure toward the front gate. My body froze, coming face to face with none other than Beelzebub. One of the three demons I didn't want to run into. This slithery snake had his nose far up Lucifer's ass, and he would turn me in without a second thought.

"I'm surprised to see you here, Lord Dagon," he smugly remarked, smiling with thin lips.

The foul creature always chose the creepiest forms humans gave him for whatever reason. He paraded around as a frail, old man with long, thin hair, hollow cheeks, and a hunched back. His power was similar to mine, although he had limits. He could only turn into nightmares, taking on the forms given to him by frightened dreamers. I could turn into anything, including the same nightmare he chose to take the form of.

"I needed a bit of R and R," I replied, rolling my eyes.

He tilted his head, grin still firmly in place. "You really think me a fool?"

I crossed my arms. "I've always thought you were a fool."

His neck swiveled from side to side as if he were looking for something. "You will fail in your quest."

My eyes narrowed. "Why don't you kindly fuck off and leave me to my business?"

His head snapped back in my direction. "I can't let you go through with this.. it will throw off the balance of the world."

I bit my lower lip. What did he think I was up to? My plan wouldn't throw off any balance.. in fact, my plan would eventually help balance the human world out. "Again, I ask you to kindly fuck off."

The little creep took a step toward me. "I will kill her before she reaches the gate, and, I will kill any other you try to bring through. The balance must be kept. You failed before, and you will fail again."

Scowling, I manifested my trident. "Back off, Beelzebub. I'm not in the mood for your bullshit."

The old demon laughed, starting to transform and shift into a hideous beast. He stood as tall as the palace itself, resembling a massive centipede made entirely of bones. His head, or heads rather, were the only things that looked out of place. They appeared as three large human skulls with burning red eyes. He wrapped his lower body around me, picked me up, and threw me far out into the Lake of Fire.

JAZZERA

CHAPTER 40

I screamed as Dagon's body was flung to the other side of the lake. Climbing out of the boat, I raced along the shoreline, hoping to see a glimpse of him, but a rumble behind me caused me to stop and turn, staring up in paralyzing fear.

"Jazzera, get out of the way!" shouted Ermek.

I tried, but my feet were frozen. The bone creature squealed a devilish shriek and whipped its bony tail toward me. I lifted my sword above my head, eyes squeezed shut, and braced for impact. Ermek tackled me to the side, and we barely evaded being battered by the gigantic tail.

The beast readied for another attack. Ermek drew back an arrow and let it loose, but another demon knocked away the clean shot. It was an immense dragon-like beast with dark purple skin and sprawling black wings. The creature had three heads, each with a massive jaw.

They clamped down on the bone demon's tail, snapping it like a twig. The bone demon lunged forward, clenching its teeth down on one of the dragon's necks. It pulled back until it severed the head from its body with an awful tearing sound. The dragon snarled and backed off until three more heads burst from the stub's torn flesh.

"A hydra!" cried Ermek.

I had heard of hydra creatures before, but I always assumed they were nothing more than fairy tales, a story of an almost unkillable beast. For every head cut off, another three would grow in its place. Another head was gnawed off.. moments later, three more grew from the stub. All seven heads attacked the bone demon at once.

"Stay behind me!" it shouted. The hydra was Dagon!

Pulling my sword, I tried to find a good place to attack the bone beast, but nothing presented itself. How would I ever be able to damage such a creature in its own domain?

"She will die. They will all die!" roared the monster. "You are bound to her, and you will perish with her!"

The creature wrapped its bony limbs around Dagon's body, puncturing his skin. Black blood oozed from his wounds. The creature didn't want Dagon. It didn't even seem to care about Ermek. It wanted me. It must know why I am here, and, what did the beast mean? We were bound together, and we would die together. Did demons perish if their Priestess did? No, of course not. My death only meant Dagon's freedom. Another head was ripped from Dagon's body, the lifeless appendage falling only feet from me. Its dead eyes stared out into the distance, and I couldn't take it anymore. I couldn't watch Dagon be tortured because of me. Without the bond, Dagon would not be compelled to protect me.

The demon may stop focusing on him and turn its attention to me.

Grabbing my hair, I put my sword to it and whispered, "Indissolubili vinculo frangitur." *The unbreakable bond is now broken.* I sliced through my hair, letting the strands fall to the ground. The fight paused for a moment, and one of Dagon's heads looked back at me.

"What did you do, you idiot? I can't even feel any of this!" he shouted. "Now I can't sense you!"

Ermek grabbed my arm, and we both dashed for cover. The bone demon fought to escape, trying to follow me, but Dagon seemed too strong. The beast ripped off another head and used that opening to lunge for Ermek and me. I readied my sword, but it was unnecessary. The monster was only feet from me when it curled up in agony, shrieking so loudly that I had to cover my ears. Dagon was also screeching as if tortured by some invisible force.

I backed up and stiffened when I hit something solid behind me. I turned around and saw the most beautiful man I had ever seen. He had short, black, wavy hair with bangs that fell just above large, dark-brown eyes. His skin was a light brown, and stubble shadowed a strong, square jawline and full lips.

"Welcome Jazzera Fukumoto and Ermek Johnson. To what do I owe the pleasure of your visit?"

"What are you doing to them?" I stammered, tearing my eyes from the beautiful man and back to Dagon and the other demon. Both had changed forms again.. Dagon was back in his human form, and the bone monster was a shadow, squealing in pain.

"What fun is fighting with no pain?" theorized the man calmly.

"This isn't just pain. They look like they're being tortured," voiced Ermek.

The man smiled. "You are such a kind soul. First, you show compassion to the souls of the damned, and now to a couple of misbehaving Demon Lords."

"Who are you?"

Dagon's suffering and cries of agony were almost too much for me to handle.

"I have several names. One of them is The Morning Star, but most of you humans know me as Lucifer." He bowed slightly, and his handsome smile grew larger.

I held my breath. I was standing in front of the devil himself. Every fiber in my body begged me to run, but my brain knew I had nowhere to go, and, no matter how badly I wanted to flee, I couldn't leave Dagon behind like this.

"Please. Make it stop. Stop hurting him."

Lucifer chuckled, the smile never leaving his face. "Young love is so precious. Dagon will survive. It's been centuries since he has felt pain like this. Let's allow him to soak it all in. After all, you came here to close the Gates of Hell. This pain may be the last thing he feels for centuries to come."

"You know why we came here?" Ermek's voice shook as if terrified.

"I know more than you think, mortal. Let us go inside, and perhaps we can have a discussion."

I begged, "Let him go, please."

Lucifer took my hand and began pulling me through the palace door. "If those two imbeciles wish to act like children, they will be treated as such."

When we stepped through the threshold, the doors closed tightly behind us, and I could no longer hear the shrieks of either Dagon or the other demon. The palace's interior was nothing like I pictured in my mind. It wasn't dark like Dagon's home.. it was brightly lit with white marble floors and stonework shaped into elegant pillars and spirals. Flowers of all colors were placed tastefully in vases around the room. A grand, white throne with dark blue cushions stood at the end of the long room. Letting go of my hand, Lucifer walked up to the throne and sat down, legs crossed.

"I'm amused to think Dagon thought this little plan would work, that he genuinely believed he could make it through Hell without being detected."

"What are you going to do with us?"

Tapping his finger on his lips, he looked in deep thought. "You have nothing to fear from me, Jazzera, I assure you. Nor does your friend here." He paused, then looked over to Ermek. "And as long as you keep that compassion in your heart, you will find no place for you in Hell."

As if a weight had suddenly been lifted from Ermek's shoulders, he stood taller and prouder than I had ever seen him before.

"Then, if I may, what do you want from us?"

Lucifer's eyes darted back to me. "I want you both to realize the consequences of your future actions, no matter what you decide. Remember, my demons were promised seven hundred years to walk among the living. So far, it has only been two. Neither of you humans could fathom the amount of loyalty each of my demons has shown toward their duties. They gave up Paradise to keep the wicked in chains, and most did it out of love."

That last sentence caught my attention. All Dagon had done in Hell was help torment the souls of the damned. How was any of this done out of love?

Lucifer smiled. "Pardon my intrusion into your thoughts, my Lady. Nearly every Demon Lord once loved a human or loved their parent so much they decided to go to Hell rather than leave them. Baal, a beloved god, chose to go to Hell rather than be torn from his father, Dagon, who was also loved on Earth. Adam betrayed Lilith, and even I lost the woman I loved to the violence of mankind. Each sacrificed Paradise because they knew the wicked should never be allowed through the Gates of Heaven."

I reflected on his words.. I had never looked at it from that perspective before. Peeking over at Ermek, I searched for a cue on some way to respond. When he gave me nothing, Lucifer's eyes softened. "My demons aren't without their flaws. They caused quite a stir on Earth when they were allowed to walk the lands in physical form. Dagon is mentioned in the Bible a couple of times. Like many others, he was worshiped as a god by primitive man. He went by many names worldwide, Loki, Prometheus, Mercury, and of course, by his proper name. Wars were fought in his name, and sacrifices were offered to him. God stopped the angels and demons from taking physical form to allow humankind to grow independently, without divine interaction. If you were to leave the gates open, would the chaos continue? Or would my demons work on correcting their mistakes? In the end, Jazzera and Ermek, the choice is up to you. I will let you continue your quest and allow Dagon to accompany you."

Lucifer didn't move from his spot as the large doors opened independently. Dagon and the other demon walked down the center of the room until they reached the throne and kneeled before their king.

"So please, Lord Dagon, tell me why I shouldn't banish you to the bottom of the lake for millennia? Why I shouldn't let the fires burn your body while the weight of the molten rock crushes you?"

Dagon got to his feet. "Well, for one, he started it." He sneered at the other demon. Beelzebub's red eyes glared back. "Secondly, I am waaay too pretty to have my skin melt off." He cracked a grin, and Lucifer didn't seem pleased. "I suppose aside from that, I have no excuse."

Lucifer clasped his hands together. "Luckily for you, I wish to see how this chain of events plays out, and I will allow you to join the humans on their quest."

JAZZERA

CHAPTER 41

With a blast of blinding white light, swirls of color wrapped around me like paint mixed by an artist. The colors spun faster and faster until I nearly lost my balance, leaving me dizzy as the spinning finally stopped. A chill worked down my body as a cool breeze swept the ground, picking up grains of sand that scraped softly across my feet. It was nighttime, and the stars shined brightly. Ancient ruins loomed in the distance, standing testimony to the passage of time.

Large pillars made of sandstone, cracked and beaten by countless wind storms, created a perfect circle around the dais on which I sat. Between the two tallest pillars stood a translucent door that radiated an orange glow and intense heat. In front of the door stood a waist-high post with an odd-looking circular recess and ancient symbols gouged into the stonework—the Gate of Babylon.

With my sword at the ready, I waited for an attack, Ermek at my side. The gate's aura was heavy and impeded any demonic signatures.

Dagon placed his hand on my blade and pushed it down. "That won't be necessary." His voice was calm, almost detached.

It was curious.. he said several times that we would face one of the nastiest Demon Lords of Hell. How would my sword not be necessary?

"Dagon, what's going on?"

His face remained blank. "They should be here any moment."

"I thought you said they would be waiting for us." Ermek crept closer to me.

"I said a lot of things."

Anxiety raced through my blood. "Dagon?"

He stood silently, arms crossed casually in front of him.

I stepped toward him but froze when two figures materialized. One was a demon I knew all too well. I wasn't expecting Lilith.. her appearance here confused me almost as much as Dagon's lack of emotion. She wore a black leather catsuit and her signature golden makeup, which shimmered in the portal's light.

The other demon, the infamous Legion, was in the form of a pale man with glowing green eyes that focused intensely on me. Their hair was styled in a tight ponytail that fell just above their calves. They wore a flowy, white jacket-like garment tied at the waist with a rope belt and loose-fitting pants that looked almost like a skirt.

I stepped into a fighting stance, glaring at Lilith. "You may have bested me last time, but now you are outnumbered."

She snorted. "Are we, though?"

"Put the sword down, Jazzera. You're the one outnumbered." Dagon spoke in a flat, emotionless

313

tone. My eyes widened in disbelief as Dagon walked to the other demons.

Lilith cackled. "She doesn't know? I thought you two were lovers?" She smirked, looking over at her son.

Dagon's eyes wouldn't meet mine. "She would have never gone along with it if I had.. the result would have been the same as with Jade."

Ermek loosed an arrow toward Dagon, but he swiftly knocked it from the sky as if it were barely moving. "You betrayed us? Are you turning us in to them?"

"I'm not turning anyone in, Ermek. Nobody has to die here. Not you, not her, not me. I just needed Jazzera here."

I feared the answer, but I had to know. "Dagon, what is going on?"

He took a few steps toward me, arm outstretched beseechingly. "I'm not going to close the gates, Jazzera. I never was. I need you to destroy the key. As long as it exists, some stupid mortal or angel will try to seal the gates again. Seven hundred years isn't enough. Lucifer would have tossed me into the Lake of Fire for longer than that."

He lied to me. It was all a lie, a trick. I should have known. I had been warned my entire life that demons do nothing but lie, trick, and destroy everything around them.

"You lied to me," I whispered.

Dagon shook his head as he walked closer. Warmth radiated from his body. "You said that you didn't want to close the gates and wanted to be with me. Well, this is how you be with me."

My heart ached with every word. Was any of it real? The gentle touches? The kind remarks? The intense way we made love?

"But God allowed you seven hundred years, not an eternity! This wasn't God's plan!"

Dagon scowled, and the other two demons scoffed. "Destroy the key, and let's find out. If God is so against it, he will smite me where I stand."

He placed his finger gently under my chin, and I violently pulled away. I didn't know what to believe. This entire time he was using me. After everything we had been through, I was nothing more than a means to an end—a pawn to be sacrificed for his gain.

"We could be gods, Jazzera. The real God can't come to Earth. It would be destroyed, overwhelmed by his power, but we can right the wrongs that have been done to this world. God thought that removing us would make things better, but it hasn't. It made them worse. Together, you and I can help change everything."

"How can I trust you?" The words slipped from my lips. I wanted to hurt him and tear his body apart, but no matter how badly I wanted it, I couldn't attack.

Lilith interrupted, "Enough games, Dagon. Make her destroy the key, or I will make her destroy the key."

"Your mother is right. We will find another Nephilim to destroy the key if you cannot deliver. We have little use for you." Legion manifested a golden whip at their fingertips.

For a second, I stared at the long-haired demon. They sounded like several voices at once, and it was utterly terrifying.

"Why do you need me? I freed you. Why break my heart like this?" Tears fell from my eyes, and I loathed each droplet as they dripped down. I didn't want Dagon to see just how badly he hurt me. "Why don't you break the key?"

Dagon ran his finger along my cheek, wiping the tears away. I wanted to pull back, but I stayed still and let him touch me. "No angel or demon can break the key. Or it would have been broken eons ago.. only a celestial with human blood can break the key."

"Enough of your babbling!" Legion lashed their whip toward me. I raised my hands in defense, but the golden strand wrapped around my arm. Ermek shot at them, and the demon moved swiftly to the side with inhuman speed, the arrow flying past their head. I tried to pull away, but they yanked the whip, sending me tumbling to the ground. I lost my sword in the process.

"Let her go, Legion!" Dagon demanded, manifesting his trident. He went to lunge at the demon, but Lilith slammed into his body, tossing him across the ground like he were nothing more than a rag doll.

"Dagon, stop being such a drama queen. When this is over, you can get yourself a new toy." Lilith manifested her sword.

I tried to work my wrist free from the whip while the white-haired demon pulled me toward them. The more I fought, the harder Legion tugged. A cackle of voices cut through the air as I thrashed about, trying desperately to get my feet underneath me where they belonged. Ermek ran at the demon but was blocked by Lilith. She swung her sword toward him, and he quickly raised his bow to stop the deadly blade from hitting its mark.

At Legion's feet, they yanked me upward, pulling me against their body, which pulsated heat. I cringed at their closeness and fought, but their grasp stayed firm no matter what I did.

The demon manifested an object in their hand. "Use your power to destroy the key!"

I looked at the key, a circle with three notches cut into it. In the center, three square cubes jutted out from the surface.. it was the perfect fit for the circular hole gouged into the small pillar.

A trident impaled the demon directly in the head, forcing them to let me go. They fell back, loosening the whip from my arm. Dagon pulled the trident from the demon's head and thrust the prongs deep into its back.

Ermek was busy dodging Lilith's blows, but he couldn't outmaneuver her forever. I retrieved my fallen sword, ran at her from behind, and sliced her in half with the angelic-powered blade. She stilled, in shock, holding her sword in the air just over Ermek's head. Her upper half slid off and hit the ground with a sickening thud. Screams of rage or agony, I couldn't tell which, rent the air. Shortly after falling, she began crawling toward her lower half.

"Get the key!' roared Dagon.

Snapping my attention back to Dagon and Legion, I realized that Legion now had the upper hand. They had managed to pull free of Dagon's trident and wrap their whip tightly around Dagon's neck. Frantic, I raced over to where the key had been recklessly dropped. A sudden warmth seeped into my hand when I picked it up.

"Close the gates!" cried Dagon, still trying desperately to free himself. Ermek shot an arrow, striking Legion in the side, but the demon barely flinched. They kept their focus on Dagon.

Taking a steadying breath, I ran to the small pillar, fiddling with the key until it finally fit in the hole. The keyhole's dial was turned all the way to the right. If I turned it left, it would close the gates, and all of this would be over. My hand shook as I slowly moved the key. When I heard the first click, I paused and looked at Dagon.

"Close the gate now! It's the only way to stop them!"

I stared in horror as flakes of skin began drifting from Dagon's body into Legion's.. they swirled around like sand in the wind before being absorbed. Legion was trying to consume him. I put my hand back on the key. Dagon would be safe in Hell. Lucifer wouldn't allow him to be killed, would he? But if I closed the gates, I would never see him again, but Dagon betrayed me.

Closing my eyes, I shook my head. No. Dagon betrayed the demons. With a cry, I focused on my mark and used every ounce of strength to fuel its power. The energy surged through my body and rushed into the key, which began to glow a bright blue. The key cracked, bursting into glowing dust that fluttered through the air.

Everything went silent. I turned to the group.. Legion and Dagon were frozen in place, and even Lilith stopped trying to fuse her body together.

"What have you done?" asked Ermek.

A tear slid down my face. "I can't lose him."

JAZZERA

CHAPTER 42

The prolonged stillness was fraught with tension, as if every being in the group was waiting for something to happen. Perhaps we were waiting for God to bring his hand down and crush us all for what I had done. When no cosmic consequence happened, Legion released Dagon, pushing him away violently. Dagon staggered for a second, walked over to his mother, and helped her piece herself together. All three demons stared at me.

Legion nodded to me before vanishing. Lilith glared at me and gave me a once-over as if she were appraising me. Eventually, she smiled. "Good girl." She, too, vanished as Legion had.

Dagon was now the only demon left, and I wished he would say something, but this was complicated. I couldn't believe I had gone through with it. There was no going back after this. I wasn't the girl who had closed the Gates of Hell and saved humanity. I was now the selfish girl who kept the gates open because she fell in love with a demon.

"I'm sorry," he finally muttered.

"Why didn't you just tell me the truth?"

He sighed heavily and kicked at the dirt. "I was afraid you would be like the last one." I waited. "There was a Priestess...A Nephilim. Before the Rapture, Nephilim could see angels and demons. The marks formed only a month before the end of everything, and, I was being my typical, selfish self." He gestured to the small pillar. "When the gates opened, if you placed the key in the keyhole, the notches could be aligned in a specific way. If the middle notch was up top, the gates would be open until the timer ran out, seven hundred years, for example, but if you turned the key to the right, the gates would stay open. If the key was destroyed, then the gate could never close." He turned to me. "I tried to manipulate Jade, but along the way, I gained feelings for her. I told her what she needed to do. That when the gates opened, I would be in physical form, and we could be together."

He ran his hand gently through my hair. "But my baby mama decided to intervene. She hates me because my eldest son stayed with me in Hell when the gates closed, and, she wanted to punish both of us. She wanted Jade to close the gates the moment they opened. 'To save humanity.'" I could tell he was rolling his eyes. "I guess Jade couldn't decide who to believe. So she didn't close the gates or keep them open. Instead, she left them be and hid the key with another Nephilim. In a rage, my ex-lover murdered her. The only time I got to feel her was when she died in my arms, just as the gates opened." He stared into space for a moment. "With her dying breath, she told me I would get my seven hundred years as promised." He caressed the side of my face. "You are a good person, Jazzera. So was she. I was worried that you would make the same decision she did if I told you, and I thought that if I kept it from you, maybe I could force your hand,, and that maybe, over time, you would forgive me."

I was overwhelmed with emotion. I loved Dagon.. I had nothing to compare it to, but I knew it was real. These feelings I had for him greatly outweighed the feelings I once felt for Ermek.

"Was anything you told us the truth?"

He smiled. "Yes. The Followers are still full of shit. God doesn't care who you fuck, and you're allowed to eat pork, but I am telling you this now... I love you, Jazzera. More than I have loved any being. Had Jade been in your place, I would have sacrificed her to get what I wanted, but I wasn't willing to sacrifice you."

Every part of my body wanted to wrap itself around him, but I held back. He may have tricked me into coming here under false pretenses, but he fought Legion to ensure I wasn't hurt. He fought a demon he had expressed fear of from the very beginning. In the end, he had told me to close the gates, not for his own safety but for mine. He was willing to go back to Hell to save my life. Also, instead of vanishing like the two other demons, he stayed behind to face my wrath.

Perhaps all of that was worth giving him another chance. Dagon was free of the bond and no longer under my control. We could start fresh.

I swung at him, balling up my fists and connecting with his jaw. He staggered back before rubbing his face. "There, now we can start over."

Dagon frowned. "I felt that one, you know. You hit pretty hard for such a little thing." He focused on

321

Ermek. "Well, go on. If you want to hit me too, go ahead."

Ermek didn't hesitate in the least.. the force he threw behind the punch caused Dagon to fall to the ground.

"You deserve much more than that," Ermek gritted through clenched teeth.

Dagon rubbed his face and slowly got up. He kept his hands over his nose until I heard a popping noise. For a moment, Dagon glared, but it morphed into a grin as he brushed his hair from his shoulder.

"Well, now both of you get to brag about the fact that you broke my nose."

"So, what do we do now?" inquired Ermek.

"I say we head to Heathen country. Neither of you wants to return to the Followers, and you can make a living as Demon Slayers. There is good money in ridding settlements of pests. One day, we can try to get the demons and angels to work together. If we band together and show people the truth, things may turn out alright. War will never stop since there will always be those who feel they can escape Hell's grasp, but in the long run, we can make a difference. We just have to get past our egos."

I smiled, wrapped my arms around him, and kissed him hard. He was right. The world may not be perfect, but we could try to help change it the best we can. After all, we had the rest of our immortal lives to do it.

EVALYN

CHAPTER 43

Snowflakes drifted lightly through the air and melted when they hit the warm ground. It wouldn't be long before they began to stick, covering the world in a blanket of white. This was the first sign that autumn was over and winter was pushing its way in.

As I walked through the courtyard of my unfinished castle, I glanced over at the numerous demons locked tightly in their cages. Many were deadly sin demons, while others were puny imps and shadow dwellers. My own demon walked along beside me. It wasn't a good conversationalist, but it kept me well protected. Most Priestesses would never attempt to capture a wrath demon, yet here it was, stalking slowly on my right-hand side. From time to time, I wondered what this demon had done in its past life to become such a monster. Were they a serial killer? A mass murderer, perhaps?

Whatever it had done, it claimed that it couldn't remember its life as a human.

A parade of armed guards made their way down the long path toward me. I recognized most of them, two of them being my most trusted men. They escorted a filthy little Priestess with long, matted red hair. I didn't bother to meet them halfway.. instead, I stood there waiting for them to tell me their business. When a few of the newer soldiers hesitated upon seeing my demon, I smiled.

"Such a small girl needs this many soldiers to accompany her?" I questioned as the group of men stopped in front of me.

The men saluted, and my most loyal soldier, Vlake, stepped forward. "There was a massacre at the stadium near the Missouri border, my Queen."

I tilted my head to the side. "Were there any survivors?"

He shook his head. "None of our men made it out alive. All of the Priestesses scattered with their demons. All except this one here." He gestured toward the tiny redhead.

I shifted to the young woman. "And why would you stay?"

She glanced down. "Where would I go? My Demon Slayer was killed, and I have no skills to survive in the wild. I came with these men willingly.. to serve you."

Her words made me want to roll my eyes. "And what happened? How did the men at the stadium die?"

The girl hesitated as if contemplating her answer. "They captured a Priestess. She was with two men and a demon. She fought Jose, and her demon killed him. A female demon came and slaughtered every man there except the Priestess' companions."

Raising an eyebrow, I walked around the girl, giving her a once-over. "Why would a demon spare her and her companions?" The girl shrugged.

"Tell Lady Evalyn about the male," instructed Vlake.

"He was a Demon Lord."

I stopped and stared into her eyes. "A Demon Lord? And it was under the control of this Priestess?" The girl nodded. "What was the demon's name?"

The girl had to think for a moment. "Dagon, my Lady."

Turning to Vlake, I commanded, "Fetch my mother. Tell her to meet me in the throne room, and, get this girl some food." Vlake nodded and disappeared while the other soldiers escorted the girl to one of the side entrances. I hurriedly made my way down the path, through the front doors, and up to my throne. Plopping down, I waited for my mother to make an appearance.

It seemed like ages until she decided to grace me with her presence. She always looked so elegant as she strode along the stone floor, her blue velvet dress swishing gracefully. To me, my mother always looked otherworldly. It wasn't until I was near adulthood that I understood why. My fairness was only a shadow of hers because she was an angel, and I was only half.

"You requested my presence, my Queen?" she murmured, then made a small curtsy.

I smiled slightly. I had never called myself a queen, but she insisted I was destined for greatness.

"Tell me of the Demon Lord Dagon." Her smile turned into a frown. "You know of him?"

"Of course, I know of Dagon.. it's hard to forget the demons that once paraded around as gods." Her tone was pensive.

"How powerful is he?"

"He is a Demon Lord, so his power will surpass your own, but he was born on Earth, so many demons are physically stronger than him. In the celestial world, age makes a demon stronger, not weaker. Dagon may be thousands of years old, but he is still quite young for a demon."

"A girl from the stadium told me that he had been captured by a Priestess."

My mother grinned. "Well then, this is perfect. Dagon could be the perfect specimen to test the power of the Crown. One thorn should be all it takes. If he is bound to a Priestess, he cannot leave her side for very long. If you find this Priestess, you will find Dagon."

I turned to Vlake, who appeared by my side. "Send word out through the realm. Find this Priestess and bring her to me, unharmed."

"How will we know this Priestess?"

My mother chimed in before I could. "I still have connections to Heaven and Hell, and I'm sure I can find out who this Priestess is. We will find her by the time the snow melts. This, I promise you."

~Until We Meet Again~

About The Author

DW Sheneman is a writer who surrounds herself in open-world RPGs, favoring the morally gray hero. She strives to bring a touch of villainy to each of her characters. With a dark yet lovable sense of humor and obsessions with surviving a survivable doomsday leaking into her tales, DW is on the path to becoming The Queen of Dystopian and Apocalyptic Romance. It's time to escape your everyday life and question everything because all is never what it seems when you are dealing with a Queen.

Stay Up to Date
Social Media Links
Newsletter

Made in the USA
Monee, IL
03 April 2023

30580910R00192